the
favourite
child

BOOKS BY EMMA ROBINSON

the favourite child

emma robinson

bookouture

Published by Bookouture in 2025

An imprint of Storyfire Ltd.
Carmelite House
50 Victoria Embankment
London EC4Y 0DZ

www.bookouture.com

The authorised representative in the EEA is Hachette Ireland
8 Castlecourt Centre
Dublin 15 D15 XTP3
Ireland
(email: info@hbgi.ie)

ISBN: 978-1-83618-036-4
eBook ISBN: 978-1-83618-035-7

For my mum
For being amazing

ONE

ERICA

I didn't know what a mother's worst nightmare was until it happened to me.

To this day, I still don't know what woke me that night. The heat? The smoke? The sound of fire eating away at the house around us? Despite being alone in bed, I still reached for Andrew before remembering that he was at work. Then realisation hit and adrenaline propelled me from the tangle of sheets towards the children. 'Mollie! Benjamin! Wake up.'

My bedroom door – and one ear – was always open for the children, but Benjamin's door was shut. He had the box room, the smallest bedroom, and liked to feel enclosed and safe. I wrenched it open, while still shouting for my daughter. 'Mollie? Wake up, baby. Come out here.'

As always, Benjamin was curled up with his knees tucked into his chest. There was no time for our usual routine of waking – gentle, slow and clear – we had to get out of there. I shook his arm. 'Ben. You have to wake up. We need to leave.'

Mollie's voice came from behind me. 'Mummy, what's happening? Why is there smoke?'

Don't frighten them, I told myself. *They're only small.* 'I think there's a fire, sweetheart. But we'll be okay. We just need to get outside.'

Mollie was bright and sharp, and eight was plenty old enough to know what *fire* meant. 'Where's Daddy? I want my daddy.'

It's funny. Although I was the one who did pretty much everything for the twins – and I would be the one they came to if they wanted feeding or comforting – when Mollie was scared, it was always Andrew that she wanted. Who could blame her? His six-foot, broad-shouldered confidence had been my refuge too, once upon a time. And that was before you added in the effect of his police sergeant's uniform.

I tried to keep my voice calm, just as the teachers at Benjamin's school had shown me. 'Daddy's not here, sweetie; he's at work. We'll call him once we're outside.'

Benjamin wasn't stirring. I shook him harder and he woke with a yell and pushed me away. 'No!'

My efforts at calming Mollie were no better. She shouted at him. 'We have to go, Ben! We have to run!'

Mollie's fear and anxiety were entirely appropriate for the situation, but unlikely to work on her brother. There was no time for me to crouch down to his level, give him the instructions one at a time, explain the reason we had to go, and go fast. Instinct made me grab him; terror made me strong.

Perhaps it was the shock of me lifting him from the bed that made Benjamin relax into me as I held him close, his head resting on my shoulder, something I hadn't been able to do for years. With my left arm wrapped around the top of his legs, I reached for Mollie with my right. 'Let's go.'

We didn't get far. Across the landing, we looked down to where the fire had taken hold. At the bottom of the stairs, smoke licked at the carpet, ready to consume us. What else could I do but take them through it?

Benjamin started to wriggle and moan in my arms. Beside me, Mollie whimpered. 'I'm scared. Mummy, I'm scared. Where's Daddy? I want Daddy.'

Her final words ended in a fit of coughing. The smoke was getting thicker. We had no choice but to go.

What were you supposed to do in a fire? My mind was a complete blank. All I could remember was the stop, drop and roll that Mollie had learned at school the year before. A vague memory of her trying to instruct a bemused Benjamin that, if he caught on fire, he should stop running, drop immediately to the floor and roll to put out the flames. I prayed it didn't come to that.

'We have to go down there, Mollie. You need to be a brave girl for Mummy.'

She pulled my hand backwards. 'No, Mummy! No! It's dangerous. Don't go.'

Benjamin must have caught her fear or maybe it was just a twin thing. He began to push his fists into my chest, trying to leverage himself out of my hold.

Like me, Mollie was small and slight. Ben had Andrew's build and had been stronger than me by the time he was six. I tried again to calm him. 'No, Ben. Mummy is taking you outside. Don't hurt Mummy.'

With the smoke beginning to rise, I didn't have the luxury of negotiating with either of them. Holding tight to Mollie's hand, I started the descent. 'Trust Mummy, Mollie. Be a good girl. We have to get outside where it's safe.'

How I didn't fall down that staircase is a miracle in itself. Benjamin pushed at me, Mollie pulled away from me and, all the time, I was using every particle of strength in my body to drive them towards what looked like hell on earth.

The smoke got thicker; both children were coughing. I tried to keep low, out of the densest part of the cloud of smoke, but it was impossible. Benjamin's fists were getting harder, Mollie's hand was twisting in mine. What could I do? What should I do?

And then it happened.

TWO

Five years since they'd moved here and fenced off the front garden and Erica still hadn't mastered the child-proof lock on the front gate. Fiddling with it, she tore the edge from her thumbnail. 'Damn.'

Through luck and effort, rather than skill, she wrenched it open and it scraped the gravel path as it squeaked back on its hinges. The small front lawn had been freshly cut – Andrew's Saturday morning regimen must still be in place – and the sweet grassy smell tickled her nose. She breathed it in, storing it away in her lungs.

Unkempt and overgrown, the flower beds at each side had not had the same attention as the grass. June is a crucial month for rose care and it broke her heart to see the bushes sagging with the weight of their tired blooms. All they needed was a little pruning and restraint – a piece of string, a cable tie – and they'd display their beauty for all. Staring at them, she jumped when she heard a voice.

'Hello, love. How are you? I like the new hair.'

Her hand on her new, shorter, easier-to-manage cut, Erica turned to her left. Over the fence, Lynn was on her knees, weeding her own side of the wall.

Since the last time she'd seen Lynn, she'd let the grey in her own hair thread further into the blonde and it suited her. 'Thanks. It was getting too difficult to manage. I'm good. How are you?'

As she sat back on her haunches, Lynn gave Erica a smile of welcome that she hadn't had here for weeks. 'Can't complain. How's our Benjamin?'

They'd arrived at their house on this new estate at the worst time in their lives. Though Andrew had wanted to be closer to town, she'd been determined that this place would be a fresh start for them. A new build would be pristine, modern, electrics checked and functioning. The day they'd arrived, after weeks living in an Airbnb, she'd breathed a sigh of relief.

Lynn had been there to greet them that day, having moved in the day before. From that moment on, she'd been a tower of strength for Erica. Lynn had always had that gift of being there without ever intruding. In that first week, Erica had expected her neighbour's judgement at the screams and yells – often hers – that rang out of their back door, but she'd been nothing but kind to all of them. For Mollie, she'd been a replacement grandparent for Erica's own mother back in the States, teaching her to knit and make banana loaf and letting her set up her paints and crayons on her dining room table where they wouldn't be swiped by her twin brother every few minutes.

Ben hadn't been as interested in spending time with Lynn, so it was kind of her to ask after him. 'He's doing well. He loves the new school. They're really great with him.'

The lines around Lynn's eyes deepened as she smiled. 'That's good, love. It doesn't seem five minutes ago that you all came here. Where does the time go, eh?'

It had taken a while for them to settle. Obviously, they'd not been able to go back to the other house after the fire: it hadn't been safe for any of them. Relocating was difficult at any time, but doing it with young twins, hospital appointments, and a husband who could never be a hundred per cent sure what time he'd get home, made it all the more difficult. Nevertheless, she'd grown to like it here. This house had been a sanctuary from the uphill struggle of the outside world and – despite knowing that it was the right decision for Ben – it'd been such a wrench to move out. She missed it terribly. And, she realised now, she'd missed having a neighbour like Lynn terribly, too.

After Lynn lost her husband three years ago, she'd been a whirlwind of activity, throwing herself into anything that kept her busy, refusing to give in to grief or age. She'd always have a friendly word for Erica on her way in or out somewhere, and dropped by often with a cake or a story in the evenings when Andrew was working late. In the ten weeks since she'd moved out, Erica had learned how long and lonely the evenings could be without anyone close by. With barely any social contact at all. Lynn's smiling face brought a lump to her throat. 'How are your roses doing? The garden looks great.'

Scanning the neatly tended flower beds, Lynn sighed with contentment. 'They're coming on a treat. Your Andrew did my lawn this morning, love him. The mower is getting a bit much for me now.'

Her gut twisted. Could she still call him 'her' Andrew while they were living apart? When the only conversations they had were short, stilted and centred on the two children? Not knowing how much he'd told the neighbours – and still hoping the situation was temporary – Erica didn't correct Lynn. 'That's good of him. He might want to give his own garden a bit of attention, too.'

Maybe Lynn had worked it out for herself, because she narrowed her blue eyes and tilted her head. 'When are you coming back? I know the last couple of months have been rough on you, but we miss you around here. And the kids must miss one another, don't they? And you and Andrew are such a lovely couple. I don't want to pry, love, but I'm worried about you both.'

Another twist to the gut. The last couple of months hadn't just been rough, they'd been unbearable. The worst part about being back here was the danger of encountering anyone who knew what'd happened at Easter. The real reason Erica had left. Not Lynn, she was kind, but what if she bumped into any of the parents from the school? Living in that apartment an hour away might be lonely, but at least no one knew her there. And as for coming back to the house where her husband and daughter lived... How could she answer that question when she really didn't know? Would they ever be able to get back to the way they'd been?

None of this was suitable conversation over a garden wall. She forced a smile and a breezy tone. 'Logistics are tricky. Ben's school is close to where I'm living now. It's an hour away from here. You know how he is in a car for more than about ten minutes.'

There'd been enough seatbelt battles out the front here over the last five years for Lynn not to question that statement. Instead, she took a pause and looked Erica dead in the eye. 'What about Mollie?'

The challenge in her tone was uncomfortable. Lynn had always been supportive, not judgemental. Where had this come from? What did she expect her to say? It was out of her control. 'Mollie wanted to stay here, you know that. She's doing so well at her secondary school and her friends are all here. To be honest, I think even seeing me on a Sunday is too much. Or is this a gentle complaint about her saxophone practice?'

Her attempt at humour hadn't landed well. She thought she'd got the hang of British irony after sixteen years in the country but Lynn wasn't smiling. In fact, there was something on her face that Erica couldn't read. Maybe it wasn't judgement. Was it... concern?

'Look, love. It's not my place to stick my nose in where it's not wanted. But Mollie's only thirteen. A girl that age needs her mum around.'

Guilt nibbled at Erica. As far as she knew, Mollie was doing great. So great, in fact, that she barely had the time to chat in the evenings and – last weekend – she hadn't been here at all. Looking at Lynn, she just wanted to get inside and see her. 'I think she's fine. But I'll see how she is today.'

The usual expression of kind benevolence returned to Lynn's face. 'That's good. I didn't want to upset you.' She paused. 'I'm worried about Andrew, too. I don't know if you already know this, but he's—'

'I'm really sorry, Lynn, but I need to get inside. Ben's carer is only there for a few hours today and I want to make the most of my time with Mollie.' Though she felt bad for cutting her off, it was true, she really did only have a few precious hours to spend with her daughter.

Lynn waved her apology away. 'Of course, I'm sorry for wittering on. You go, love. I'll catch up with you another time. I need to make a cup of tea, anyway.'

She waited for Lynn to ease herself to her feet and close her front door behind her before knocking on her own door. Though she still had keys, it didn't feel appropriate to just let herself in now that she wasn't living here. She certainly didn't want Lynn to witness her embarrassment if the door went unanswered as it had last weekend. That time, when she'd come to collect her daughter for their regular day out together, Andrew had finally opened the door and merely shrugged at her. 'She's not here.'

'What do you mean? I've been coming here at eleven on a Sunday for the last two months. Where is she?'

That shrug again made her want to reach up to Andrew's

broad shoulders and shake him. 'Out. With her friends. When I got up this morning, she'd left a note and asked me to tell you.'

It'd stung like a slap. Not only did her daughter not want to see her, but she hadn't thought to call or text her herself? Erica would've understood. Mollie was thirteen. It was to be expected that there were Sundays that she would rather hang out with her friends than her mom. Even if that was the only time they got to be alone together at the moment. She'd tried to speak to her on three separate occasions this week, but Mollie had ignored Erica's calls, sending a vague text back after the third attempt instead.

I'm fine. Just off to my sax lesson. Can't talk.

Erica hadn't been able to stave off a feeling that she'd done something to upset Mollie but didn't know what it was. And now Lynn's words of caution had thrown petrol on the spark of concern. She needed to see her daughter's face. Mollie had never been able to hide it if something was going on.

Taking a deep breath, she held her knuckles to the door. Before she even made contact, it opened to reveal Andrew dressed in a crisp shirt and jeans with a back draught carrying the citrus of his aftershave; all of which was incongruous for a Sunday at home. 'Finally! I've been waiting for you to get here.'

She pushed down her irritation and the desire to tell him that it had only just turned eleven. The time she always came. 'Is she ready to go?'

Her heart sank when he shook his head. Another week where she wouldn't be able to see her daughter? She couldn't let this go on.

Then he surprised her by opening the door wider and standing back to let her through. 'She's in the shower. Come in. She needs you. It's serious.'

THREE

When they'd bought this house five years ago, it'd been the hall which had immediately sold it to her. The solid black and white tiled floor had that feeling of permanence and safety she'd craved after the terrible night of the fire. On the second viewing, they'd taken the children and Ben had been transfixed by the floor. Mollie had been more taken with the bedroom with a window seat that they'd told her was hers to decorate however she wished. Glancing around on the way in, though, it looked so very different to Erica now. It wasn't home.

Andrew held out his hand for her to go through to the kitchen. 'Do you want a drink while we wait for Mollie? Coffee?'

He was a good-looking man, she couldn't deny that. In fact, he was better looking now than he'd been when they met. She was the one who'd encouraged him to go to a proper barber and suggested he wear his hair a little longer, who'd bought him fitted shirts and well-cut jeans instead of the baggy student clothes he was still wearing when they first met. It wasn't just his clothes, though. Age suited him, too. It was so unfair. 'Yes,

I'll have a coffee, thanks. What's going on? Why does Mollie need me?'

The anxiety that'd prickled when she was talking to Lynn in the garden now ratcheted up a notch. All manner of terrifying possibilities flashed through her mind. Andrew was frustratingly evasive. 'Let me make you a drink first.'

Clenching her hands into fists, she breathed through her need to immediately know what was going on. From experience, her husband did not deal well with being told what to do. As he turned towards the counter, she noticed a large new chrome coffee machine. It wasn't like him to spend money on household appliances. 'That looks a bit posh.'

In the past, he'd have laughed at her use of such a quintessentially English word; now he merely blushed as he turned to her. 'Yeah, well. Thought I'd treat myself.'

Rubbing at his face, a slight stubble scratching against his fingers, he gave her that smile which had disarmed her from the first moment she met him. But all she could see was the pale white mark on his finger: he wasn't wearing his wedding ring. Reaching instinctively for her own, her stomach lurched. When had he taken it off?

Twirling the plain gold band around her finger, she kept her lips tightly pressed together. They'd always looked like a mismatched couple. His height and breadth compared to her five feet two and size four feet. His thick dark hair, her blonde waves. Perhaps that's why the twins had always looked so different. But their differences had always been what made them fit together. His practicality and her soft skills. His discipline and her sense of adventure. Despite coming from very different families – and completely different countries – they'd been a good match. A happy couple. But now? They lived in separate homes with a child each and he was buying coffee machines and taking off his wedding ring. She feared it was really all over between them.

Feeling like a visitor in her former home, she perched on a stool by the breakfast bar. 'Andrew. Can you just tell me what's going on? What's happening with Mollie? Even Lynn suggested that I need to check in with her.'

Steam hissed from the machine. Andrew reached for a cup from a selection stacked on a chrome stand – also new – before he turned around to face her. 'I had to collect her from school on Friday. She's been suspended for two days.'

Erica nearly fell from her seat. Suspended? Mollie? She hadn't had so much as a detention the whole time she'd been at school. Top marks in all school reports for effort, attitude and behaviour: the archetypal perfect student. There must be some mistake. 'That's ludicrous. What possible reason could the school have for suspending her? And why didn't you call me straight away? You waited two days to tell me? Not only am I Mollie's mother, Andrew, but I could've done something. I used to work there. I know who to speak to. I could get to the bottom of what's going on.'

Behind Andrew, the stupid machine gurgled and he turned to slot a cup underneath a chrome tap. Tweaked something. 'Well, firstly, I didn't call you because she asked me not to. She was mortified. Secondly, I'm not sure what you think you could do when you're not even working there at the moment. And, lastly, the reason she was suspended was because she was caught stealing.'

The not-calling would have to be argued about later. Stealing? Mollie? The girl who'd made her drive back to the bakers because she'd discovered three Yum Yums in the paper bag and she'd only paid for two. 'Did you ask them for proof? There must be some mistake.'

Andrew slid her coffee across the breakfast bar. He'd attempted something artistic with the foam. 'That's what I said, but apparently not. She was caught red-handed with the teacher's purse in her hand.'

Erica choked on the scalding coffee she'd sipped too soon. 'The teacher's purse?'

Even though she still wouldn't have believed it, she'd assumed the accusation of theft would be something belonging to the school. A book. Or a set of pens. Before Easter, when she'd been teaching there, there'd been a spate of kids stealing the remote controls for the classroom projectors which could completely sabotage the next lesson.

Andrew sighed, leaning against the counter with his coffee in his hand, shaking his head. 'You can imagine how I felt having to face being told that about my own daughter. To make it worse, the call came to me at work and I had to have the meeting with the deputy head wearing my uniform.'

An age-old irritation dug its fingers into Erica. Was he more worried about how this looked for him as a Detective Inspector than he was about their daughter? That felt unpleasantly familiar. 'I can't believe any of this. Are they sure it was her? Was she doing it for a dare or something?'

No matter how she turned this around in her head, it didn't make sense. She wasn't one of those parents who thought her child could never do wrong, but Mollie? Stealing from a teacher? Really?

Andrew shrugged. 'Definitely her. Like I said, she was caught red-handed. It was break time. Her English teacher left the room and, when she came back in, Mollie had taken her purse out of her handbag and was taking cash from it.'

This made even less sense. Mollie's English teacher – Miss Martin – was her favourite. Mollie adored her. Erica felt sick. This was not the way her daughter had ever behaved. 'I can't believe the school just suspended her. Did they not try and find out why she was doing it? They know that she's a good kid. A really good kid.'

Her throat was tight with the injustice of it. Generally, the behaviour at Mollie's school was good, but there were still kids who were in trouble all the time. And didn't she know better than anyone where that could lead?

She shuddered and pushed that thought from her mind. Mollie wasn't one of them. Her heart ached picturing her poor girl in the head's office being told that she was being excluded from school for two days. She could only imagine how devastated she would feel. This didn't happen to kids like her.

Andrew frowned. 'That's what I spent the whole of last night doing. Trying to find out why she was taking money. But she won't tell me. She won't say a thing.'

She couldn't bite her tongue a second time. 'And yet you still didn't think to call me?'

He raised a mocking eyebrow. 'I interview suspects for a living, Erica. If I can't get her to tell me, I don't fancy your chances much. Why would she be any different with you?'

Erica took another sip of the bitter coffee in an attempt to swallow down the desire to yell 'because I'm her mother' at him. Arguing with Andrew wasn't going to help this situation one bit. Plus, she didn't want to give him the opportunity to remind her that Mollie hadn't wanted to see her for over a week. It was painful enough that her daughter was pushing her away; she didn't need to hear it from him too. Instead, she turned the tables. 'Ben's fine, by the way.'

The clench in his jaw showed she'd hit the target. 'I know that. I saw him on Wednesday, didn't I? And we both know if he'd as much as broken a fingernail you wouldn't be here to see Mollie.'

That stung. Is this what they'd come to, taking pot-shots at each other? This wasn't the right time for them to air their grievances. All she wanted was to see Mollie and hear her side of the story.

From the room above, as if in answer, the mournful strains of Mollie's saxophone scales bled through the ceiling. Andrew strode into the hall and shouted upwards. 'Mollie! Your mum's here. Come down now, please!'

Instantly, the music stopped and Andrew returned to the kitchen. Something else occurred to Erica. 'What are we going to do about her being off school? She can't be on her own all day for two days running.'

Andrew shrugged. 'She's thirteen. She'll be fine. And I can ask Lynn to keep an ear out for her.'

Ordinarily, Mollie was more than capable of looking after herself – she let herself in from school every day and was alone until Andrew got home – but present circumstances made Erica uneasy. 'I can't come back here tomorrow because I've already promised to open up the shop. But I'm worried about her spending so much time without one of us here. We don't know what's going on with her. I'm scared that...'

Unsure what she was scared about, she left the sentence hanging. Andrew shook his head. 'You might have made yourself the expert in our son, Erica, but I'm the one who's been looking after Mollie for the last three months. You don't get to be the expert in her, too. She'll be fine.'

He couldn't have taken her breath more if he'd slapped her in the face. They waited in silence until there was a creak on the stairs. Leaving her coffee cup on the counter, Erica slid from the stool and waited for her daughter to come down.

She took a deep breath to prevent herself from jumping on Mollie the minute she appeared, desperate to know what was going on. Why would Mollie have stolen money when she could've asked them for it? What did she need money for that she couldn't tell them? And in what possible world had her kind, conscientious and law-abiding child been caught stealing from her favourite teacher at school?

FOUR

At thirteen, Mollie was already an outline of the woman she would become. All of the softness in her body and face had been replaced with curves and angles which made her look older than she was. For a while now, Erica had noticed the attention her daughter drew from strangers – particularly men – and had experienced a violent desire to shield her from their gaze, keep her young and innocent and uninhibited by the approval of others.

In the kitchen doorway, she was taken aback by how beautiful she was. Her warm blonde hair, still wet from the shower, had been combed back from her face, giving even more emphasis to her cheekbones, her large green eyes, the pinkness of her freshly scrubbed cheeks. Just looking at her made Erica proud. 'Hi, sweetheart.'

Mollie had the luck to have inherited Andrew's long eyelashes and she looked up and through them at Erica from her bowed head. Erica knew this expression of old. The conflict on her face between anger and tears. Trying to be grown up. Fighting to hold it all in. Her face crumpled and she fell, sobbing, into Erica's arms.

She held her only daughter tightly, pressing her cheek into the top of Mollie's head, waiting for the sobs to stop their juddering through her body. If she could've picked her up and held her like a baby, she would have. But she wasn't a baby and Erica couldn't make this go away like a bad dream. 'Shall we go and sit on the sofa and you can tell me what happened?'

Behind her, she could sense Andrew's judgement at what he saw as her being 'too soft' on the children. She could only imagine what he'd already said to Mollie about the theft. But she knew that this was so out of character for their daughter that there must be some mistake.

Nothing had changed in the living room in the last three months, although there was an air of it being unused. Holiday photographs of the children on the cherry-wood sideboard still smiled at her as she followed Mollie across the wooden floor. Even the mustard cushions in various prints, which Andrew had thought ridiculous and unnecessary on their overstuffed navy sofa, were still there. Mollie clutched one of these to her chest – plain side towards her body, large blooms facing away – as she eyed Erica from the corner of the sofa.

'What's going on, sweetheart?'

Whatever need had thrown Mollie into Erica's arms had clearly been sated and their brief moment of reconciliation seemed to be over. Mollie pulled her legs up in front of her and held her knees wrapped in her arms like a line of defence. 'I don't want to talk about it.'

Coming from behind, Andrew's voice made Erica jump. 'You don't have a choice in that, Mollie. You could be prosecuted for stealing. You have to tell us what happened. Did someone tell you to do this? Are you being bullied?'

Each question seemed to make Mollie recoil further into herself. Andrew treating her like a suspect in his interview room really wasn't going to get them anywhere. Erica gave him a tight smile. 'Maybe we should give Mollie a chance to talk?'

He threw up his hands in the *why-do-I-bother* mime that she knew of old. 'I'll be in the kitchen.'

It was a relief when he left, but she still needed to get Mollie to open up. 'Right, your dad's not here. It's just you and me, Mollie. What is it? What's happening?'

If she'd thought Andrew's exit would help, she was wrong. If anything, Mollie shut down even further. 'Nothing. I just took it. That's all.'

Over the years, when she was teaching, Erica had had to speak to many students about their behaviour while attempting to get to the bottom of what had gone on. But this was like trying to talk to a brick wall. 'You have to see our confusion, Mollie. This is just not like you. You're not a thief.'

Mollie's eyes flashed with something she didn't recognise. 'How would you know? You're not here. How would you know who I am?'

The sharpness of her words cut through Erica like a knife. If only she knew how much of a wrench it had been for Erica to live separately from her. How much it had hurt in the last couple of weeks when Mollie had told her not to bother to come, that she was too busy to see her, or to see her own twin brother. 'I'm here as much as I can be. It's difficult when I'm over an hour away. You wanted to stay at the school. You can't commute from where I am. We went through this months ago.'

Guilt chewed at her even as she reminded her daughter that it'd been her choice to stay at the house. Because she shouldn't have had to make that choice at thirteen, should she? And, in truth, there'd been an element of relief when Mollie opted to stay with Andrew. Mainly, but not exclusively, because it would've been a tight squeeze for the three of them in that tiny one-bedroom apartment. She'd have made it work, though. It really had been Mollie's choice to stay where her friends were.

But this explanation seemed only to make Mollie angrier. 'Well, you can't really have a go at me for getting suspended when you're suspended from the school too. When do you have to go in for your panel? Maybe they could do me at the same time.'

The nasty edge to Mollie's tone nearly made Erica gasp. This was not her daughter. This was anger talking. Hurt. Fear. But why? 'My panel hearing is on Thursday, but this is hardly the same thing, Mollie.'

Instead of replying, Mollie's scowl deepened and darkened.

She'd have to try a different tack. 'What did you need the money for, then? Is there something you want? You know you can ask me and Dad if you need anything.'

With Ben's fees and two properties to pay for, money wasn't exactly flowing through their bank accounts. But they would always find funds if the children needed something. Even if it meant that her coat was coming apart at the seams and she hadn't had a new pair of shoes in about three years.

Mollie's face was a blank page. 'It's fine. I don't need anything.'

Fine. Was there a more frustrating word in the English language? Fine meant *not good enough* or *you're wrong* or *I'm ending this conversation now.* And it meant nothing. It told her nothing.

It was so much easier when Mollie was younger. The constant chatter on the walk home from school, the nights she'd sneak into Erica's bed with her latest book, the mornings spent swinging her legs at the breakfast bar, alternating questions with mouthfuls of Cheerios.

'You have to talk to me, sweetheart. My brain is coming up with lots of explanations but I haven't got a clue which one is right. I can't help you if I don't know what's going on.'

That clench in Mollie's jaw mirrored her father's. 'I didn't ask for your help.'

Where had this aggression come from? When she'd seen her last, Mollie had seemed perfectly happy. Admittedly, they'd only had four hours together and Mollie had spent half of that replying to text messages from her friends, but there'd been no clue that this was going to happen.

How she envied the women who had lots of time to hang out with their daughters. Social media was full of their coffee dates and shopping trips and sometimes even 'girls only' weekends away. She'd tried to make the time to do these things with Mollie but, with Benjamin's needs and Andrew's job, it never seemed to work out. Since the move, she was concerned because they wouldn't even get their snatches of time together at home. Which is why she'd started these Sunday visits without Benjamin. So that she and Mollie could get some time on their own together. Mollie got to see Ben once a week when Andrew would visit him. Although that was in the evening and not ideal. Originally, Andrew had suggested that that could be an evening where Erica got a break to do something for herself, but so far she'd stayed at the house when they were there, not wanting to waste an opportunity to see her daughter a little more.

'Mollie, I don't want to get cross, but I'm exasperated. You've been suspended from school. You've been caught stealing. Five minutes ago you were in floods of tears and now you're looking at me as if I'm the enemy. I don't know what to do here.'

'There's nothing you can do. Nothing. This is pointless. You wouldn't understand, anyway. Just forget it. This has got nothing to do with you.'

The force of her anger made Erica's head spin. What wouldn't she understand? What was the 'this' that had nothing to do with her?

Before she could even formulate a response in her head, her phone rang in her pocket and, as a reflex, she pulled it out to check the caller. It was her home number. It must be Jade. 'I just need to get this. Two minutes.'

Move over Helen of Troy: the look on Mollie's face could've

sunk a thousand ships. Erica knew she was angry at the inter-
ruption, but it wasn't as if she was actually telling her anything.

'Hello? Jade?'

'Hi, Erica. Sorry to interrupt your time with Mollie. I'm
sure I'm using my father's eyes as my mum would say, but I
can't find Ben's cup and I'm making his lunch.'

Jade had worked with them long enough to know that Ben
would flatly refuse to drink anything unless it was in his lime-
green cup with a straw. Erica's brother had sent it over from the
States and – despite him going back to the same store and her
frequent scouring of the internet – they hadn't been able to
source another just like it. 'Have you looked in the dishwasher?'

'Yes, sorry. Already looked there. And the cupboards and
his room. Any other ideas? I mean, he doesn't take it out to the
car, does he?'

Erica's heart sank. No. Usually he did not take it out to the
car for reasons just like this. But yesterday, he'd wanted to finish
his drink and they'd needed to get to the supermarket before it
closed so she'd let him. 'Dammit. I think it's on my back seat.'

'Oh, okay. I'll try and persuade him that another cup will
work.'

Jade knew as well as she did that Benjamin would flatly
refuse. Which meant that he wouldn't have anything to drink
until she got home with his cup later. Not only that. He
wouldn't eat his lunch either. Which meant he wouldn't have
his medication. 'It's okay. I'll come back.'

'No, it's fine.' Jade was such a brilliant help. Her calm practicality a wonder in a girl who was half Erica's age. 'I'm here
with him. I don't want you to cut your day short. We'll figure it
out together.'

But Erica knew that it wasn't as easy as that. It might escalate if Ben got upset. And she couldn't risk losing another carer
or she wouldn't be able to come out alone ever again. 'It's my

fault for taking the cup. It's okay. Honestly. I'll be there in an hour.'

She ended the call and faced Mollie, whose anger had hardened in her face. 'You're going already?'

Erica's heart sank to the pit of her stomach at the tone of her voice. 'I'm so sorry, love. You heard the conversation. I need to get back to your brother. Come with me. We can talk in the car on the way there. You can see your brother. And, as you haven't got school in the morning, why don't you stay overnight with me? We can talk about all of this. I want to understand.'

Getting to her feet, Mollie threw the cushion on the sofa. 'No, thanks. It's fine. Just go. Your favourite child needs you.'

FIVE

MOLLIE

Grey concrete with blue doors, my old school was not particularly pretty, but I loved it there. My classroom was full of bright displays and a dark-blue rug with squirrels and foxes on it where we'd sit at the end of the day and listen to our teacher – Miss Hewitt – as she read aloud. It was my favourite time of the day. Everyone was quiet and still and listening. Sometimes I would close my eyes and pretend that I was in the story somewhere far away.

Miss Hewitt was my favourite teacher ever. She had short dark hair and always wore trainers with trousers, sometimes with a matching jacket. Whenever I finished my work, she would notice and smile and give me something even harder. When I completed that, too, she'd widen her eyes and tell me I was 'amazing'. She liked Doctor Who and drinking coffee from a mug that said 'Don't Speak to Me Until This is Half Empty'. She had a smile that was real. It didn't come out every minute like some teachers, but when it did, you knew she really meant it.

Every day, when Mum was late, Miss Hewitt would wait

with me at the door as I tipped my foot from the step onto the tarmac of the playground. 'My mum isn't late,' I would tell her. 'She has to collect my brother first.'

Her voice would be tired but kind. 'I know, Mollie. It's okay.'

I remember a particular day when I was really impatient for my mum to arrive. On my blue school jumper – on the top right next to the school badge – I had the white sticker I'd been waiting all year to get. Student of the Week. It felt like everyone had had it except me. I'd tried so hard for it. Putting up my hand for every question, staying last to tidy up the classroom after craft time, helping others when they didn't understand the work. But it had never been my turn. All the boys had had it. Even Simon Carpenter and he was always naughty.

Maybe my excitement at showing my mum the award was why it felt we'd been waiting a really long time. Balancing with my toes over the edge of the step, I was worried that Miss Hewitt would be thinking the same thing. 'She'll be here soon. Sometimes she gets stuck in traffic. All the other cars get in her way.'

Miss Hewitt looked up from the papers she'd been reading and smiled at me with her kind eyes. 'It's okay, Mollie. I know your mum has to get your brother first. I know Ben, remember?'

Ben used to go to my school, too. When we were younger. He'd had to go to another school because it was too difficult for him here. Not just the work. The playground, too. He used to walk around the edge of the tarmac on his own and I would get this weird tearing feeling in my stomach because I wanted to stay and play with my friends but I didn't like him to be on his own.

The playground was empty now. The last of the children had gone home with their mums or dads. Sometimes my dad would collect me from school if his shifts worked out. That would be good because I got to leave with everyone else. I liked the hustle and bustle and calling goodbye to my friends, my hand safely in my dad's and his undivided attention as I explained what we'd learned about the difference between fish and mammals and how Miss Hewitt had made us laugh by asking us which one a mermaid would be.

Today, though, I was glad it was my mum. She knew how important it was to be Student of the Week because she was a teacher at the big school a little way away from here. She was the one who told me the secret that sometimes the best children don't get the award first because the other children need it more. I told her that I understood, but really that's not fair, is it?

Miss Hewitt must've seen the way my fingers kept going to the top of the sticker where it had peeled away from my jumper a little bit. It felt nice to play with the top of it. 'Be careful, you'll make it fall off.'

I knew this was one of her jokes, but I stopped playing with it just in case. I wanted it to look perfect when Mum and Ben got here. To protect it, I wrapped my coat over the top, before pulling up my socks and making sure that they matched either side.

'Here she is.' Miss Hewitt sounded almost as pleased as I felt to see my mum hurrying through the dark-grey gates onto the playground.

'I'm sorry. I'm so sorry. Ben had a... it doesn't matter, I'm sorry.'

With her hand still clamped on to Ben's arm – sometimes he didn't like holding hands – she reached for me and pulled me in for a hug but spoke over the top of my head. 'I really appreciate you waiting for me.'

Miss Hewitt smiled. 'I know what it's like. See you Monday, Mollie.'

Miss Hewitt winked at me and a fizz of excitement rose in

my belly at the thought of the news I had for Mum. With the sticker safely hidden under my coat, I decided it would be better to wait to tell her until we got home, where I could get her full attention.

'Sorry I was late, sweetheart. Your brother has had a tricky day.'

She didn't go into detail, but I could tell by the way he was wriggling against her, fighting her when she tried to get him into the car, pushing her away, that he was upset about whatever had happened. Once she'd shut the door on him, she closed her eyes for a moment as if she just wanted to go to sleep.

It was horrible when this happened in public. It wasn't Ben's fault, I knew that. Mum said that he just got overwhelmed sometimes. Noise or crowds or smells or heat or anything that felt too much to him would make him upset. At home, we could help him. But when we were outside, people would look at us, stare at Ben, frown at Mum like she was doing something bad and it made me want to scream at them to stop.

When we got home, things didn't get any better. Ben had worked himself up into a real meltdown. He was shouting and slapping his hands on the floor, on himself. Mum was trying to soothe him but he wasn't paying any attention. It wasn't working. Why didn't she just leave him to it? 'Mum, I want to show you something.'

She didn't even look at me. 'Not now, love. Let me sort Ben out and then I'll come and look.'

My throat felt tight. I wasn't going to cry. I wasn't. This was supposed to be my moment. She was supposed to be looking at me. I took my coat off and stood in the sitting room, waiting for her to notice my sticker, to ask me what it was for. But she didn't even seem to notice I was there. 'It's okay, Ben. You're home now. It's all okay.'

I couldn't wait any longer. 'Mum, look at—'

'Go and take your uniform off and get yourself some juice, Mollie. I can't come right now.'

The sharp tone to her voice was enough to prick the tears from my eyes. I ran to the bedroom, peeled the sticker from my jumper, screwed it up in my hand and threw it in the bin.

SIX

ERICA

On a quiet Sunday afternoon, Erica could get from her old house to her new apartment in fifty-eight minutes. Clutching the steering wheel tightly, she cursed herself for forgetting to take Ben's cup back inside before she left. Mollie's anger had been more worrying because it was cold. It wasn't the heated petulance of a teenage hissy fit. She'd been seriously upset. At the traffic lights at the end of her street, Erica banged the heel of her hand onto the steering wheel. Why had she forgotten the cup? Idiot. Idiot. Idiot.

At least there was an empty bay on the street for her to park in and she didn't have to waste time looking for a space. The small modern apartment was on the second floor of a white painted block of six. Her front door was dark green which opened onto an oatmeal carpeted hallway with doors to the bedroom and bathroom to the left and right respectively. The bedroom was Ben's so that he had his own space and enough room for his toys. At the end of the hall was the living room: a pale-grey rectangle with space for a TV, a sofa bed and a fold-down dining table with two chairs. From there, a small kitchen led off to the right.

The living room was where she spent most of her time. Though she'd intended to make sure she unfolded the sofa into a proper bed each evening, invariably, she'd fall asleep in front of the TV with her head on the arm of it and would end up staying there for the night, curled up under the large blanket she left folded over the back. When she hurried in, Jade was sitting on that same sofa, while Ben paced up and down in front of her, flicking his hands on either side of him.

Though Erica didn't know her exact age, Jade couldn't be more than nineteen. From the moment she'd started working with them, she'd wanted to feed her up: there was nothing of her. Skinny black jeans and t-shirts from bands Erica had never heard of were a constant. The colour of her hair was not. When she'd turned up this time with some kind of blue-green tint, the look of wonder on Benjamin's face had been a picture.

'You didn't need to come back, Erica. I just called in case you knew where the cup was.'

It amazed Erica that Jade could stay so calm when Benjamin was so agitated. Every inch of her own body was taut with the need to soothe his stress. 'I could hear he was upset, so I wanted to come and calm him down.'

Jade twisted a bright-green lock in her fingers. 'That's what you're paying me for. He's okay. He's safe here. He just needs time to work it through. Have you got the cup? I'll pop to the kitchen and get him some of his juice.'

She knew that Jade was caring, but – once Benjamin got himself upset – Erica was the only one who could soothe him. She passed the cup over to her and turned to her upset boy.

Ben was beautiful. His floppy blond hair – in need of a cut she kept putting off – curled at the ends so that it kissed the tops of his ears. Despite the height and breadth he'd gained in the last year, his face was still that of the little boy whose hand she'd always held so tightly. Especially at the times the world had been cruel. The people who stared at them in supermarket aisles when he was heartbroken because they didn't have his favourite flavour of yogurt, the children who wouldn't play with him at the park because he couldn't speak to them, the mother at the school gate who'd loudly told her friend it was 'such a shame' that a boy as handsome as him was 'y'know, different'. If only he were still small enough to be held in her arms and kept safe from the world. If only they both were.

'Hey, baby. Mum's here. I've brought your cup.'

Jade emerged from the kitchen with the cup of juice – Morrison's Summer Fruits, of course – and she passed it to Erica.

Ben made a grab for it and glugged it down as if he'd just emerged from a week in the desert. Guilt ripped at her heart. 'He must've been really thirsty.'

Jade indicated the cup of juice on the coffee table. 'I did offer him a drink, but...'

'Oh, I know.' Erica smiled at Jade. She didn't want her to feel bad. The fault wasn't with her; it was with Erica. 'I should've checked it was in the kitchen before I left to go to see Mollie.'

Jade shrugged her tiny shoulders. 'I was happy to persevere. I bet he would've had a drink eventually.'

Erica wasn't so sure. On top of his fixation on the green cup was the stubborn streak he'd inherited from his father. But she didn't want to get into that. Ben had had a drink, he was calmer. The dark clouds had dispersed before the full force of the storm could hit. 'Did you find his letters?'

On her way to Mollie's this morning, she'd sent a text to Jade to tell her that Ben might want his letters to play with. He'd become so fascinated by the ones they were using at school that she'd bought him a set for home. 'Yep. They were exactly where you said they'd be. You've got them now, haven't you, Ben?'

Sure enough, Benjamin's left hand was clenched full of the

plastic magnetic letters, his thumbs rotating as he stroked them. Ignoring Jade's question, he held out his cup for another glass of juice.

It was obvious that he wanted another drink, but Jade didn't move. 'What do you want, Ben?'

Erica pushed herself up from the sofa. 'He wants more juice. I can go and get it for him.'

She held out her hand for the cup, but Jade was still looking at her son who was rocking from one foot to the other. 'What do you want, Ben?'

Irritation prickled. Erica was home now. Jade could leave. She knew what her son needed. But, as she opened her mouth to say that, Ben brought the back of the fist holding his letters onto the palm of his right hand.

'More! You want *more* juice. Great signing, Ben. I'll go and get you some *more* juice. Great work.'

Swallowing down what she'd been about to say, Erica smiled at her son. 'Great signing, honey. Shall I get the board out so that you can put the letters on it?'

Without waiting for him to react, she opened the drawer beneath the TV and brought out an A3 magnetic whiteboard. She held it out to him, but he was pacing again as if she wasn't even there.

This was probably one of the most difficult parts of looking after Ben. When she couldn't find the way to bring him back to her. It was like a shutter went down between his world and hers and she didn't have the password to get through. He only stopped pacing when Jade returned with another cup of juice, which he emptied in about three gulps.

When people talked about autism as a superpower, they didn't see what it was like when her son was having a full-on meltdown. How heartbreaking it was to see your child in mental anguish and not be able to help them. When your child is at the profound end of the spectrum, there was nothing 'super' about it.

Mollie's accusation that Benjamin was her favourite child had cut deep. It'd felt wretched to leave her back home, but what else could she do? If Benjamin had wound himself up into a real upset, it would've taken hours to bring him down again. Mollie knew that as well as she did. Mollie was brilliant with him. She loved him. So where had those bitter words come from?

Once Jade had gone and Ben was happily arranging his plastic letters onto the board, she tried to call Mollie. As was becoming the norm, she didn't answer. Erica sent a text.

I'm sorry I had to leave, sweetheart. Ben is settled now. Can I call you?

Though she checked her phone in the next fifteen minutes – seven, eight, nine times – there was no reply. So she texted Andrew instead.

Can we talk?

Though it was at least immediate, his reply was brief.

Sorry. I've had to go into work and sort a few things out. Talk tomorrow.

She frowned at his words on her screen. He hadn't mentioned anything about working today when she'd been there earlier. He didn't work shifts any longer since his promotion, so why had he had to go in? Or was he lying about work? More importantly – why was he leaving their daughter alone on a Sunday afternoon when she was clearly upset?

Lynn's words in the garden came back to her. *I'm worried*

about Andrew, too. I don't know if you already know this. What might she already know – or not know – about Andrew? What was going on?

For a moment, she considered calling Lynn to find out what she'd meant. At the same time, she could ask her to check in on Mollie. But that would make Erica look pathetic and would make Mollie even more mad at her. The worst thing you could do to a teenager was treat them like a child. She closed her eyes and leaned back into the unyielding sofa bed. Exhausted and worried and baffled as she was, she still needed to get the energy from somewhere to make dinner for Ben. She opened her eyes to watch him with his letters. *You had no choice.* She told herself. *You had no choice.*

It was around the twins' second birthday that Mollie started to pull ahead of Ben in her milestones. When Erica had voiced her concerns, Andrew wasn't much help. 'You're overthinking it. They're just babies still. He gets there in his own time, doesn't he?'

He had been walking and playing, it was true. 'He doesn't point at things. Mollie points at what she wants. And she's stringing words together.'

He'd shrugged and laughed. 'Mollie's just forward for her age. She's clever. Like her mother. And why does he need to point? The women in his life pander to his every whim because he's handsome, like his father.'

Then he'd winked and kissed her and pulled her close. He'd made her think that it was all in her head. That she was worrying about nothing. He'd scoop up the children and make them giggle and she'd try to put it out of her mind that Mollie was picking up a little handbag and filling it with the things she wanted, chattering away to them and making tea with her little tea set while Ben preferred to sit with his blocks, lining them up, stacking them, getting upset if anybody tried to move them or him away.

However much Andrew tried to reassure her, however much she wanted to be reassured, she knew there was something different. It was always there, that nagging voice in her head. When she watched Ben, played with him, fed him, loved him... she just knew.

After watching him for a while, trying to gather her strength, she took a deep breath and pushed herself upwards out of the couch. 'How about a pizza, Ben?'

True to the way this day was going, there were no pizzas in the small freezer compartment. Though she had no spare cash to be splashing around, she couldn't leave Ben alone, so she'd have to order in. Before she could locate the menu for the local pizza place, her phone rang in the other room.

Flying back into the lounge, hoping it was Mollie, she snatched it up from the couch. When she saw the number, however, her heart sank. She didn't have the time or emotional energy to speak to her mother right now. She cancelled the call and let it go to what – she knew – would end up being a very long voicemail.

SEVEN

It wasn't until she woke the next morning at 6 a.m. that Erica remembered she needed to call her mother in New Jersey. It would be the early hours of the morning for her so she couldn't call now. Another black mark against her name. Since her father had passed away, she'd really tried to make peace with her mother. But why should she always be there to listen to her when her mom hadn't supported her?

When the twins were young, she'd been so envious of the women who had their family around them to help. Her mom was thousands of miles away and telephone conversations were always stilted and tricky. She didn't know why she'd even asked her opinion on Ben's development, but that's what mothers are supposed to be there for, isn't it?

As expected, hers hadn't even considered her concern. 'It's normal to worry when you're a mom. He'll be fine.'

'It's not just worry. I've checked the book and he should be walking by now.'

Her mom had just laughed. 'Put the book away. That was always your problem. Nose stuck in a book rather than the real world.'

Irritation bubbled at the age-old criticism she'd endured from her parents until the day she'd left college. Anyone else would be proud of their daughter for being the first in her family to go further than high school. 'Even without the book. Mollie is practically running around and he just watches her.'

There was another dismissive response to this. 'He's a boy. They're always lazy. He'll catch up and then he'll be away. You'll enjoy being a mom so much more if you just relax, honey.'

Relax? She'd wanted to say. Like you did?

As usual, Ben was already up and tipping cornflakes into a bowl. While he was occupied, she could grab a quick shower before getting him ready for school. Even though getting both kids ready for school and then going to work herself had been tough, when they moved here, she'd missed having something to get dressed up for herself. That's why she'd started volunteering at the local charity shop, although today she wished she could just go to Mollie. She couldn't let them down at the last minute, but she'd have to say she couldn't do tomorrow. With everything that had been going on, she'd totally forgotten about the Teacher Misconduct Panel she had to face on Thursday, too. She'd have to tell them that she needed the rest of the week off.

By the time they left the house, the sun was trying to push its way through clouds that looked as if they'd been spread across the sky with a child's paintbrush. 'Look at the clouds, Ben. Aren't they pretty?'

He followed her pointed finger upwards then resumed his focus on the ground ahead, his trainers thudding on the pavement with a steady beat. At thirteen, he was already taller than she was. With his father's solid torso and broad shoulders, it was like taking a man to school. His height and breadth made the world even more difficult. People assumed he was older than he was, so their expectations of his behaviour were always higher than even a child without his complex needs could live up to.

For Ben, with his limited speech and non-neurotypical way of processing social cues, it was impossible.

Today was the first day of Mollie's suspension. Once Ben was safely in school, she fired off a text.

Morning, sweetheart. How are you feeling?

When her phone pinged with the response a few minutes later, she was absurdly grateful to get a reply, even if it was a cursory *ok*. Parenting a teenage girl sometimes meant you had to make do with the crumbs of affection that were offered.

Because she walked there straight from school drop-off, Erica was always the first one at the shop each morning and they'd given her the keys to open up and get the kettle on. It suited her. This morning, she took the opportunity to call Andrew for an update. 'How's things? Is Mollie feeling any better?'

'She stayed in her room all last night. We had the opening to "Careless Whisper" about forty-seven times.'

That made Erica smile. When Mollie had decided to take up the saxophone, that was the one thing she'd asked her to learn. 'I'll look forward to hearing that. Has she said anything? Told you any more about the money?'

She still didn't want to use the word 'theft'. Not in connection with Mollie.

'Nope. I tried a couple of times last night and she just shut down. I've come into work this morning to clear anything urgent, but I've explained that I need to take the rest of today and tomorrow off for a family emergency.'

No way would he have told them the nature of the emergency and admit that his daughter had been suspended from school. Erica tried to keep the surprise from her voice. 'I thought you went into work yesterday afternoon? Couldn't you have done it then?'

There were a few beats of silence. 'Okay, Miss Marple. I wasn't sure yesterday that I was going to take the time off. On reflection, I think you were right, she does need someone at home.'

Had he just admitted she was right? Wonders would never cease. Although she wasn't convinced with his explanation about yesterday. It had seemed strange at the time that he'd gone into work on a Sunday. Had he not gone into work at all? But where had he gone? And why would he lie about it? 'I'm glad she's not on her own.'

'Actually, I was thinking I could bring her over to yours tonight. She could spend some time with Benjamin. That might soften her up a bit. Get her to talk.'

Another surprise. 'Good idea. And then maybe you could sit with Ben, and I could go for a walk with Mollie. She might open up more if we're not staring her in the face.'

It was an old technique she'd used as a teacher. When you had a child in for a detention and you wanted to get them to open up, the last thing that worked was to sit and look at them, waiting for a response. Far better to be tidying your classroom around them, giving them space to talk when they were ready.

She could almost hear him frown down the phone, imagine his heavy eyebrows hooding his dark-blue eyes. 'Do you think that's a good idea? If Mollie and I turn up together and then she leaves and he's left with just me, I don't think he'll be too happy. You know he doesn't like being left with me.'

Here he goes again, Erica thought. Why couldn't he understand? It wasn't that Andrew didn't spend time with Ben, it was that he seemed to expect their son to respond to him in the same way that Mollie did. It'd always been awkward between them and, now that they didn't live in the same house, it was even more difficult. 'You have to be the adult, Andrew.'

The sarcastic tone returned to his voice. 'Thanks, Miss. I'll try that.'

It irked her in the extreme when he accused her of talking to him as if he was one of her students. Especially when he was more likely to talk to her like a suspect. 'I'll see you later.'

'Actually, wait. While you're on the phone, have you seen this email from Ben's school?'

Of course she'd seen it. In fact, she'd seen it on Friday when it actually arrived. 'Yes, don't worry about that. I've already told them he can't go.'

There was a silence on the other end. 'What do you mean, he can't go? It's just a trip to the local café. Why can't he go?'

It annoyed her that he was still trying to be involved in decisions when she was the one living with Ben day to day and knew what he was capable of. 'I know what the trip is. But I don't think I'm allowed to do anything involved with schools or students at the moment.' Surely he realised this. Or was he just trying to make her say it?

'Hold on, let me read it again.' There was more silence while he brought up the email on his phone. 'Yep, I thought so. It doesn't say that parents have to be there.' He began to read aloud. 'This is the first in a series of trips for our next unit Living and Learning where students will be encouraged to complete independent daily tasks guided by their teachers and support staff.'

Sometimes he was so frustrating she could scream. 'I know what it says, Andrew, but I don't want Ben going out on a trip without one of us there.'

'It's a trip to a local café, Erica. What do you think is going to happen?'

How could he even ask her that question? He knew as well as she did why she was so concerned about this. 'If it's just a trip to a café, why is it so important to you that he goes?'

He spoke to her as if she'd lost her mind. 'Because as the letter says it's a step to becoming more independent. I'm assuming they'll take him into a café, show him how the menu works, teach him how to order what he wants.'

Was he for real? 'Are you listening to yourself? How's he going to order what he wants when he can't speak, Andrew?'

His voice turned as hard as steel. 'I'm pretty sure the teachers wouldn't be taking him if they didn't think he'd get something from it, Erica. Isn't that the whole point of us sending him to that school and paying those fees so that he can have experiences like this?'

Was it that he couldn't, or that he wouldn't, understand what she was trying to tell him? 'You know why I'm worried about this, Andrew. Don't make me spell it out again.'

'I do know why, oh, believe me, I know. But you can't continue to let your fear hold him back, Erica. What happened with that boy—'

'I don't want to talk about what happened with that boy!' Rehashing this with him again was the last thing she wanted to do. She lowered her voice. 'I have to go. The other staff are arriving. Just come over with Mollie tonight. She's our priority right now.'

His laugh was unkind. 'Oh really? Well, that'll be a first.'

After cutting the call, she banged her mobile phone up and down several times onto a pile of paperwork. Why was it always like this? Going around and around and back and forth and him never seeing things from her perspective? What was it going to take for him to realise that she was right about Ben?

EIGHT

Benjamin had been at the window, looking out for Mollie, for the last hour.

These were the moments when she felt cruel for keeping them in different homes, but the conversation with Andrew earlier reminded her how untenable it had become for them both to live together. As the rows got more frequent, her energy to fight had reduced until she just wanted to conserve whatever she had to focus on the children.

She knew they must have pulled up outside when Ben started to jump up and down, his excitement at seeing his sister palpable.

'Come on, then, Ben. Let's go get her.'

Though she didn't jump or flap her hands like he did, Mollie was just as pleased to see her brother. She held out her arms to him and gave him a brief, but tight, hug. 'Hi, Ben. What shall we do?'

She always greeted him like this, and he would take her hand and lead her away to show her his latest collection of pebbles or any other treasure that he'd collected since they were last together.

Andrew, forgotten on the doorstep, held up a hand which he waved at their disappearing backs. 'Hi, Ben. It's Dad.'

Erica stood aside to let him into the hallway. 'He's only got eyes for Mollie, you know that. Do you want a coffee? Only instant, I'm afraid.'

Why was she trying to make him feel better about being ignored? It wasn't as if he made the biggest of efforts to encourage Ben to want to spend time with him. Whenever he came to see Ben, she had to act as an interpreter, reminding Andrew how to approach things with him, what he liked to do, how best to communicate. Each time, it was as if Andrew expected him to have changed since his visit the previous week.

He followed her through to the kitchen. A tiny square of grey linoleum surrounded by white cupboards. Even if she'd had a posh coffee machine like his, there would've been nowhere to put it.

Propped up against the corner cupboard, his legs stretched halfway into the kitchen as he watched her fill the kettle and put it on. 'How was your day?'

'Okay. Quiet. But okay.'

'I can imagine. Only so many cardigans you can sell to old ladies. Are you missing teaching?'

'Yes. I am. Being in the classroom is... energising, I suppose. Hard work, but I like it.'

He nodded slowly. 'So, you'll go back? If everything goes well at the panel on Thursday?'

Before she could answer, Mollie appeared in the kitchen with Ben trailing behind her. 'Ben needs some biscuits.'

Though she was supposed to be in trouble, Erica couldn't help but smile. This is what Mollie would do when they were little. If she wanted something, she would say that Benjamin 'needed' it, learning quickly that Ben's needs were often top of their consideration. She reached behind her into the cupboard and brought out a packet of chocolate digestives – Ben's favourite – and passed them over. Then the two of them disappeared again.

A smile played on Andrew's lips. 'She misses him.'

Was he trying to make her feel guilty? She wasn't the one who'd suggested splitting the two of them up. 'I know. He misses her, too.'

Andrew looked down at his hands. Again, she noticed that he wasn't wearing his wedding ring. Should she have removed hers? Was that what you did when you were separated? It was such a fundamental part of her that she hadn't even considered removing it. 'How was *your* day?'

He shrugged. 'I couldn't stop thinking about this business with Mollie. I just don't understand it. I've dealt with enough petty thieves in my time: she's just not the type, is she?'

He wasn't going to get any arguments there. She'd been trying to work it out, too. 'If it was because she needed money, surely she'd ask one of us? I mean, what could she want to buy other than clothes or Frappuccinos?'

'That's what I don't understand. I tried to ask her again today but she just clams up. Won't say a thing. I've never seen her like this.'

'Let's go and sit with the kids, see if Ben can work his magic on her.'

In the living room, Mollie and Ben were sitting on the floor together and he was watching her braid some lengths of wool that he'd brought home from school. From when he was tiny, he'd loved any kind of thread or yarn. Even her pairs of tights weren't safe from him. He liked to tie them onto the door handles of the living room.

Watching the two of them together like this, Erica could taste the bittersweet nostalgia for when they were small. These days, especially with them living apart from one another, it was easy to forget that they were twins. Physically, they were pretty different.

Mollie's slim frame had started to change with puberty, but she was still tiny compared to Ben's solid, broad boyishness. Sometimes, though, in their smiles, she could see the connection between them.

Had they done the wrong thing in living apart? Seeing them side by side, she couldn't help but think that they might've done. But the school Ben was attending had been so good for him. And their residential buildings could provide somewhere for him to live someday when they could no longer care for him. When *she* could no longer care for him.

Mollie got to the end of the braid and Benjamin clapped then held out his hands for it. Watching her pass it over, Erica remembered how kind and generous Mollie had always been when they were small. Giving Ben first choice of their breakfast bowls, or picture books, or toys. Andrew used to get annoyed with Erica for not stepping in if Ben took something belonging to Mollie. But Mollie never seemed to mind. 'It's okay, Mummy. I can get another one.'

Andrew cleared his throat. 'What's that you've got, Ben. Can I take a look?'

Ben cupped the bright wool braid between his hands so that Andrew couldn't see it and shook his head.

Andrew looked at Erica for help and she tried her best. 'Show Dad, Ben. He wants to see how pretty it is.'

Mollie raised an eyebrow. 'If you're that desperate, I'll make you one.'

Erica assumed she was making a joke, but Andrew didn't seem to take it that way. 'I'm trying to talk to your brother, Mollie.'

Heading an argument off at the pass, Erica stood up. 'I didn't make you a drink, Mollie. Come out to the kitchen with me and I'll fix you something.'

Mollie looked so much calmer than she had yesterday that Erica didn't want to ruin the moment by asking her again about the money she'd taken from her teacher's handbag. But there wasn't really a choice.

'You know we need to talk about this, right?'

Mollie's face darkened. 'Can we not just leave this today?'

It was tempting. 'No. We can't. You have to talk to us at some point, Mollie.'

'I don't know what you want me to say!'

Never before had she raised her voice like this. They weren't a family who shouted at one another. Moody, stroppy, hormonal, yes; she could be all of those at times. But not this. Erica fought to keep her voice calm. 'We want to know why you took the money.'

'Because I needed it! Why else would I have taken it? I needed it, okay?'

Blazing with anger, her eyes burned into Erica, as if she were the one in the right here. How could she think that this was okay? *Stay calm. Stay calm.* 'And what did you need money for that you couldn't ask me or Dad to help with?'

'You wouldn't understand! Just let me sort it out for myself!' Mollie slammed her mug down onto the counter and left the room.

Erica closed her eyes and leaned against the sink. She was completely out of her depth here. How was she supposed to manage this? What wasn't Mollie telling her? Fear about what she might need that money for made her heart thud hard out of her chest. She was only just thirteen. Wrestling her mind away from the dark thoughts that threatened to overpower her, she tried to be rational, to not let her fear 'imprison' her as Andrew had accused her of once. This was Mollie. Their bright, beautiful, clever, kind and *sensible* daughter. All of the reasons a young woman might need money couldn't apply to her, could they? *Please God, don't let it be drugs or pregnancy or anything that could hurt her.*

She could feel Andrew's presence before she opened her

eyes. He closed the door behind him before he spoke. 'How did that go?'

Throat tight, eyes stinging, she threw up her hands in defeat. 'She won't tell me anything. It's like she hates me. The way she spoke, the look in her eyes...'

Her hand flew to her mouth to catch the sob she couldn't hold in. Seeing her tears, Andrew softened his voice. 'She won't talk to me either, Erica. It's not just you. I've tried everything I can think of to get her to open up. I got nothing.'

The paper towel she tore from the holder was rough and hard on her face as she blotted her tears and blew her nose. 'She did say that she needed the money. But she wouldn't tell me what for.'

In detective mode, Andrew's eyes narrowed. 'What exactly did she say?'

Closing her eyes to try and remember, all Erica could see was the red anger that'd come her way, burning her heart like fire. 'She said that she took the money because she needed it. That I wouldn't understand and that she needed to sort it out for herself.'

When she opened her eyes, the look on Andrew's face – Confusion? Dread? Fear? – made her even more terrified. He looked back in the direction Mollie had just gone, as if trying to trace her thoughts along the path of her footsteps. 'This could be really serious, Erica.'

If she'd had anything in her stomach, she probably would've thrown up right then and there. Unlike her, Andrew didn't jump to conclusions. He didn't let his mind unravel to the most catastrophic of outcomes. Even when he was wrong, he was absolutely one hundred per cent sure of himself. If he thought this was something really bad... She swallowed the acid in her throat. 'So what do we do now?'

He brought his eyes back in her direction. 'If she won't tell us anything, we have to find someone who might know. Her friends? Her teachers? Anyone else she might talk to?'

He was right. They couldn't just wait for Mollie to open up. If she wasn't prepared to tell them about the stealing, they were going to have to find another way to get to the bottom of it. 'Celeste is still at the school. She's on the Senior Leadership Team. I've told the shop that I can't come in tomorrow, so I can call her first thing and arrange a meeting?'

Andrew frowned. 'Celeste? I know she's your friend, but is she the right person to speak to?'

That was a strange thing to say. 'She'll know what's going on. I'd rather talk to her than anyone else at the minute.'

He pulled out his collar as if it was too tight. 'Do you want me to do the meeting? I mean, are you even allowed on the premises? You haven't been back there since...'

She shook her head to stop him speaking. 'This is different. I'm there as a parent. I want to go. But you can come with me if you like?'

An anxious expression crossed his face. 'I don't think we both need to be there. That might be overkill.'

She didn't agree, and she was nervous about setting foot in the school and who she might see, but she was more concerned about getting to the bottom of what was going on. Mollie had needed money so desperately that she'd stolen it from her teacher's handbag. Why hadn't she come to them? What could be so awful that she didn't think they'd understand? Whatever it was, Erica was going to find out and then she'd make it okay.

Even if that meant she had to walk back into that school again – the mere thought of which made her want to throw up on her kitchen floor.

NINE

MOLLIE

No one knows this, but the day Mum left I cried face down on my bed for about two hours.

Mum and Dad never argued in front of me, but that didn't mean I didn't know about it. One night last year, I could hear their voices coming through the ceiling into my bedroom. 'You're not listening to me,' Dad kept saying. 'You're not listening.' I don't know how Mum could not be listening because he was so loud.

We all went to look at Ben's new school together. It took ages in the car and Ben kept taking his seatbelt off. In the end, Dad pulled over and Mum came to sit in the back between me and Ben. It took forever to get there and I couldn't understand how they would be able to get him to school every day. Then a horrible thought hit me. 'We're not moving again, are we?'

When she shifted her position to look at me, Mum's eyes were full of tears. 'We're just going to look.'

That wasn't a no. 'I don't want to move again. I like our house. I don't want to go to another school.'

A new boy had joined our school a few months before and I'd felt so sorry for him, trying to fit in and find friends. There was no way I wanted to have to do that. And I did like my school. Especially now Mum didn't work there. I mean, it was okay when I first started – nice even – to have her around. But when all that stuff was going on with that boy and his parents, everyone was talking about it. Talking about her. People I didn't know – even some of the older kids – kept asking me where my mum was and why she wasn't in school. Had she been suspended? Arrested? What was happening? I got so sick of it.

'No one is talking about you going to another school.' Dad's voice from the front answered my question but seemed to be directed at Mum. She chewed at her lip rather than answer him.

It still wasn't enough. I wanted to hear it from her. Last time we moved, it had been her decision. I'd heard that through my bedroom floor, too. 'It was your choice to move here, Erica.'

'There was a fire, Andrew. It wasn't safe.'

I leaned forward in my seat so I could turn and look Mum in the face. 'We're not moving, are we?'

She shook her head and did that fake smile I hated. 'No one is going to force you to move anywhere, sweetheart.'

I didn't take in much about Ben's school apart from the fact it was big and bright and the classes only had about six children in them. The whole time we were being shown around, all I could think about was the prospect of moving again. Every part of me felt sick at the thought. I'd lose my friends, my teachers, my bedroom. No. I wasn't going to do it. I'd have to tell them that it wasn't fair.

And that's what I did. Back in April when Mum and Dad sat me down to explain what was happening.

Mum leaned forwards on the sofa, her hands together like she was praying. 'Ben needs a different school and we think the one we visited will be perfect for him.'

Immediately, I knew what was coming. Ben already went to

a different school from me, so there would be no need for this obvious set up to talk to me about him. 'Okay.'

'The school is an hour's drive away and you know how difficult he finds it to be in the car for long periods of time.'

Dad made a strange sound, but when I glanced at him he said nothing. Just continued to sit to the side of Mum and watch her speak, face like a stone. I turned back to her. 'What are you saying?'

Mum's eyes were really shiny and she chewed at her lip. It was getting more difficult to remember her as a teacher who would stride around school checking in on students, sharing a laugh with them. Ever since that school trip at Easter, she'd looked like this. As if she was scared of something. Even her clothes had changed. She used to wear bright floral dresses with trainers or skinny jeans with a shirt. These days she was never out of leggings and long shapeless t-shirts.

Now she glanced back at Dad before she got to the real point of why we were here. 'I'm going to rent an apartment, close to Ben's new school. I'll have to be there all the time for the first few months until he's settled in. And then maybe I'll go back and forth. It's all a bit up in the air at the moment. This place has come up for Ben and we needed a quick solution.'

Then Dad joined in. 'Mum will be able to come back anyway. At the new school, Ben can stay overnight sometimes so that we can do things together that we can't do when he's here.'

Mum stiffened. 'Not right away, obviously.'

Back and forth, each time they spoke my stomach felt tighter and tighter. Mum was leaving? 'Are you getting a divorce?'

'No, sweetheart. No. It's nothing like that.' Mum reached out for my hands. 'This is just something we need to do for Ben right now. It's not forever.'

Dad said nothing.

'I don't want to change schools. I don't want to move away.'

I was looking at Mum, but Dad answered. 'You don't need to. I'm staying right here. Nothing needs to change.'

But everything would change if Mum was gone. I searched her face to try and get to the truth. I could see how hard this was for her and I didn't want to make it worse, but... 'Do you really have to go? Is this because you're suspended?'

She swallowed. Then shook her head. 'No, it's nothing to do with that. It's because it will be so good for Ben. He needs this. You can come and stay with me whenever you want. I'll Face-Time you every night and I'll come back every week to visit you. I'm sorry, sweetheart. I know this is a lot, but I think we have to give it a try.'

The day she moved out, I couldn't watch her drive away. I gave her a hug and a smile and then told Dad I needed to go upstairs and I just laid down on my bed and cried.

Mum promised me that nothing would change, but it did. I couldn't think of anything to say when she FaceTimed me; it was so awkward. Things that I might've mentioned to her if she was here felt... weird to talk about when I was staring at her face on the screen.

Which is one of the reasons that I didn't tell her about Luca. When his friends told my friends that he fancied me. Or when he asked me out at the end of one lunch break. Or when I said yes and he became my boyfriend. Luca. Dark eyes, wide smile and that confidence that meant all of my friends were totally jealous that he wanted to be with me. That he'd chosen me from all the girls that wanted to be with him.

It felt really good to be someone's favourite.

TEN

ERICA

Tuesday was the second day of Mollie's suspension. There was already a standard 'Return to School' meeting booked for Wednesday morning, but when Erica had called Celeste last night, she'd said she had a free period just before lunch and told her to come in.

Erica hadn't been inside the school since before Easter. Before the residential trip. No one had told her explicitly that she couldn't set foot on school grounds, but she'd been suspended on full pay until the outcome of the investigation. How ironic that her suspension would be decided either way this same week.

Parking in the visitors' section felt strange, having to speak to the office on the intercom even stranger. The squeak of the heavy wooden door into reception was familiar, but the smell of paint and carpet adhesive was new. The entrance had had a refit since Erica was last there. The royal blue carpet and grey walls had a very corporate feel that she wasn't hugely keen on. From her seat on a square grey armchair, she scanned the newly displayed photographs for any students that she might recognise. It was a blend of nostalgia and self-torture, her stomach clenched in the hope that she wouldn't see him in any of them.

It was a relief that the receptionist was new and wouldn't recognise her. She was able to smile and take a seat rather than endure a polite catch-up on everything that had happened since she'd left. 'I'll let Miss Winters know that you're waiting.'

She and Celeste had arrived at the school at the same time – Erica taught English, Celeste taught computer science – and they'd hit it off straight away. Celeste had a sharp sense of humour that'd had Erica's shoulders shaking like they were two badly behaved students in their induction meeting. Back then, Erica hadn't had children, and they'd both been a regular feature of the group who decompressed after a week at the whiteboard with a visit to the local pub. Sometimes Andrew would come and meet her after work; he and Celeste got on well, too.

Since Erica had had the children, Celeste had been promoted twice and was now a member of the Senior Leadership Team. It was funny to think of her being so important. If Erica hadn't had so much to deal with at home, would she have been promoted in the same way? Would she have even wanted it?

The door to the side of reception swung open and Celeste flew through with her arms ready to engulf Erica in a tight squeeze. 'Hello! Sorry, I was meant to be waiting to welcome you.' She lowered her voice. 'Are you okay? Is it weird being here?'

Erica smiled as she released her. 'Very. Thanks so much for seeing me on such short notice.'

'Don't be silly. I've been meaning to call you about something, actually, but time just runs away, doesn't it? Let's sign you in.'

Following in Celeste's wake to her office, Erica couldn't help but admire her friend. Celeste was one of those women who always have everything under control, never look stressed, always have a smile for everyone. Her long blonde hair ended in a perfectly straight line at her shoulders. Her make-up was subtle and flawless, crisp suit and black wedges plain but probably expensive. It wasn't surprising that she'd been made responsible for overseeing the pastoral team working on student behaviour: no student was stupid enough to take her on. More importantly, she was so universally liked that they didn't want to.

Her stride was almost twice Erica's and she spoke as fast as she walked. 'So, how have you been?'

'I'm holding it together. Well, I was until this happened, too. I'm sorry I haven't been in touch. Things have been tough.'

She waved away Erica's words. 'Don't apologise. You've had more than enough to be dealing with. How's Ben? Does he like the new school?'

Celeste was glancing left and right as they walked. Maybe Erica wasn't supposed to be here? 'He's doing great. Look, I'm not going to get you into trouble by coming in, am I?'

A shake of the head was followed by a blush that contradicted it. 'I did double-check with the head that it would be okay. I've had to promise not to talk about anything other than Mollie.'

Nerves at being here weren't helped by the corridors that brought back a host of memories as they made their way to Celeste's office. Photographs of smiling students on the wall wearing science goggles or throwing javelins or painting on canvas. As they turned the corner, she spotted one of Mollie.

The photograph had been taken in her first year. Only two years ago and yet she looked so different. This Mollie was a child, bright-eyed and enthusiastic. The Mollie of now was pushing firmly on the door of womanhood and, this week at least, looked as if she'd had every ounce of enthusiasm squeezed from her.

Celeste's office was small but she'd managed to stamp her personality onto it. The walls were purple and all the stationery on the desk in the centre of the room matched it perfectly. 'How the heck did you get John to paint it this colour?'

John, the site manager, was well known for his firm belief that there should be one colour palette throughout the school: a kind of orangey magnolia not seen anywhere else on earth. The door clicked shut behind them. 'I didn't ask him. I just did it myself. Do you like it?'

'It's great.'

Erica took the seat she was offered and Celeste slid into her own on the other side of the desk. 'So. How's Mollie doing? Has she told you anything else about the incident?'

Celeste was being very tactful by using the word 'incident' rather than 'theft'. Now it was Erica's turn to blush. 'No. She won't talk about it at all. I really don't know what to do. She's just completely closed off about it. What do you think happened?'

Last night in bed, she'd gone through all the possible reasons that Mollie might need money. Now she was fully expecting to be told that Mollie was having friendship issues, or maybe even a problem with a boy. She'd been a teacher; she knew what happened at this age.

But Celeste shook her head. 'I asked around her teachers and there's nothing. No evidence of anything changing. She's a model student. Working hard. Polite. Engaged. Everything you could want.'

It made no sense. Erica knew that there weren't always tell-tale signs when a student was going through something. Girls, in particular, were very good at putting on a brave face and pretending to the world that they were fine. Still, this didn't help her to uncover what'd been going on. 'Really? No one? Not even her English teacher, Miss Martin?'

Mollie loved her English teacher, would often hang around

after class to tell her what she was reading or show her the latest poem she'd written. That's what made it even more incredible that she was the one Mollie had stolen from. Of anyone, Erica might have expected that Miss Martin would know what was going on behind Mollie's smile.

But Celeste was shaking her head. 'No, I asked Sarah Martin and she was just as blindsided as everyone else. No one can believe that Mollie stole the money. Sarah offered to speak to her, but I said to hold off until I'd met with you.'

It might be a good idea, but the way Mollie had looked last night, now was possibly not the right time. 'What about the other teachers? Is there anything going on in Mollie's cohort?'

Celeste raised an eyebrow. 'There's plenty going on in that cohort, but not to do with Mollie. The only thing that we can think of was that Mollie seemed pretty disappointed that she didn't get the school council role.'

School council? That didn't make sense. 'But she's too young. Why would she be applying for that?'

'It's one of the ideas from the new deputy head. He's trying to address some of the lethargy by giving the younger students some status and responsibility.'

Mollie hadn't mentioned that at all. 'I didn't even know that she'd applied.'

Surprise flashed across Celeste's face, but she spoke quickly to smooth over the hurt in Erica's voice. 'It was only a couple of weeks ago. Maybe she hadn't got around to it. Look, it might be a good idea for you and Andrew to come and talk to her tutor. Between the three of you, maybe there's something we're missing. You'll have a back-to-school interview tomorrow morning, won't you?'

Again, Erica felt her face redden. Back-to-school interviews were for the misbehaving kids. Not for her Mollie. 'Yes. I think that was on the letter that Andrew showed me.'

Celeste narrowed her eyes. 'How are things between you and Andrew?'

How to sum it up in a word? 'Civil?'

Celeste sat back in her chair. 'And are you... I mean... Tell me if I'm prying, but are things really over between the two of you? It was all so sudden. You moving out with Ben. Is that really the end of your marriage?'

If she was surprised by the directness of Celeste's question, she could understand it. Every time Celeste had seen them, Andrew had been the model husband. In many ways he *was* a model husband. Then she thought about the way he'd spoken to her yesterday. The fact that he wasn't wearing his wedding ring. 'To be honest, I don't know what's happening right now.'

Celeste nodded. 'Look, I've wanted to tell you something, not known quite how to raise it.'

The serious look on her face increased the temperature in the room by a few degrees. But before Erica could ask what it was, there was a knock on the door and Celeste raised her chin and the volume of her voice. 'Come in.'

The door was pushed open roughly and the face that came around it made Erica gasp. It wasn't possible. Mussed dark hair, untucked shirt: the boy's sullen stance was echoed in his voice. 'Miss Clarke says I have to come and work with you.'

Unable to tear her eyes away, Erica held her breath. No. It couldn't be him. It couldn't. Her eyes must be playing tricks on her.

Celeste pointed back out of the room. 'Okay, Michael, you can work at the desk outside. I'll come and speak to you in a moment.'

He didn't move to go. 'She said I was being rude but all I said was—'

'Michael.' Celeste's voice was firm, but not unkind. 'You can see that I'm in a meeting. I will come and speak to you, but you are going to have to start work and I'll be out there shortly.'

His scowl took Erica right back to that day. Once he'd closed the door, she stared at Celeste, waiting to be told that she'd imagined it. 'That boy...'

'His brother. They're like clones of one another. In every way.'

Erica felt cold. 'And is the mother...'

'Still a nightmare? Yes. She has a new boyfriend at the moment, so we haven't seen much of her. Michael is having a rather tough time here, although he does have to make his own dinner every night and he's up on his Xbox until the early hours so it's not surprising that school and following rules is rather a struggle.' She paused. 'Obviously, I shouldn't have said any of that. Old habits die hard with you in here.'

Erica smiled weakly; her heart rate was still slowing down. 'Looking at him... it just brought it all back.'

Celeste tilted her head to the side sympathetically. 'I can imagine. I'm sorry. Just really bad timing.'

Now the shock had left her, Erica felt a coldness she couldn't shift. 'It's Thursday, you know. The panel.'

Celeste had already said that she couldn't talk about it, but she leaned forward and lowered her voice. 'It wasn't your fault, Erica. You know that, right? Whatever they say, it wasn't anyone's fault.'

Her head knew that, but her stomach didn't. Even the thought of what happened that day made a shiver run down her spine. Swallowing down the lump in her throat, Erica tried to smile. 'Well, I'd better go and leave you to speak to him. What was it you wanted to talk to me about?'

For the first time, Celeste looked uncertain and nervous. 'Actually, it's not important. I really should get to Michael. Shall I call you in the week? Maybe we could go out and have a proper catch-up?'

Who knew when she'd be able to get a night off? But she

smiled. 'That would be great. Maybe you could come to me? It's difficult for me to get out because of Ben.'

Celeste frowned. 'Has he stayed over at the new school yet?'

She shifted in her seat: she hadn't come here to talk about Benjamin. 'Not yet. He's not ready.'

'What about you? Are you ready?'

Her friend knew her well. 'You're beginning to sound like Andrew.'

Pushing her chair back on its wheels, Celeste held up her hands. 'Ignore me. I just miss my pal.'

'I miss you, too.'

And she missed being here. She missed having a life when she was just 'Erica' and not someone's mum or estranged wife. But seeing that boy outside Celeste's office was a stark reminder. She'd seen what could happen if you took your eye off of someone else's child and she couldn't risk that for Ben. He needed her and that's where she had to be.

ELEVEN

Children were flooding out of the doors of the building as she left. A sea of smiles and shouts and girls with linked arms and boys kicking footballs. An hour for lunch to decompress before going back to their classrooms.

How different would their lives have been if Benjamin had been one of these boys? If her day had consisted of just dropping both children off together in the morning, feeling confident that they would have a good – or at least satisfactory – day? Having been a teacher all her life, that's what she'd assumed school would be for her kids. Ordinary. When she'd found out they were expecting twins, she'd actually congratulated herself that school logistics would be a walk in the park.

She'd never forget the look on Andrew's face when he discovered she was carrying twins. Absolute shock, his mouth a perfectly round circle of disbelief, followed by a smile that spread across his face like jelly.

'Twins? Oh my... that's amazing. It's amazing, right?'

He'd looked at her for confirmation that she was just as pleased as he was before reaching across her gel-covered stomach to kiss her. She had no idea what the sonographer thought of that. But Erica hadn't been able to stop smiling either. 'Yes. It's absolutely terrifying, but it's amazing.'

When they discovered in a later scan that not only was it twins, but that they were expecting one of each, he'd been even more ecstatic. By then, Erica was getting heavier and more tired, so she was less ebullient, but it was really exciting. If only she'd known then how different her two babies' lives would be.

'Erica?'

She turned in the direction of a soft voice to see Mollie's best friend, Amelia. 'Hi. How are you?'

Amelia shuffled from one foot to the other, clearly embarrassed to be talking to an adult in the middle of the courtyard. 'I'm okay. How's Mollie? I was worried when I heard about... you know.'

Maybe she didn't want to mention the suspension, but Erica was surprised at the question. 'Haven't you spoken to her?'

Amelia shook her head. 'She won't answer my messages.'

Another layer of anxiety wrapped itself across Erica's shoulders. Mollie was addicted to that phone. Surely she would want to speak to her friend? Although there might be a reasonable explanation. 'Maybe her dad took her phone. I'm not sure.'

Amelia looked relieved at the possibility. 'Oh, that makes sense. Can you say hi to her for me? I've got to go now. I need to see my food tech teacher before the next lesson because I've forgotten my ingredients.'

'Of course. She'll be back tomorrow and I'm sure she'll be really pleased to see you.'

Amelia didn't look convinced of that, but she gave a little wave and a small smile as she left. Erica wanted to ask her what she knew, or suspected, about the money Mollie had taken. But she didn't want to fuel gossip by talking to her about it in front of all these other students. For a start, Mollie would be mortified and it was also probably a child protection issue to have an adult grilling one of the students on school premises. She wasn't a teacher here at the moment.

Before pulling out of the car park, she called Andrew with an update. No answer. Why wasn't he waiting for her call? Then she tried Mollie. Same thing. Were they in the middle of something?

Across the road, an older woman was pushing a stroller with a young child in it. She must be the grandmother. Erica watched as she smiled and chatted to the child who was wriggling and laughing. Envy squeezed at her. How much easier might her life have been if she had a bigger support network here. If she had family. It was her choice to move over to the UK all those years ago and the freedom of being away from home had been intoxicating to begin with. Her American accent had ensured that it was easy to spark up a conversation: people were always interested in where you were from and why you were here. And then she'd met Andrew and decided to stay.

But she hadn't reckoned on how isolating it would be to have twins with no family around to help out. Andrew's mother was elderly and lived two hours away with his sister. His father – also a police officer – had passed away before the children were born and, in the sixteen years she'd lived in the UK, Erica's parents had never been to visit.

The main reason that she and Andrew had decided on such a small wedding – his family, some of their friends, a registry office and then fish and chips at a local restaurant – was that her parents had decided not to come. Her father was a flat refusal; her mother had mentioned something about throwing them a party 'when you're back home'. It didn't seem to matter how many times she'd said that England was her home now. Erica had been grateful that her brother, Joe, had made the trip, but the poor guy had had to field questions from everyone as to why their parents hadn't come.

In a slightly freakish coincidence, her mother chose that

moment to call again. Regardless of Erica's greeting, and the caller display, she started the telephone conversation as she always did. 'Hi, Erica, it's only me. Mom.'

Waiting for Andrew to call her back, Erica wanted to leave her line open. 'Hi, Mom. I'm kind of in the middle of something right now. Can I call you later?'

There was a dramatic sigh at the other end. 'You're always in the middle of something. What am I supposed to do if I need to speak to you?'

Maybe the same thing as I had to do when I needed you, she wanted to say.

As soon as she'd had the first scan, and found out that she was expecting twins, she'd called her mom. Even though she'd sounded pleased and excited for her, as soon as Erica had asked about her parents coming to visit near the time of the birth, the hesitance was back in her voice. 'Oh, honey. It's such a long flight and you know that travelling is tricky for your father these days.'

Under normal circumstances this would've been irritating; pregnancy hormones made it likely that she'd burst into tears with disappointment. Erica had tried to not let her mother hear that. 'You could come on your own if Dad can't make it?'

In fact, that would've been preferable. Without her father there, her mom could've helped out, shown her the ropes of having a baby, rather than just sat on the sidelines telling her that she was doing it wrong, which had always been her father's standard position for any of them.

Her mom's voice had taken on that conciliatory tone she'd heard so many times before. 'Well, we'll see how it goes, shall we?'

Immediately she'd known that that'd meant *no*. That day, it was like a door shut in her heart. She'd managed to make her peace with them not attending her wedding. But if her parents couldn't come when she was having a baby – having two babies

– then she'd needed to face facts. Other than her brother – who had moved to the other side of the States by that time and was understandably busy with his own wife and kids – Andrew and the children were her only family now.

Despite all of their history, she still felt guilty when her mother called. Even more so since her father had passed away. 'What is it you need, Mom?'

The deep sigh at the other end of the line made her grip the phone tightly in frustration. 'Your cousin Ruth tells me that you're not coming home for her wedding.'

She'd been expecting this call. 'I can't, Mom. I have the children.'

'Bring the children with you. I'd love to see them. It's been years, Erica.'

It'd been twelve years. The only time her mother had seen the twins was when they were fourteen months old and she and Andrew had endured a transatlantic flight with them only to be treated like an irritation in a house that was governed by her father's preference for order and silence.

'The children are in school and Ben won't be able to cope with the flight. You could come here if you want to see them?'

By this point, it was practically a rhetorical question. Any hopes she'd had that, after her father passed away, her mom would make the trip to see them had quickly been quashed. As it was today. 'You can't expect me to travel all that way on my own.'

She bit her lip to prevent herself from saying that her mom had been more than capable of flying across the country to stay with her brother, because her mom sounded upset and she wasn't cruel. 'It's just not possible for me to come right now. The children need me. I'm sorry.'

Her mom sniffed at the other end of the line. 'I'm sorry, too. Since your father passed, I need support. When he left you that money, I thought you'd use some of it to come home.'

The emotional blackmail was so obvious it almost had subtitles. The money her father had left her in his will had been a welcome surprise. Without it, they'd never have been able to afford the fees at Ben's school. For a while, she'd carried the guilt of not returning home for his funeral. But Ben hadn't been on a plane since they'd made a trip to Spain when the twins were five. It'd been disastrous. Ben's ears had hurt him the whole way there. He'd moaned and kicked his legs and the looks – and comments – from other passengers had been excruciating. No, there was no way she could fly back to the US with the twins and no way she was leaving Ben while she flew there alone. Just as she wouldn't now. 'Can't you call Joe?'

'Your brother is very busy. You know how demanding his job is. He works for the government, Erica. He can't just drop everything.'

She definitely didn't have the energy for the Joe PR Tour. It was a good job that he was such an easygoing nice guy, or her mother's obvious preference would've made her hate him. Thankfully, her phone beeped to rescue her. 'Mom, I have another call coming in and it might be Mollie. I'll call you later on, okay?'

The incoming call was Andrew and he sounded distracted. 'How did you get on at the school? What did Celeste have to say?'

'Not much. They're just as perplexed as we are. Up until the theft, there was no indication that she was struggling or unhappy and they've not picked up on any rumours from the students of anything going on.'

That was often the best way to find out what was happening. Teachers who had good relationships with their classes were often privy to information that was doing the rounds. Sometimes students would talk about it in your classroom in the hope that you would overhear and ensure matters were taken in hand without them having to snitch and tell you about it directly.

'What do we do now, then? Just keep her grounded until she tells us what's happening or why she did it?'

That sounded draconian and counterproductive. Their daughter was as stubborn as a mule. 'We need to sit down with her together. We've only got this afternoon and evening because she's back at school tomorrow and I want to get to the bottom of this before we have the meeting with her teacher in the morning.'

She was dreading sitting in the back-to-school meeting looking like a clueless parent who had no idea what was going on in her daughter's life. Even if she actually was a clueless parent who had no idea what was going on in her daughter's life.

'Actually, I've had to pop into work.'

'What? You said you were staying home with her?'

'I know. But I'm a Detective Inspector, Erica. Something important came up and I had to come in. I can't just drop everything right this minute. I'll speak to Mollie tonight.'

His comments set her teeth on edge like a dried-out marker on a whiteboard. She knew – oh, she knew – that he had an important job. She was the one who'd had to give up all hopes of promotion in her own career to fit her life around the children, around Ben. Andrew's progression through the ranks had continued, uninterrupted by appointments with doctors and teachers and specialists. It was an effort not to weigh down her words with irritation. 'I think we should do it together.'

'Look, I need to go, Erica. When I get home, I'll call you.' He coughed. 'Did Celeste mention anything else?'

There was something behind this question that she couldn't grasp. 'Like what?'

'Nothing. Just making sure that I'm up to speed on everything. And, seriously, if you need me to talk to Mollie on my own tonight, it's fine. I know how difficult it is for you to drop everything.'

Anyone else might think he was being thoughtful, but there was no mistaking his tone. 'I'll be there later.'

He'd gone before she'd had a chance to ask whether he'd heard from Mollie in the last hour and whether she had her phone. She tried her one more time before throwing her own phone onto the passenger seat, pulling out of the car park and heading for the motorway.

She'd pick up Ben from school, then go straight to the house to see her daughter. If she wouldn't open up, Erica would have to take her phone and see what was on it. Call her friends. Do whatever it took to get to the bottom of all of this.

TWELVE

Collecting Ben from his new school was a far nicer experience than when he'd been in a mainstream setting. Back then, she'd often have the dreaded walk to speak to his teacher at pickup time. More than once, when he was wriggling to get out of her iron grasp, arms or legs flailing, she'd heard another mother whisper, 'You'd think a teacher would know how to control her kids.'

Here, the other parents were quite possibly the least judgemental people on the planet. And there were fewer of them. Class sizes were smaller and a lot of the students came to school on a minibus from towns around the area. Erica hadn't got to know any of the other parents yet, but she knew from listening to conversations on the playground how many of them were single moms. Raising a child with special needs was not exactly easy on a marriage. Look at what had happened to hers. Sometimes, in the middle of the night on that uncomfortable sofa bed, she'd play the last thirteen years as a film track in her head and try to work out the point it happened. When did it start to go wrong?

The day she and Andrew brought the children home to

their small starter home, the sun had shone like a blessing. Helping Erica from the car first, then returning to collect the twins – tiny in their brand-new car seats – Andrew was practically bursting with pride. She honestly didn't think it was possible for a human being to be happier than she was that day.

As she'd already guessed, looking after two babies at once was no walk in the park. No new mother is prepared for the life-changing whirlwind of a newborn. But having twins added another dimension. There was no 'sleeping when the baby sleeps' or 'pick up and put down' or any of the other trite advice people threw at her when she staggered through those first weeks like a bleary-eyed zombie with a hangover. There were times that the twins would tag team all night, seemingly hell-bent on ensuring that she didn't get more than a handful of snatched minutes of sleep.

But at other times, when the stars aligned, she'd feed them both simultaneously and then sit in the glow of the night light – a precious baby in each of her arms – and marvel at the perfection of them. Cupped in each hand, their warm heads with a soft down of hair, their spines running along the inside of her arms, their diapers – or nappies as she was learning to say – soft in the crook of her elbow. They were so beautiful. Shadows cast by the night light accentuated their delicate features. Long eyelashes brushed the tops of their cheeks, button noses that begged to be kissed, the cupid's bow of their perfect pink lips.

Andrew was great back then. As soon as he got home from work, he'd be itching to be with the children. But there was so much he couldn't do. Even though it'd been tough, Erica had been determined to breastfeed both of them. The birth hadn't gone the way she'd hoped. After Mollie had been born, there'd been some complications and Ben's heart rate had dropped. They'd had to rush her in for an emergency C-section. Even now, she thought about that. Did it make any difference to him?

Because of that, she hadn't given up on the breastfeeding,

even when she was so sore one evening that she'd just cried and cried.

Andrew had tried to help. 'Why don't I make up a bottle? Just for tonight?'

'No.' She wouldn't hear of it. 'I have to do this.'

'What about if you express some milk, then? At least that way I can do the night feed tonight? You can get some rest?'

She hadn't wanted him to get up in the night. He'd had so much on back then, studying for his sergeant exams and working ridiculous hours. She hadn't wanted him getting up with the children when he had to drive the next day. After all, she had the luxury of a whole year's maternity leave. Although, the word 'luxury' seemed a misnomer some days.

Mostly, though, she remembered the joy of that first year. The first smiles and giggles. The knowledge that, however upset they were, she could make things better just by holding them close. And sometimes – when they were asleep together on the rug, curled together like a pair of parentheses – her heart was so full that it pushed warm tears from her eyes.

If only it was that easy to keep them both safe now.

The main school doors opened onto the playground and the younger students flooded out first. Then it was time for the older classes. Ben was the third one out. Head down, he plodded towards Erica's smile and held out a large piece of paper. His teacher was right behind him. 'Ben wanted to bring his work home to show you.'

Meeting the teacher at the end of the day held no fear here. It was always a positive exchange, even if Ben had had a difficult day. The teachers here were looking for progress in different ways; not confined to the measurements she'd been used to as a teacher in a mainstream school. 'That looks great, Ben!'

He passed her a sheet of paper with pictures of food cut from magazines. His teacher explained, 'They're the things Ben wants to buy when we go to the café next week. We're looking forward to it, aren't we, Ben?'

Anxiety fluttered in Erica's stomach. After seeing Celeste today, she felt even more worried about letting Ben go on a school trip without her watchful eye. It wasn't that she didn't trust the teachers – they were amazing – it was that she knew all too well how easily things could go wrong.

Taking Ben's hand, she smiled at the teacher. She had time to sort out the details of this trip another day. 'Thanks. That's great.'

They were halfway home from school when Erica's phone buzzed in her hand. They'd reached the house with the pebbledash wall which Ben loved. He would run his fingertips over the stones stuck into the concrete, transfixed by the sensation of the smooth stones in their rough setting. She used to worry that the owner would come out and ask what he was doing, but they'd never seen anyone and it wasn't as if Ben was doing any harm.

When she picked up, Andrew sounded annoyed. 'Hi, it's me. Have you collected Mollie from the house?'

Her heart skipped a beat. Had she said she'd do that? 'No. Was I supposed to?'

Ben's focus was still on the stones, his face a picture of innocent enjoyment. At moments like this, it was impossible to see him as anything but a vulnerable soul who needed to be protected from the world.

'No. But I've got back home and she's not here.'

That was a relief; at least she hadn't failed again. 'Maybe she's gone for a walk?'

He sounded irritated. 'I expressly told her she had to stay home. She can't be grounded and then be swanning around with her friends.'

The way she'd looked yesterday, Mollie didn't seem as if she wanted to be swanning anywhere. It was understandable that she might need some fresh air, something to do. Still, it was unusual for her to go out without permission. Or was it? In the last three months, those rules had been down to Andrew, not her. 'She's probably just having a walk around the block. Have you checked the Life360?'

When Mollie had first started to go out with her friends a few months ago, they'd installed an app on her phone so that they could see where she was. It'd felt terrifying letting her go out to the park without any adult supervision – unfortunately for her, having a teacher and a police officer for parents meant they'd seen and heard too much about the dangers for young girls in the local area – but they knew that they had to let her build her independence. The app on her phone had been a compromise.

An exaggerated sigh at the other end of the phone conveyed Andrew's annoyance at the stupidity of her suggestion. 'Of course I've checked it. She's got Battery Saver on.'

Knowing that this might incur further ridicule, she still had to ask. 'What does that mean?'

'If she's turned on Battery Saver, the app can't access her location.'

That didn't sound good. 'Do you think she's done that on purpose?'

His humourless laugh was a dry cough. 'It's quite a coincidence if she hasn't.'

Icy fingers of fear clutched at Erica. 'Why would she do that?'

Another sigh. 'I assume it's because she doesn't want us to know where she is. Why else?'

But that made no sense. There was nowhere she could think of that Mollie would go that she'd want to keep a secret from them. The only places she was allowed to go were the park or to her friends' houses and they wouldn't be home from school yet, would they? She tried to breathe through the creeping anxiety. 'She must be on her way to Amelia's house. Or to meet her from school. Or one of the others.'

Amelia had said that Mollie wasn't returning her calls. But if she wasn't speaking to her, who would she be speaking to?

Andrew practically growled. 'She'd better not be.'

As always, he was coming at this from the opposite direction, more concerned with Mollie's disobedience than her safety. 'Let me call Amelia's house. She's probably over there right now.'

She hoped that she was right. Yet somewhere in the pit of her stomach, instinct told her that there was more to this than met the eye. Why was Mollie not telling them what was going on? Surely this couldn't all be about her missing out on a place on the school council?

And where was she?

THIRTEEN

MOLLIE

All week, I'd been waiting for the results to come out. First, they said it was going to be Wednesday, then Thursday, then it was Friday morning and I got a text from Amelia to say they were definitely going to be out today.

My stomach flipped over in anticipation. Since I'd started at the school, I'd wanted to be on the school council. No one knows this, but I've kept a notebook with everything I've ever achieved – hockey captain, academic colours, test scores – so that I had a list of things ready to put on my application when I got to that stage. Plus, I've helped out at every school event that asked for volunteers, I always hand in my homework early and I've never ever had a detention.

Dad was fiddling with his mid-life crisis coffee machine when I got downstairs and he glanced up at me. 'All ready for school? I can drop you on my way to work if you like?'

He doesn't know that I applied to be on the school council. Neither does Mum. I nearly told her on the phone last night. She was asking about school and how things were going. I gave her the usual reply – 'It's fine, nothing new' – and crossed my fingers that there would be news today. If she'd asked again, pushed a little more, I might've told her. But immediately she moved on to telling me about Ben and how well he was getting on at his school. As she talked, I imagined coming home with the school council badge on display on my uniform, waiting for her amazement that I'd been selected when she knew nothing about it.

Dad was still looking at me, waiting for an answer. 'No, I'm fine thanks. I want to walk in with Amelia.' I grabbed a pastry from the cupboard and let him pull me in to kiss the top of my head before the hiss of the machine made us both jump.

Amelia met me halfway between our houses and she threaded her arm through mine. 'I bet you've got it. You're so clever, they're bound to have picked you.'

Was it bad that I thought she was right? I'd never have admitted that to anyone. No one likes a girl who pushes herself forward, do they? I had to pretend not to care about it when I did. I really, really did. 'No, it'll be you. All your sports and drama stuff. It'll be you.'

We practically ran into the school gates to find the results that'd been posted on the student news noticeboard. I was so nervous for the result. I know that everyone thinks that school is easy for me because I get high marks. But I have to work so hard to stay at the top. Whenever we have a test, everyone in my class expects me to get the highest score. No one even says well done anymore. But if I slip up? Everyone is there for it.

Except Amelia. She gets it. She knows how much I work. Which is why it hit me so hard when we saw the list of school councillors, scanning the list until we got to her name. Amelia had been selected.

Within moments, a small crowd was wishing her well. Telling her congratulations. I just stood there, like an idiot. Frozen to the spot.

I know that I should be happy for her. She's my best friend. What does it say about me that I was so jealous that I just wanted to stamp my feet and cry? What does she have that I don't? My grades are better. I work harder. Is it because she's much prettier than me? She has this perfect smile and great skin and her eyelashes look like she's curled them even when she hasn't. She'll look great in all the photos that go up in reception. Better than I would.

Of course, I pretended to be happy for her. I grinned like a loon and hugged her and bit into the side of my cheek to stop myself crying. I don't think anyone realised how awful I felt inside. It was such a relief when Luca arrived. His smile made me feel a little better. He must've realised how disappointed I was as he whispered in my ear, 'They should've chosen you.' I'm so glad I have him. At least I am someone's favourite.

When I got home that night, Dad was already there. He was distracted about something, waiting for a phone call, he said. I wanted to make a call myself. To Mum. However preoccupied she was, I knew that she'd understand how I felt about the school council. Once I'd got changed out of my uniform, I planned to go downstairs and get a snack, then call her.

Fifteen minutes later, I had my foot on the top stair, about to go and see what was in the fridge, when I heard Dad on his phone. Something in his tone made me pause, hold my breath. Listen. And what I heard changed my mind about everything. From then on, Mum was the last person I wanted to talk to.

FOURTEEN

ERICA

It'd taken a lot of persuasion, and the promise of ice cream at home, to move Ben away from the pebbles in the wall. The ice cream had the added benefit – when combined with his favourite cartoons on the TV – of keeping him occupied so that Erica could speak to Amelia.

Though she missed Mollie dreadfully, and hated this tiny apartment, it was actually easier to look after Ben on her own. Andrew had always pushed her to react differently, expecting too much from their son. For a long time, he wouldn't even accept that Ben had additional needs. He kept saying that he just needed more time to catch up. He'd try to push Ben to do more and then wonder why it ended so badly. Now, when it was just the two of them here, she could make things work so that Ben could cope. And once Ben was okay, that gave her some freedom to do the things that other people took for granted. Like make a phone call.

Mollie and Amelia had spent enough time at each other's houses for Erica to have her mom Kirsty's telephone number stored. In another life, she and Kirsty – a no-nonsense Scot with a sharp sense of humour – may have been good friends. But

Erica had had to turn down offers of a glass of wine whenever she collected Mollie because she always needed to get back to Ben in the car.

Still, she seemed pleased to hear from her. 'Hi, Erica. Long time no speak. How's things at your new place?'

Either Amelia hadn't told her about Mollie's suspension – unlikely – or she was being very tactful. 'I'm fine, yes, thanks. I'm actually trying to track down Mollie. Is she with you?'

The one beat of silence confirmed it had been tact. 'No. I thought she was... at home.'

Home. A word with such a simple meaning yet such huge implications. Erica had no idea where her actual home was these days. 'Yes, she was, but she's decided to take herself off somewhere and we don't know where she is. Would you mind if I had a quick word with Amelia? Just to find out if she might have any idea where she's gone?'

It was excruciating. Admitting that she had no clue where her daughter might be. At least Kirsty hadn't been one of that group who'd discussed – pretty openly – how awful they thought she was for leaving her daughter. On a WhatsApp group, apparently. With no mention of the fact that her daughter was actually living with her father. He, according to the one mum who'd told her what was said, had been praised for being such a great dad.

'Of course.' She could hear Kirsty's breath change as she walked the phone to wherever her daughter was. Probably safely in her bedroom. 'I'll just find her for you.'

Girlfriends could be tricky for some teenagers. Over the years, Erica had seen first hand how best friendships could implode quite quickly – and nastily – and cause a lot of hurt. When Mollie met Amelia, they got very lucky. Not only was she both kind and polite, she had the kind of outgoing person-ality that really brought Mollie out of her shell. The two of them had been inseparable since their first day at school and it wasn't long before they were meeting up at weekends, arranging sleepovers and texting back and forth late into the night. If anyone knew where Mollie was, it would be Amelia.

There was some mumbling at the other end and then a hesitant voice came on the line. 'Hi, Erica.'

Erica tried to keep her own voice upbeat and light, not wanting to worry the girl. 'Hi, Amelia. It was nice to see you earlier. I'm actually looking for Mollie. I don't suppose you've seen her?'

On the phone, her voice sounded like that of a little girl. At thirteen, they all thought they were grown up, but they really weren't. 'No, sorry. Like I said earlier, I haven't heard from her since... since she left school on Friday. After I saw you today, I tried to call her again, but she's still not answering.'

Erica didn't want to panic her, but she was starting to feel pretty worried herself. 'Do you know anyone else she might have gone to see?'

There was a pause, then Amelia sounded confused. 'I thought you said she was grounded?'

There was no time for pretence. 'She was. But she's gone out and we're not sure where she is. If you've got any idea, we'd be very grateful.'

Again, Amelia hesitated, before stuttering. 'No... I don't think there's anywhere I can think of.'

The hairs rose on the back of Erica's neck. There was definitely something that Amelia wasn't telling her. Not for the first time since Andrew had informed her that Mollie had left the house, Erica wondered if there was a boy involved. In her experience of teenage girls, a boy could often be the catalyst of a bad turn of events. But Mollie was only thirteen and she'd never mentioned any interest in boys. 'Are you sure? Any other friends she might have gone to visit?'

'If she was going to see anyone, I thought it would be me.'

The hurt in Amelia's voice was palpable. Erica had to

remember that she was only thirteen. 'Of course. I know you're her best friend. She loves you.'

There was some more murmuring at the other end of the line. Erica glanced over at Ben who was still happily watching his cartoons. Her hands were clammy with fear. What was it that Amelia was keeping from her?

When she spoke again, Amelia's voice was heavier, as if it was weighted with the secrets she'd been trying to keep. 'Mum says I should tell you that I've been a bit worried about her this week.'

Erica clutched the phone tightly in her hand. 'Really? Why?'

There was another pause. More murmuring from Kirsty before Amelia's words tumbled into her ear. 'I don't know if you know that she had a boyfriend. But he finished with her last week and she's been very upset about it.'

Erica swallowed her shock. There *was* a boy involved. Did Andrew know about him? He was with her every day. How had he missed it? That's where being 'more relaxed' and 'not being imprisoned by fear' got you. 'I see.'

Now that Amelia had decided to open up, it all came out in a rush. 'And I worried how she'd react after we found out that I got the school council thing. I know that Mollie must be disappointed but she was so nice about it. She said she was proud of me and everything. Do you think that's why she hasn't come to see me? Do you think she's just been pretending and that she's actually angry with me about it?'

The wobble in her voice betrayed how upset she was. Teenage girls and their desperate desire not to upset anyone. How did it start so young? This need to please. To be liked. To not rock the boat. 'I'm sure it's not that. She would've been thrilled for you. You'll be great. She's probably just gone for a long walk or something. She'll get back home and be cross with me for worrying about nothing.'

It didn't feel like nothing, though. With everything that Amelia had just told her, Erica was starting to build a picture of a very unhappy teenager and that was without the suspension from school. Watching Ben with his ice cream in front of the TV, she ached for the days when she had her two babies in one place, safe under her own eyes.

She could hear more murmuring at the other end from Kirsty and, when Amelia spoke again, she sounded more confident. 'Shall I send a message out to our friends and see if anyone has heard from her?'

Mollie would be furious if she knew that Erica had instigated this, mortified that all her closest friends would know that she was being treated like a child, but what choice did she have? 'Yes, please, Amelia. That would be great.'

'Okay, I'm handing you back to my mum.'

Kirsty's voice was kind. 'Can I do anything, Erica? What do you need?'

How long had it been since anyone had said that to her? She nearly cried. 'If Amelia can send a message to her friends, that would be great. I might be worrying unnecessarily, but—'

'But that's what we do? It's our job to worry, right? I'm sure Mollie's absolutely fine. But as soon as Amelia hears anything, we'll let you know.'

'Thank you.'

Once she'd ended the call, Erica sat with her mobile in her hand, wondering how it had got to the point where she knew so little about what was going on in Mollie's life. The application for school council, the boyfriend, the possible fallout with her best friend: she hadn't had the faintest clue about any of it. Mothers and daughters were supposed to be close, to share what was going on. She should've been there to help Mollie navigate the pitfalls and disappointments of these bumps in the road. Was this all her fault for leaving her behind?

Despite the hour it took to get from her new apartment back

to the house, she'd tried so hard to make sure that living separately wouldn't pull her and Mollie apart. She called every day and visited every Sunday. She sent little texts during the day, even just silly memes to make her laugh. It'd been so difficult being away from her, but she'd managed to persuade herself that this was best for them all.

But it wasn't true, was it? Ben was thriving, it was a relief not to be butting heads with Andrew every day, but she'd failed her daughter, hadn't she? Their relationship, their connection, had been torn in two. Mollie had had her first boyfriend, first heartbreak, first big failure at school and she hadn't wanted to speak to Erica about any of it. Panic gripped her in its claws. What was going through Mollie's head right now? Where was she? Why hadn't she answered her phone?

As she pressed Andrew's name on her phone screen, she sent up a silent prayer that he'd have good news.

FIFTEEN

MOLLIE

Being dumped is like having your heart pulled out of your chest and then having someone stamp on it. When you're still at school, and everyone knows about it, you have to pretend that you don't care and just smile and shrug and hide the fact that you just want to run away and not come back.

That weekend was tough. First the disappointment that Amelia got the place on the school council and then over-hearing Dad's conversation about Mum. Maybe I did text Luca a lot, but he's my boyfriend, isn't he? He's supposed to want to talk to me. By Sunday morning, I was going crazy stuck at home and I asked him if he wanted to meet up, but he was busy with his friends. Late on Sunday night he dumped me by text, telling me I was 'too needy' and 'too much'. I crawled into bed and curled up into a ball. There was no one for me to talk to. I've never felt so alone in my whole life.

Monday morning, I tried to tell Dad that I was sick but he said I had to go in. At least he offered to drop me there, but I still had to walk through the gates on my own and endure Luca's friends smirking at me on the playground. Not caring that I'd barely replied to her messages all weekend, Amelia took my arm and told me to not even look at them. She took me to the toilets and let me use her Bath and Bodyworks spray and said that I could do so much better than him. She was really great. I was angry with myself that I'd let my jealousy about the school council get in the way, but I still couldn't get over it. And then it got worse.

After lunch, I heard the two girls behind me in Spanish whispering that they'd heard that Luca was interested in Amelia. Like they'd punched me in the back, I felt winded. I couldn't breathe. I stared down at the page of vocabulary I was supposed to be translating and it blurred in front of my eyes as I listened to them say that they thought he only went out with me to get to her. A big fat teardrop rolled down my nose and smudged the page below. Did they actually want me to over-hear? It hurt so much. I really thought he'd liked me. That he'd chosen me. For me.

As soon as the bell went for the end of the day, I grabbed my things and hurtled towards the school gate, not waiting for Amelia like I normally would. It's not her fault if Luca likes her but it's just too hard. She has everything. She's pretty and smart and everyone likes her. She's already the teacher's first choice for school council, she doesn't need Luca to choose her, too.

What is it about me? Why am I never anybody's first choice? What do I need to do to get someone to notice me? That's all I could think about all the way home, hot tears rolling down my cheeks until I got back to an empty house, threw my bag at the bottom of the stairs, ran up to my bedroom and let myself sob until I had nothing left to cry.

I wanted my mum so badly; I wanted her to put her arms around me and tell me everything was going to be okay. But she wasn't here. She was miles away. With the child she chose. The one who always came first. Her favourite.

Feeling like that, I suppose it's no surprise that I ended up doing something really stupid. Making everything so much worse. I was desperate for someone to notice me. To choose me.

If only I could turn back the clock. Not pick up my phone. Not answer that message.

Not ruin my whole life.

SIXTEEN

ERICA

Erica's heart thudded with every one of the nine rings until Andrew picked up. 'Have you heard anything?'

After her last two calls, he'd said that he'd contact her as soon as he had anything to tell. It'd only been eight minutes since they last spoke but she couldn't wait any longer. 'No. I've been to all the local parks and places that teenagers hang out and I can't find her. Any luck from her friends?'

Amelia had already called back to say that she hadn't been able to track Mollie down. Apparently, she hadn't replied to any of the messages Amelia sent and she hadn't been on any of the Snapchat groups, either. Amelia had asked other friends to message Mollie – in case it was just her she was avoiding – but she wasn't answering anyone else's messages either. 'No. Nothing.'

Up until now, Erica had comforted herself with the thought that Mollie was punishing them for grounding her at home, but now she was really starting to panic. The Life360 app was still showing 'Battery Saver' for Mollie's phone, which meant that she had either – as Andrew believed – purposely disabled their ability to track her, or her phone was genuinely low on battery. Erica wasn't sure which of those was the most frightening.

'You have to call your colleagues. We need the police out looking for her. She's a missing person.'

Andrew sighed at the other end of the phone, his voice laced with irritation. 'It's only four o'clock in the afternoon and she's been out of touch for less than two hours. I don't think we need to bring in the flying squad just yet.'

Was he more worried about losing face with his colleagues than locating his daughter? 'We need to find her, Andrew. She's obviously not thinking straight. This is so unlike her.'

'I'll go out again and then, if I can't find her in another hour, I'll call it in.'

Erica wasn't anywhere near satisfied with that. She needed to be out looking, too. In her head, at the very least, Mollie was upset and alone somewhere. And at the worst... she couldn't even bear to think about that. Ben was settled playing with his letters. Maybe Jade could come over and sit with him while she scoured the streets for her daughter?

When she called Jade, however, she could barely understand her over the phone. Her voice was thick and sounded like it was coming from behind a blanket. 'Hello?'

'Jade, it's Erica. I'm sorry to ask you at the last minute, but is there any way you can come over and sit with Benjamin for me? I wouldn't ask, but it's a bit of an emergency.'

'I'm sorry. I've got a terrible migraine. I'm in bed.'

Erica's heart sank. 'Not to worry. It's fine. I'll ask someone else.'

She didn't want to make Jade feel bad, but there was no one else. She couldn't even call the agency Jade worked for and ask them to send someone. It wasn't fair to Ben to just leave him with a carer that he didn't know. With Jade, Erica had stayed the first time she came to make sure that Ben was comfortable – and, to be honest, so that she could see what she was like – and then she'd only left him alone with Jade for an hour or so the next time. She had no idea how long she was going to be out looking for Mollie.

Hoping desperately for good news, she called Andrew again. 'Anything?'

His voice echoed. He must be using the handsfree this time. 'I've literally just pulled out of the car park, Erica.'

She knew that she wasn't helping matters, but the fear and guilt of just sitting here were intolerable. 'Sorry. I'm just desperately worried. I wish I could be there looking with you.'

'Then come.'

He made it sound so easy. 'I haven't got anyone to sit with Benjamin.'

'Just bring him with you.'

Again. So easy. 'He's taken a dislike to being in the car for longer than about ten minutes. And he's got all his letters laid out so moving him now might prompt a meltdown.'

There was a long silence at the other end. A silence dripping with all the old arguments they'd had on her 'coddling' of Benjamin. *You're not doing him any favours. He needs to learn how to behave. You make him worse.*

She knew what Andrew would say next before he said it. 'What about the school? Why don't you call the residential part and see if he can stay there tonight?'

Benjamin's school had a residential section, like a boarding school. Children came from all over the UK to stay there and they also had bedrooms where the day students could stay for just one or two nights at a time. Though it was almost three months since he'd transferred to the school, she still hadn't felt as if he was ready for a whole night away from her. It still required a lot of effort and persuasion to get him to clean his teeth at night, wash himself effectively, get himself dressed. She couldn't send him somewhere else to stay until she was sure that he could do it. It was difficult enough for her to help him with those things now that he was older and bigger and puberty was changing him from boy to man. She didn't want him to need this kind of care from a stranger.

Still, it was a fair suggestion. 'I could call them. But it's all a bit sudden and last minute. We've never left him before.'

'We?' he coughed out a sarcastic laugh. 'I don't think *we* have ever decided anything for Benjamin. That's your domain.'

She bit on her tongue rather than his words. His passive aggressive dig wasn't the point right now. 'He needs to feel safe.'

'He will be safe. I know you still think about that boy on your school residential, Erica. But this is a completely different situation.'

She closed her eyes to try and block out the memory of that day. Over three months ago now, but it could've been yesterday.

She'd managed to avoid school residential trips since she'd had the kids. Life was a struggle to get everything done. Often, she'd be marking at the kitchen table until eleven or twelve at night and then Ben would be awake at five, wanting to go downstairs. There were always younger members of staff who were keen to go. But this particular time, the head had asked expressly for her. 'We need someone with experience. And first aid training.'

When she'd reluctantly agreed, she hadn't known why they'd wanted her to go.

Andrew had been really annoyed. 'How can you be away for five days? What am I supposed to do about work?'

'You'll have to take the time off. There's nothing else for it. I don't have a choice, Andrew. It's my job.' There was a tiny part of her – a teeny tiny part among the anxiety about being away from the children – that was almost pleased that he'd have to do everything for the kids while she was away. Let him see what it was like to be on alert every minute of the day.

At her school, there was a rule that children with a certain amount of behaviour points would not be allowed on school trips. There was always a push-back from parents on this. Reasons why the school were discriminating against their child whose additional needs meant they were more likely to be excluded from these trips. She understood their feelings – she was a Special Needs mum herself – but she also understood that the teachers were already taking on a huge amount of responsibility looking after other people's children on holiday. Residential trips – any school trips – were a very different situation to the school environment. If kids misbehaved, there was no back-up, no one to call, nowhere safe to put them.

The boy's name would forever be etched on her mind. Vinnie Fisher. He was the child who was always in detention on a Friday night, whose record on the school behaviour system was longer than three people's arms. He wasn't always badly behaved – no child is – but he consistently pushed boundaries, was rude to staff and had a mother who would back him up whatever he did. According to her, it was never his fault.

Vinnie wasn't invited on the trip. When it was announced at the beginning of the school year that they were going to the Lake District that March, they'd been told that they had to have less than twenty behaviour points. By the time of the cut off, Vinnie had thirty-seven.

Behaviour points were given for various reasons: lateness, lack of effort, no homework, disruption. Vinnie's were almost all for persistent disruption and inability to follow instructions. Both of which would make his attendance on a school trip an absolute nightmare for staff.

But his mother had – as always – marched into school and accused the head of discriminating against her son. She'd also started slating the school on a local Facebook group, garnering support from other local parents who loved to jump on to posts like this and use it as a way to pile on their own frustrations with the school. Truth and an understanding of the complexity of these situations had no place on these online courts where the disgruntled parents set themselves up as judge and jury on any decision the school made.

Eventually the head caved. Vinnie was going to be on the trip. And he would need someone to monitor him closely throughout. That person was going to be Erica.

With a shudder, she shook the memory from her head. She couldn't think about that right now. This time, Andrew was right. She didn't want to leave Ben, but she had to be out there looking for Mollie. What other option did she have? 'Okay. I'll call the school and see if he can go there this evening for a few hours. Then I'll drive up and help you look for Mollie.'

'Good. Call me when you get here and I'll let you know where I've already covered.'

Before she called the school, she took a minute to think this through. Right now, Ben was content, with one eye on the letters on his board and the other on the TV. His dinner – a beige banquet of nuggets and oven chips which she knew he'd eat without complaint – was just about to be ready. She'd have to pack him a bag while he ate. Then hope that she could make him understand why he had to go back to school when he hadn't been to bed yet.

At thirteen, she didn't want to leave him for a moment. But Mollie was only thirteen, too. And she was out there some-where alone. Erica had no choice but to call the school and see if they had any capacity for Ben to stay overnight. Even though she felt sick to the stomach at the thought.

SEVENTEEN

MOLLIE

Once I'd stopped crying about Luca dumping me, I just lay there for a while. I thought again about calling Mum, but I knew she'd be busy with Ben. Still laying there, I started thumbing through my phone. Almost as if I wanted to torture myself, I went onto Snapchat to see if anyone was talking about it. There was only a message from Amelia, asking why I didn't wait for her. I couldn't face even replying to her. Not yet.

Then I saw that someone called Roman had added me. I didn't recognise that name. For a couple of minutes I thought he might be a friend of Luca's and he was going to say something mean. But I couldn't remember anyone at school with that name. One of his football mates maybe?

Mainly for something to do, I replied and asked him who he was and why he'd added me. He said he'd seen my picture on my friend Amelia's account and that he recognised me. He thought that he and I had gone to the same school years ago when we were younger.

Amelia and I hadn't met until I came to this school. Me and my family had had to move after there was a fire at our house when I was eight. Someone at my dad's work thought that the fire happened because of someone he'd arrested so we had to get a new house and start at a new school. To be honest, I don't really remember the place we were in before. Or much about the school I went to back then.

Anyway, the school he said he went to wasn't that school so I told him he'd made a mistake.

He was so embarrassed that I felt sorry for him. Like, he was mortified. Kept saying that I probably thought he was a complete idiot. He was so polite. He even asked if it was okay to send me a picture of himself that showed how embarrassed he was and I know it was stupid – but I said yes. The picture he sent me was really cute. It was him with his fingers in front of his eyes and he'd written 'Dying' on the back of his hands.

I told him he really didn't need to worry about it. Then he said that I was kind and that he was surprised because *I always think girls as pretty as you are going to be mean.*

I told him to shut up. But sent a picture of myself pulling a face afterwards. Immediately after I sent it, I felt sick. He'd probably think I was so stupid. What did I do that for?

He just replied, *Wow.*

When Dad came home, I had to go and have dinner, but when I came back to my phone, he was still there. We spent the rest of the night chatting, even after I was supposed to be asleep. It was so nice to talk to someone who didn't know anything about me or my family or about what was going on at school. In my lessons the next day, I was so tired.

Tuesday morning, I was going to tell Amelia what happened, but – by then – the rumour was everywhere that Luca fancied her and was just waiting for me to 'get over' him so that he could ask her out. Can you imagine how that felt? I mean, I know it's not Amelia's fault, but it didn't make me want to talk to her about Roman. I wanted to keep him to myself. A secret just for me.

While my history teacher droned on about the Battle of

Hastings, I was writing Roman's name in different styles in my notebook. Roman. Roman. Roman. Made me think of 'romantic'. Which is really stupid but I'd never had a boy be that nice to me. When I got home, he'd sent me about twenty messages. Saying he'd been thinking about me all day at school. We chatted again all night. He was so kind. Every so often he would say something about how beautiful I was. And that he'd be stumbling over his words if we met in real life.

He sent me more pictures of himself. Without his hands in front of his face this time. He was so much better looking than Luca. I had this stupid fantasy about him turning up at the school to collect me and everyone's jaw hitting the floor, Luca realising that he'd been a complete idiot for letting me go.

All the time Roman was saying nice things to me, he was putting himself down. When I told him about Luca, he said that he'd been dumped recently, too. He said he thought it was because he was too skinny. It's mad, isn't it? Boys worry about being too skinny and we worry about being too fat.

That's not what I worry about though, I said to him.

What do you worry about? he asked.

I have scars.

Scars?

From a fire. When I was eight.

And he was so kind about it. So gentle.

Maybe that's why I did it.

It was on the Wednesday, the third night that we'd been talking. I'd already sent Roman three or four pictures. I'd done my make-up before calling him. Dad doesn't like me wearing a lot of make-up outside the house, but I love doing tutorials on YouTube. I'm really good at contouring. I had a lot of pictures on my phone that I'd sent to Amelia, so I sent him some of those.

I guess I'm lucky that the scars from the fire aren't on my face. Mainly, they're on my right arm. The doctors think I must've reached into the fire for something. There are a few curls of red on my right shoulder and I can't wear a top that shows my collarbones, otherwise you'd be able to see them.

Roman had a big scar across his chest from an operation he'd had as a child. He didn't go into too much detail about what the operation was, but he said, *I get it. I really do. I hate getting changed for PE at school. Everyone just stares at it.*

It was so good to be able to talk to someone who knows what it's like. *It's exactly that,* I told him. *And they pretend not to be staring but they really are. It's awful. My scars are so ugly.*

I thought I'd upset him for a while. He didn't reply for about ten minutes. My thumb hovered over the keypad. How could I say sorry? I didn't mean his scars would be ugly. Had I been as insensitive as those girls in the changing rooms whose eyes skimmed my body before they jerked their faces away, repulsed?

Then a picture arrived. A well-toned body with a long scar that started at his breastbone and ended just above his belly button. A thick white rope of skin, puckered in places, which stood out against his toned torso.

Pretty bad, right?

No. I typed as quickly as I could. *Not at all. It's a neat line. Mine looks like an angry rash across half my body.*

I knew what he was going to ask.

Can you show me?

I took a deep breath and pulled down the neck of my t-shirt

over my right shoulder. Took a photo of the dark-red bumpy stain and sent it.

That's not as bad as you said it was. I feel a right idiot now for sending you my chest.

I felt like I'd let him down. And, anyway, the pictures on Snapchat are deleted as soon as you send them. I pulled off my t-shirt and took a picture of my whole body. Sent it to him.

His reply was almost immediate. *You are so beautiful.*

On Thursday, I felt so much better in school. Roman's reaction had made me feel like a confident woman. I know that sounds stupid. Talking to him, sharing all my worries about the way I looked and whether that had caused Luca to finish with me, I can't explain it; it was like I felt more seen than I had been in such a long time.

Sometimes after school, we'd hang out on the high street for half an hour before walking home, but I wanted to come back and talk to Roman, so I made my excuses and came home.

He wasn't online straight away, so I looked at some Snapchat groups. There was a picture of Luca and Amelia laughing together over a Frappuccino. The way he was looking at her made it obvious that the rumours were true. He was so into her. I scanned any other photos that people had taken after school. In the background of one of them, Luca had his arm across Amelia's shoulders. Were they together?

Anger fired across my chest. Just as a Snapchat came in from Roman.

Hiiiiii.

I tried to focus on him.

Hi. How was your day?

Boring. I was thinking about you.

When he talked like this, it made me feel fizzy in the pit of my stomach.

What were you thinking?

There was a thirty-second gap before his reply.

I can't say.

This fizziness increased.

Come on.

I keep thinking about that picture. How beautiful you are. I'm so lucky to be chatting with you. I wish I could see you in real life.

My stomach fluttered. But I couldn't meet up with him when I didn't know him, could I?

Instantly, he sent another message.

Ignore that. It sounds creepy. Sorry. I'm embarrassed.

You don't need to be embarrassed.

I think I'm going to go. I like you more than you like me and I'm an idiot.

You're not. I knew I needed to say more. *I like you too.*

Really?

He sent me another picture of him smiling. He had no top on. If anything, the scar on his chest made him more attractive not less. I couldn't help but think of Luca and his arm around Amelia. Before I could change my mind, I took off my top and took a posed image in my bra. Sent it.

His reply was instant.

Keeping your bra on is cheating.

EIGHTEEN

ERICA

Woolifers Academy was set in twenty acres of woodland and its grand stately home exterior hid beneath it a multitude of brightly decorated classrooms, a huge gymnasium and various offices and meeting rooms. Outside, there was a pool, vegetable gardens, tennis courts and acres of space where the students could move or play or sit and run their hands through the grass: something that Benjamin loved to do.

Initially, Erica had only visited Woolifers to appease Andrew, but she'd realised within ten minutes of looking around and speaking to the staff how wonderful it would be for Ben. With her father's inheritance, and some strict accounting of their household budget, they could cover the fees. For the first time, after two years of arguing with Andrew about it, she'd begun to think that letting Ben stay overnight somewhere like this might not be the worst thing. The biggest issue had been how they would manage to get him there each day when both she and Andrew had to get to work.

Then the school trip had happened, she'd been suspended from school and they'd got a call from Woolifers to say that a place had become available for Ben straight after the Easter holidays. All in the same week.

On the one hand, it solved a logistical problem. While she had no job to get to, she could rent an apartment close to Ben's school so that she could get him there without the added stress of a long car journey. It also meant, she'd told Andrew – told herself – that they could try out an overnight because she'd be able to get to the school within minutes if he didn't like being there. Once they got to the summer holidays, they'd decided, they could see how things were going and make a plan as to how they'd go forward. Three months in, they would know whether the school was a good fit, whether he could cope with some overnights, or a long commute in the car, and whether Erica was going back to school. At Easter there had been too many unknowns to make a definitive decision.

Except now the three months were pretty much up and she still didn't have a solution.

She knew that people judged her for moving out and leaving Mollie. She would've had to have had a skin as thick as a rhinoceros not to feel the eyes boring into her when she collected Mollie from a birthday sleepover at a friend's house a few Sundays ago. The mutters and the fake smiles from other mothers picking up their daughters. She'd heard one of them tell another how she 'could never leave her child'. Even parents she knew and liked had struggled to say something supportive. If Andrew had been the one to move out, would he have had the same reaction?

It was hard every day to live separately from her daughter, but Mollie was so settled where she was. She loved her school, her friends and the house they lived in. Moving so that Ben could attend Woolifers had given him the chance to have that, too. To have a life.

For Andrew, the main draw of the school was the residential side. Even before they'd been offered a place, he'd suggested

Ben could board for a week so that they and Mollie could have a holiday abroad. That had been too much and she'd got very upset with him. 'Is that why you're pushing for this? You just want him sent away?'

'For the love of... it's not some kind of asylum from the turn of the century, Erica. You've been there. It's amazing.'

'Would you send Mollie away to boarding school?' She didn't like to use her daughter in their arguments; it wasn't fair on her. But he had to see what he was actually saying and that was the only way.

He'd dropped the tone of his voice, then. It was the cool professionalism that she hated. 'I am not saying that Benjamin should stay there all the time. Listen to me. I'm just suggesting that he stay there sometimes. Give us a break. Give you a break.'

He knew where that tender point was and he was pushing it with a sharp finger. 'I don't need a break from my son!'

These arguments weren't new. They'd been having variations of the same discussion for the last two years. She wanted Benjamin close. He wanted him sent away. The move to the apartment was supposed to be a temporary compromise. But it had been harder than she'd expected to hold up her end of the bargain.

As she closed the car door and walked up the path to the residential wing, she reminded herself that Ben was familiar with the school and the staff so it wasn't as if she was leaving him somewhere he wouldn't know. Helen – the house mother for the boys' section – was ready and waiting with her customary warm smile. 'Hi, Ben. We're really excited you've come to visit us.'

When they'd started at the school, it had been explained that there were two bedrooms left available for short-term stays. Respite weekends were a common thing. But also these could be used in an emergency situation – like this – as long as they were available. There was a cost, of course – and it wasn't cheap – but the option was a luxury that many parents didn't have.

On the phone earlier, Helen had explained that usually they would want a student to have come for some familiarisation sessions before staying overnight, but in these emergency circumstances she was happy to help out. Erica was still hoping that they'd find Mollie soon and that she could collect Ben later that evening. Helen's reply had been measured. 'Let's see how it goes. If Ben's content, it might be nice for him to stay. Bring his overnight bag just in case.'

She was beginning to feel lately that the staff were trying to gently lead her to give Ben more independence. The letter about the trip into town had filled her with a fear that must look way too overprotective to them. She wanted to let him do more, knew that it was the right thing. But every time they suggested taking him out somewhere without her, she was right back at that awful day.

Aside from reputation, she didn't know Vinnie Fisher, had never taught him. But the thought of having to keep her eyes on him for every minute of the trip filled her with apprehension. The head had been encouraging. 'You're a great teacher with lots of experience. It'll be fine. I'm paying for an extra member of staff out of another budget, so you are just there to keep your attention on him.'

The first couple of days were okay. It took them six hours to get to the Lake District on a coach and he was lively but contained. Day two, they were orienteering in a field and he was fine then too.

It was day three of the five that it happened.

They'd taken the kids into Kendal for a wander around. Some wanted to buy souvenirs and gifts to take home. Others wanted to stock up on sweets for the coach. Usually, the teachers would position themselves somewhere they could be easily found and give the students an hour to wander around on their own with strict instructions to stay in groups of three.

Rather than join the other teachers, Erica stayed outside. Following, from a discreet distance, Vinnie and the other two boys he was with.

Vinnie was a challenge, but he wasn't stupid. 'Why are you following us?'

The other two boys looked uncomfortable. One of them was in her class, they got on well, but now he was being torn between wanting to look cool with this boy that they hero-worshipped and not offending a teacher he liked.

She'd smiled at Vinnie. 'I'm not following you. I'm keeping an eye on everyone.'

Of course, she had no skills as an undercover detective so – even though she tried to keep a distance – it was only another ten minutes before he rounded on her again. 'You are. You're following us. Go away.'

It was pointless pretending otherwise now. 'You've only got forty minutes, Vinnie. Just do the shopping you want to do and then we're all going back to the centre.'

'Nah. I've had enough. Come on!'

The last was said to the two boys he was with and then he was on his toes, dashing across the street. One boy followed. The second – Luke Taylor, the boy from her class – looked at her, back at Vinnie, then dashed across the road. Directly into the path of an oncoming car.

At the time, she'd gone straight into emergency mode. Calling an ambulance, sitting with the boy until it came, making sure that someone else was counting every child – including Vinnie Fisher who had been found hiding in the park. It was later that night, after they'd had the confirmation that – apart from a broken arm and cuts and bruises – Luke was going to be okay, that she'd started shaking uncontrollably, running the moment over and over in her head. Unable to shake off the sick dread of what might've happened. There was the fear of facing Luke's parents, of losing her job, of trying to work out whether she could've done any of it differently: all of those things were painful. Worst of all, she kept seeing the face of her own little boy. His vulnerability.

It wasn't possible to watch a child every second. She was a good teacher – an attentive teacher – and a young boy could have died that day. That's why she had to be the one to look after Benjamin because she *could* watch him all the time. Why could no one understand that? Why had *Andrew* not been able to understand that? She was his mum. She was the only one who could keep him safe.

Now they were outside the entrance to the residential wing, she wanted to go and see his room. To make sure he would be okay there. Check the windows and the doors. But she needed to get to Andrew and help him to find Mollie, so she took a deep breath and held out Ben's bag to Helen. Her voice wobbled. 'Here are his things.'

Helen turned to Ben. 'Do you want to take your bag from your mum, Ben?'

As if he was determined to prove her wrong, Ben took the bag. She knew it was an overreaction, but she could've sobbed as he gave her a wave and seemed perfectly happy to follow Helen inside.

Back at the car, she blew her nose. *He will be fine.* She told herself. It was more important that they find Mollie and get to the bottom of what was going on.

It was less than an hour from Ben's school to her old house, but it took a while to navigate through the country lanes at this time of the day. Dredging up all the memories of Luke's accident only heightened her fears for Mollie. Though Andrew was correct that it'd only been a few hours, she knew that it only took a few moments for tragedy to strike. In the last few weeks, waiting for the results of the investigation, she'd tortured herself with her part in what happened. She'd wanted to speak to Luke's parents, to tell them how sorry she was, but had been advised that she should just stay away. The tone in which that advice had been given had led her to assume that they wanted her head on a platter. And who could blame them? Didn't she blame herself?

After half an hour of smaller roads, she was just pulling onto the motorway when a call came in from Andrew. Holding her breath, she pressed the button on her GPS screen to take the call. 'Hello? Have you got her?'

The reception wasn't great and he sounded far away. 'Erica? Can you hear me? Where are you? Are you nearly here?'

There was an urgency in his voice that made her heart thud. 'I've dropped Ben at the school and I'm pulling onto the main road. I'm about twenty minutes away. Have you found Mollie?'

There was a pause at the other end that made her want to throw up. 'Not yet. But something has come up. Can you meet me at work? I'm at the station.'

Now she really did feel nauseous. What was he doing at the police station rather than looking for Mollie? 'What is it? What's going on, Andrew?'

His voice was as cold as the fear trickling down her spine. 'Just come. I'll explain when you get here.'

NINETEEN

MOLLIE

Keeping your bra on is cheating.

To begin with, I thought that Roman was joking. I mean, it's a very different thing for a girl to take her top off than a boy, isn't it? I know it's sexist and it should be the same no matter what your gender, but it just isn't.

Ha, ha. Very funny.

There was no reply for a few moments and then he wrote.

I wasn't joking.

I got a little scared then. Did he really mean that he wanted to see me naked? Because no one has ever seen me naked. I mean, obviously when I was little with my parents, but not a boy.

I tried three times to get my reply right. I didn't want to upset him or embarrass him or run the risk that he didn't want to talk to me any longer. He was the only good thing in my life right now. If he stopped messaging with me, I would have nothing. Eventually I replied.

I'm not ready for that right now.

The wait for him to reply was agonising.

That's okay. I understand.

I let out a huge sigh of relief. It was going to be fine.

Thanks. Sorry.

I'm not sure why I apologised. Amelia always says I apologise too much. If someone steps on my foot or if people are messing around in the corridor and I need to ask them to move so that I can get past, I always say it and she rolls her eyes at me. But I didn't want to think about Amelia right now.

It was at least seven minutes before Roman replied.

No, I'm sorry. I shouldn't have asked. It's just that I think I'm really falling for you.

My heart thumped so hard in my chest that I could almost hear it. He was falling for me? He loved me? Before I lost my nerve I typed back.

I think I'm falling for you, too.

He sent me another picture. Still shirtless, making a heart shape with his fingers and thumbs. He looked amazing. I wanted to show every single person at school. Show them all that I didn't need Luca. Roman was so much better. And he was falling for me.

I needed to think of something to send back. Wanted to look as cute as possible. I had a bag of lipsticks and eyeshadows that Mum had let me buy with my pocket money on the express condition that I didn't wear them outside of the house. I found a dark pink, painted it on and then took a picture of me pouting like I'd seen older girls do when they took selfies. Sent it to Roman.

This time the reply was immediate.

God, you look so sexy.

My stomach felt as if it was alive with butterflies. No one had ever called me sexy before. It felt good. Scary, but good.

Thanks.

I wish I could be there with you.

I wish you could be, too.

We could meet up?

Could we? Would I have to tell my parents? Was this crazy? But I wanted to. I really wanted to.

Where, though?

Wherever you want. I could come to your house?

No way. The chances of Dad finding out were too big. I love Lynn next door, but she would definitely tell Dad if she saw a boy arriving at our house.

No, somewhere else.

*We can think of something. But I don't think I can wait that
long. I really want to see you. I want to see you.*

I knew what he meant, but it still made me scared. I had to
put him off somehow.

You might change your mind about me.

*I could never do that. But I need something that shows you feel
the same about me as I do about you. I want to see how beautiful you are.*

It was as if every part of me was on high alert. It was so
exciting to have someone want me this much. He said I was
sexy. And beautiful. He was falling for me. He'd been so honest,
maybe I could be, too?

I'm scared.

Don't you trust me?

Of course I do.

Show me you feel the same. Show me you.

I thought of Luca and Amelia.
I've always been the good one. I never get in trouble. And
where had that got me?

And this is just for you? You won't show anyone?

Why would I want to share you with anyone? You're mine.

It felt almost exciting.

It took two seconds to unclip my bra. I held the camera phone high up so that it would make me look as good as possible, turned my body to hide my scars. I stared at the picture for ten seconds, eleven, twelve. In that time, Roman sent three messages.

I'm dying here.

Send the picture.

Please.

I was almost drunk on the feeling of him wanting me so much.

I sent the picture.

TWENTY

ERICA

Fifteen minutes later, heart thudding, Erica arrived at the police station. A bleak, grey square building with no personality. The car park was almost full but she managed to find a space in the far corner.

Andrew had been fresh from the police academy when they first met. Idealistic and enthusiastic, he'd felt passionately about the positive effect that the police force could have on a community. She'd felt the same way about teaching. They'd both worked long hours back then, but had carved out time together whenever they could, often sharing the highs – and lows – of their working day.

After they'd had the twins, Andrew's career had continued to climb and now he was a Detective Inspector. She'd only been to this particular station a couple of times to drop things off that he had forgotten. After what'd happened at their last house, he liked to keep his work very separate from his family.

The heavy metal door opened onto a small reception area. Grey carpet was scuffed from the boots of officers and the variety of people they brought here. Behind a thick glass window, the officer on duty at the front desk smiled up at her. 'Can I help?'

Why did she always feel nervous in places like this? As if she was guilty of something she knew nothing about. She cleared her throat. 'Yes. Hi. I'm Erica Mason. I'm here to meet with Andrew Mason.'

For some reason, the officer blushed. Now she looked at her properly, beneath the stiff police uniform, Erica noticed that she was young and pretty.

Her eyes took Erica in with a sweeping glance. 'You're Andrew's ex-wife?'

It was the first time anyone had ever referred to her in those terms. She and Andrew had been living separately for the last three months, but there'd never been any mention – from either of them – about making that a formal thing. Anyone they spoke to these days, outside of their friends, would refer to the other as 'Ben's dad' or 'Mollie's mum' so it had never been said that she was his ex anything. But they weren't living together as husband and wife. 'I suppose I am, yes.'

For some reason, the girl's blush deepened. 'I'll just call through for you.'

Within moments, the door to her left buzzed and clicked and Andrew was in the doorway holding it open for her. He looked very different from the last time she'd seen him. In his uniform, he usually looked smart and in control. Right now – face pale, hair dishevelled – he looked as if he hadn't slept in days. 'Come straight through, Erica.' Over her head, she noticed him nod and smile his thanks at the girl on the desk before leading her through a narrow corridor towards a dark-blue door on the left.

The last thing she cared about right now was whether there was something happening between him and the young woman on reception. 'What's going on, Andrew? Why did you want me to come here? Why aren't you out looking for Mollie?'

'Give me a chance and we'll explain.'

Before she could ask what he meant by 'we', Andrew opened the door and ushered her through to a room containing four desks with a computer on each. Three plain clothes officers – two male, one female – hovered behind a fourth who was staring at the screen. The fierce air conditioning in the room made her shiver. Something felt really, really wrong. Digging her fingernails into the palms of her hands, Erica turned to Andrew. 'Tell me now. What's going on?'

Andrew pulled out a chair for her that she didn't take. Then he took a deep breath. 'When I sent out the picture of Mollie to the local forces to ask them to look out for her, I was contacted by someone from a task force set up to...' He paused, as if he was composing himself. 'A task force set up to look at the sexploitation of minors.'

As if the floor had moved beneath her, Erica's stomach lurched and she gripped onto the back of the chair, afraid her legs might give way. Nausea lapped at her throat. Sexploitation? Mollie? It couldn't be... please don't let it be...

Still holding the back of the same chair, Andrew was fighting to get his voice under control, so his colleague continued, the kindness of her voice a direct contrast to the brutality of her words. 'Criminal gangs target young people, solicit explicit photographs and then use them to blackmail the teenagers. They threaten to release the photograph or video to the victim's parents or friends.'

It wasn't that Erica was unfamiliar with the term, it was that she was terrified why they were using it in the same sentence as Mollie's name. Sliding down onto the chair, grasping with her fingernails the vain hope that she'd misunderstood, she searched Andrew's haunted face for reassurance, her tone begging him to tell her that she'd got it wrong. 'What does this have to do with Mollie?'

Andrew placed a gentle hand on her shoulder. Either she or

he was trembling. His colleague continued her explanation. 'The missing persons photo of Mollie was recognised by someone who'd just intercepted a lot of images. It looks as if Mollie sent a nude to someone pretending to be a teenage boy. He was actually a man who was part of a criminal sexploitation gang targeting teenagers.'

Erica couldn't breathe. Blood rushed to her cheeks. She felt hot, then cold, then hot again. This couldn't be true. Not her baby girl. Her voice scratched at her throat, not much more than a whisper. 'Are you sure it's Mollie?'

They must be wrong. Mollie wouldn't do that. Yes, she enjoyed playing around with make-up and dressing up in nice clothes, but she never wore anything revealing or showed any interest in doing so. Plus, Mollie knew all about things like online grooming – you didn't grow up with a police officer and a teacher as parents without being told about the dangers of sharing information online. She wouldn't have done this, Erica was sure of it. They must have made a mistake.

But Andrew's face darkened, his shaking voice heavy with grief. 'I'm a hundred per cent sure. I had to identify a censored version of the photograph. You can clearly see Mollie's scars.'

The flash of pain across his face wrenched a guttural sob from Erica's chest. This couldn't be happening. Not to them. Not to Mollie. Her precious girl. 'I'm sorry, I just can't... I just can't believe it.'

Andrew's eyes were as full of tears as her own. 'I know. I'm in shock, too. I'm sorry, Erica.'

Tactfully, the other officers slipped out of the room to give them some space. She placed her own hand on Andrew's. Of all the things she could throw at him, he was always a solid constant. When she'd had nights of not sleeping over the accident on the school trip, it'd been Andrew who always calmed her down, told her that she wasn't to blame, made her repeat it back to him until she almost believed it. Despite the fear coursing through her, she had to get a hold of herself. They needed to figure this out, they needed to find Mollie. Cogs were turning in her brain as she tried to process it all. 'This must be why she doesn't want to speak to us.'

He nodded. 'And also explains why she stole the money from her teacher. The team believe that she would've been asked for money quite soon after sending the photograph. As soon as they have something they know the victim won't want shared publicly, they ask for the money. Usually around five hundred pounds.'

She held fast to Andrew's hand as if it were the only thing keeping her from drowning. Five hundred pounds? Mollie was only thirteen. The only money she'd have access to would be her savings account into which they gave her ten pounds pocket money each week and she would also squirrel away her birthday money. 'She wouldn't have anywhere near that much money.'

'I know. I've checked her bank records and she had just shy of three hundred pounds in there until five days ago when it was transferred to an account which we're in the process of tracing. She would've been two hundred pounds short.'

All this time they had been trying to understand why she'd stolen that money, she'd never have imagined it would be for something like this. No wonder she'd looked mortified when Erica had pushed for more information. When her teachers had. Erica closed her eyes. All she could see was her precious girl's beautiful face. 'Poor Mollie. My poor sweet girl. She must've been so scared.'

A hard edge returned to Andrew's voice. 'These people are very clever at what they do. I've heard parents say that they would never have expected their child to be sucked into this but I never really believed it. I think I always assumed that they hadn't kept a close enough eye on them. That they didn't really know them.'

His face folded into a deep frown. Erica felt the cold shame of knowing she'd thought the same. Maybe it was true. Maybe they hadn't kept a close enough eye on their daughter. Especially her. She wasn't even living in the same house. What kind of mother was she? 'Do you think she's actually run away?' Another thought occurred to her. If Mollie thought that a naked picture of her was going to be shared with people that she knew, she'd be inconsolable. 'What if she does something to hurt herself?'

How could there be people in the world evil enough to think that they could do this? Now the transformation from a bright sparky teenager to a miserable, emotional, angry young woman made sense. What a weight she'd been carrying on her tiny fragile shoulders. 'We need to find her, Andrew. We need to find her quickly. She might be in danger.'

He nodded. 'Agreed.' He straightened up as he spoke, back to police mode. 'We've circulated her picture to all the police stations in the area and they'll post it on social media as a missing person. We need to list all the friends she might be with so that they can be contacted. Also, any places we think she may have gone to.'

Wanting him to stay with her in the pain she was feeling, she reached out and grasped his hand again. 'Do you think she'd do anything to harm herself? Tell me the truth. What do you think has happened to her?'

She studied his face to see if he understood what she was asking. This time he gave her no false hope. 'We just need to find her, Erica. As soon as we possibly can.'

When he opened the door, his colleagues filed back in. Given a pen and paper by one of them, Erica started to make a list of all of Mollie's friends, both those at her current school and the couple from the old school that she still spoke to occasionally. Where possible, she wrote down the numbers of her friends' parents that she had stored on her phone. The ink in the pen could barely keep up with her scrawl, her wrist ached with the pressure she was putting on the page. Another idea occurred to her. 'Shall I call Celeste? She might be able to get the school to call all the students in Mollie's class?'

Andrew nodded, his lips a tight line. 'Good idea.'

Celeste's phone went to voicemail so Erica left her a brief message with what she needed. As she recounted to Celeste what had happened, the dark implications made her shudder. Her baby girl, barely thirteen and not the most streetwise of kids, was out there alone and scared, thinking that she was about to be made a laughing stock among everyone she knew. Where could she be?

Now the list was complete, she needed to do something else. 'It's going to start getting dark. We need to find her soon. I'm going to drive around.'

Andrew glanced at his watch and frowned. 'It's only just gone six. We have a while before it gets dark. And there's trained officers out looking. Why don't you go back to the house and wait there in case she comes back. She could arrive home at any time. And while you're there, you can have a look around her room. See if she's taken anything, packed a bag. Or if there's anything else that'd give us a clue. Her computer maybe? I'll get back out there. She's got to appear eventually.'

He was at the door and holding it open before she was out of her seat. She wanted to look for Mollie, too, but this was Andrew's area of expertise. Maybe he was right that she would come home and, if she did, Erica also couldn't bear the idea that she'd find the house empty. She reached out and clasped Andrew's arm. 'Please find her soon.'

His smile was grim. 'I'll do my very best.'

TWENTY-ONE

MOLLIE

I'm not an idiot. I know about grooming and about not giving out your details online. Our teachers at school have been warning us about it for years. I know not to have location turned on when I'm gaming and everything.

So how had I been so stupid as to fall for it?

The message came through about an hour after I'd sent the photograph.

How would you feel if your friends saw this picture of you naked?

I stared at the words. My stomach prickling, face getting warmer. Why was he asking that? What was I supposed to say?

I wouldn't like it. Obviously.

The reply was almost immediate.

Then you need to send me money. Or I'll send a message to everyone you know and post this picture online.

What was this about? What was happening? It was such a shock that, to begin with, I still clung to the hope that it was some kind of joke.

What are you saying? I thought we were... friends? I thought you—

You've been so silly, Mollie. You sent the photo. If you want me to delete it, you'll need to pay.

My head spun trying to work out what was happening. Roman was blackmailing me? Ten minutes before we were planning to meet up, he'd said he was falling for me, that I was beautiful and sexy and... It was all a lie? He didn't mean it? I was such a stupid, stupid idiot. As if a boy who looked like that would want to be with someone like me.

I pushed my fist into my stomach to stop the churning that was making me feel sick. The tone of these messages had changed completely. Was this still Roman? Had someone else got into his phone? Did Roman even exist? My whole body started to tremble with shock and fear.

I don't have much money.

Then you need to find some. I want five hundred pounds.

Five hundred pounds? There was no way I could get that much money without asking my parents and even the thought of telling them... no. I didn't want anyone to know about this. Ever. Shame burned my face as I typed a reply.

I can't get that much.

I stared at my phone screen. Waiting for a response. Dad called up the stairs. 'Mollie! Dinner's ready!'

I left the phone on my bed. Covered with a blanket – the one Mum had had made for me with pictures of all of our family holidays printed onto it. Looking at all those happy faces – me and Ben eating ice cream, Dad with me on his shoulders, Mum and I trying on funny hats – made my heart ache with fear. What would those faces look like once they knew what I'd done?

I had to try and think straight. As far as I knew, he couldn't send an image to people I knew unless they added him. But it only needed one, didn't it? One person to see the photo and tell everyone. Then they'd add him to see it. Or share it themselves. Like fire, it would spread through everybody I knew. It would destroy me.

Since Mum and Ben had left, Dad and I had got into the habit of eating with our dinner on our laps in front of the TV, so it was easy to stay quiet as I pushed spaghetti bolognese around my plate. The voice of the newsreader droned in the background as I watched Dad. Should I just tell him? He could make it go away, couldn't he?

But Dad was a police officer, there was no way he'd agree to just pay the money to Roman – or whoever it was at the end of that Snapchat account. He would make me report it, wouldn't he? And then they would release the photo and my life would be over.

'Everything alright with your dinner?'

Dad nodded towards my plate where I'd moved the spaghetti into the meat. Twirling the tangled strands of pasta around my fork rather than eating it. 'It's fine. I'm just not that hungry. I had a big lunch at school.'

That was a stupid thing to say. Dad could easily check my

school meal account and see that I'd bought nothing from the canteen that day. I rarely did. It took too long to line up and wait. But Dad wasn't likely to check. Mum was the one who'd do that every so often. Nag me if I'd been skipping lunch.

Even that had changed since she left. She didn't have the time now to be checking up on everything I did. She left that to Dad. And Dad? Well, he'd been out a lot more lately. Left me alone a couple of evenings each week at least. I was on my own with this. But I was going to have to get that money from somewhere.

After I'd managed to push down enough dinner to stop Dad from being concerned, I returned to my room and retrieved the phone from under the blanket.

I can get the money. Please don't send the photo to anyone.

I hadn't planned to steal the money from Miss Martin. She's my favourite teacher – I love her English lessons and she's always got time for us if we want to chat after class. But I was alone in her room and she'd left her bag under the desk. It was open and her purse was right there. It felt like the only option I had. So I just took it and went to slip it into my bag. Unfortunately for me, she came back just as I was doing it.

It was one of the worst moments of my life seeing the look of shock on her face. There was so much disappointment there. Like I'd physically hurt her. She asked why I'd done it. Whether there was anything I wanted to tell her. My mouth was empty. I had nothing. No excuse. And I couldn't tell her the truth because then that disappointment would turn to disgust.

She had to report it. I understood that. It was weird in a way that I didn't care about being suspended from school. It was actually a relief. Not having to face anyone there. I begged Dad not to tell Mum; I just needed to buy some time before she turned up here asking a million questions. He was completely confused. Had no idea why this had happened.

On Saturday, he tried to talk to me about it, but I had to keep it all locked inside. Still hoping that I could find a solution. I sent the money I had in my account – nearly three hundred pounds – and begged 'Roman' to let that be enough.

You still owe us two hundred. Or the picture will go live.

In my imagination, they were enjoying this, torturing me. I tried so hard to think of a solution. A way to get that money. If I hadn't been caught stealing, maybe I could've invented a school trip and told Dad I needed the money. He'd been so distracted lately that there was a chance he wouldn't check, wouldn't speak to my mum about it.

Now though, he wouldn't believe a word I said. I couldn't go to him for the money. So where was I going to get it?

TWENTY-TWO

ERICA

The house felt empty and cold when Erica returned. On the side in the kitchen, a cereal bowl and a mug had been washed up and left on the draining board. Mollie was such a good kid. She'd never given them any trouble. At school, all her teachers had loved her. She had nice friends and was polite and kind and lovely.

Upstairs, Erica stood on the threshold to Mollie's room. Gone was the pale pink of her younger years; instead she'd chosen to have it painted blue and dove grey. From the far wall, Taylor Swift beamed down from her position among photographs, postcards and flyers. On her bed – a single with one of those mattresses that you could pull out from underneath for the nights when her friends stayed over and they would giggle into the early hours – her saxophone lay like a body on the blankets. What Erica would give to hear its mournful tones right now.

She opened a wardrobe door and all of Mollie's clothes seemed to be there – apart from the items slung across the back of a chair or in a heap in the corner. She sank down onto the bed. Where was she? How had she not noticed what was going on with her? For so long, she'd had her eyes on Benjamin. Worrying about his schooling, his socialising, his future. Like a fool, she'd thanked her lucky stars that Mollie was so easy. From a really young age, Mollie had been independent. From about three years old, she'd been determinedly dressing herself, wanting to pour her own cereals, looking out for her twin brother when he was upset or needed calming down. Erica had taken her for granted. Oh, she'd had moments when she realised that she needed to spend some time with her daughter. Which is when she'd persuade Andrew to spend the day with Benjamin so that she could take Mollie out to buy some new clothes or they'd go to the cinema together. She'd hoped that this would be enough to keep their mother-daughter relationship on track.

On the wall, a cork board heavy with smiling faces. Mollie and Amelia, other friends, schoolmates. At the top left, curling at the edges, a family photograph of the four of them on their last holiday together. Erica remembered that photograph being taken. Once they were posed, Andrew had set up the camera on a brick wall at the back of the beach to take their picture. Each time, before the camera took the photo, Ben would look in a different direction. The more exasperated Andrew got, the funnier she and Mollie had found it. Until, eventually, Andrew saw the funny side too and they were all laughing. Ben had looked at them as if they were nuts and the expression on his face – as if he were the sensible grown up and they were silly children – had made them laugh even more.

Those were the moments when it'd felt like they could do this. That their family would survive intact, that the children would thrive. Why hadn't they been able to find a solution that hadn't torn them apart? Since she'd started at the secondary school, Mollie had seemed to need Erica less. Preferring to spend time with her friends or practising her sax or doing her homework. She'd thought that it was natural. Didn't all teenagers pull away from their parents at some point? But was that really what she'd thought? Or had she allowed herself to accept that too readily, too easily. Because it freed her up to do the things she needed to do with Ben?

Just as she was about to turn away, she spotted another photograph. This one looked fresh. It was Mollie, sitting at the table in the kitchen downstairs, books spread in front of her as if she was revising or doing some homework. Poking her tongue out at the camera, looking happy and busy and every inch a cheeky teenager. This could've been any day in the last few months, Andrew loved to snap photos on his phone of everyday pictures. Since his father died, and they realised how few photographs they had of him, he'd taken it upon himself to capture all the everyday moments they took for granted.

Therefore, it wasn't the content of the photograph itself that surprised her. But the fact that standing behind Mollie, with her hand on her shoulder, was Celeste. Holding a mug – probably a coffee made in Andrew's flashy new machine – she looked at home in their kitchen, comfortable with Mollie, as if this was somewhere she spent a lot of time.

What was she doing there and why hadn't anyone – not Mollie, not Andrew, not Celeste herself – ever mentioned it to Erica? She recalled her meeting with Celeste earlier today. Her questions about Erica and Andrew's marriage. Pressing her to tell her whether they were still together and then – she remembered with a cold trickle of fear – saying she had something to tell her. Did this photograph have anything to do with that?

Erica refused to let her mind go there. She was being ridiculous. This was Celeste. Her friend. There were several explanations as to why she was there and she couldn't think about any of them right now. Andrew wasn't her priority. She needed to focus on Mollie.

Pushing herself back up to standing, she rubbed at her eyes and cheeks with the palms of her hands. There had to be something here that would help. Maybe Andrew should've been the one to come back here. He was the one with detective experience. She didn't even know what she was looking for. Sifting through the pages on Mollie's desk – bits of homework, sketches, photos she'd printed possibly destined for the cork board – she found a picture that Ben had drawn for Mollie a long time ago. She had no idea why it was out on Mollie's desk. It was the two of them, holding hands, and her eyes blurred as she looked at it. She should check on him, too.

As she continued to sift through the photographs, she called the residential unit and tried to sound calm. 'Hi, it's Erica. Just wanted to see how Ben was doing.'

Helen's voice was reassuringly chipper and confident. 'He's doing great. Sitting in front of the television as we speak. Thanks for remembering the DVD. That was a big help.'

At the last minute, she'd thought to slip a DVD of Ben's favourite cartoons into his bag. Though they could be found on the Disney Channel, she hadn't been sure they had access to that at the school. Plus, Ben liked the cartoons to come in the same predictable order.

It sounded as if he was fine without her: that was good, wasn't it? They'd always been working towards this. Independence. Agency over his own choices. Andrew's voice echoed in her head. *Wasn't that why we moved him there?*

After Helen had hung up, Erica gave up looking through papers and faced the computer, terrified to see what might be on it. She hadn't wanted Mollie to have a computer in her bedroom. But Andrew had bought it anyway, saying she needed to be able to do her homework in the peace and quiet of her room. If there were going to be any clues as to where she was, it was probably going to be here.

She moved the mouse. The screen came alive immediately. One of the rules of Mollie having a computer of her own was that there would be no passwords so that they could check it at any time. On the screen, a video of Mollie playing the saxophone was paused halfway through. She must've recorded herself on the webcam. For a few moments, Erica was transfixed. She was so good already.

Whenever she'd learned something new, Mollie had always been so hard on herself. 'I'm not good yet.' Where had that come from? It was the same with schoolwork. Neither she nor Andrew had put pressure on Mollie about grades, but she had always set herself such impossible targets, beat up on herself when she didn't reach them.

The first time she'd played for Erica, she'd been so dismissive of her mother's effusive praise. 'I'll sound better when I can use a thinner reed. I have to learn with this thicker one and it doesn't vibrate as much.'

Wasn't that true for parenting too? You had to learn the hard way. Put the effort in when it was difficult. Hoping that, one day, you'd find it easier, instinctive, beautiful. The difference with learning to parent is that, from day one, you were thrust into the orchestra pit and expected to play perfectly with everyone watching.

Moving the mouse again, she knocked the pile of papers to the floor. As she bent to pick them up, she found something in her daughter's handwriting that made her blood run cold.

Dear Mum and Dad.
I'm so sorry, but I don't know what else to do.

Erica's legs turned to jelly beneath her and she dropped heavily onto the seat in front of the desk. What else had she been about to write? Why hadn't she finished? Please, God, don't let this be what she thinks it is.

Hands trembling, she called Andrew but got no answer. Pressing the sides of her head with the heels of her hands she tried to think – think! – where Mollie might have gone. She checked her phone again. No one had returned her calls to say that they knew where she was. Surely she couldn't have gone far? For a start, she had no money in her account. Mollie's card account was on Andrew's phone, which was how he'd known that she'd cleaned it out. But she also had an old savings account connected to Erica's. When she checked it, that too was empty.

It was then that she noticed she'd had a notification from an old Visa card that she and Andrew had shared. They used to use it when they were eating out or for booking holidays, then they'd split the bill at the end of each month. The card hadn't been used since she'd moved out three months ago. Except, according to the notification that had popped up from the app, for today.

Though she'd been told not to by Andrew, Erica used the same password for all her banking apps, so it was easy to get into the credit card app and see what it'd been used for. There were two entries. One from the local train station and another from Booking.com.

Erica's thumbs couldn't move fast enough as she opened her Booking.com app. Sure enough, there was a booking. When Andrew had warned her about always using the same password, she hadn't thought for a second that it would be their own daughter who'd use her account.

She'd forgotten that this same credit card was linked to the Booking.com account. When she scrolled through, she could see that it'd been used to book an apartment that they'd stayed in before. In Aldeburgh. The place they'd stayed in that last family holiday together. Where they'd laughed on the beach. Then yelled at each other back at the apartment. That must be where she was.

Erica grabbed her car keys, calling Andrew's number as she strode towards the door, trying not to think about what had happened on that holiday. The day when everything had started to unravel.

TWENTY-THREE

Erica was all for driving straight to Aldeburgh from the house, but Andrew wanted her to come to the station, said he'd drive them in his car. The first thing he asked when she got there was whether she'd called the agents for the property. She found their number on their old booking and they called together from the phone on his desk. He had it on speakerphone so that they could both hear the response.

It took several rings for the agency to pick up, the shrill ring each time tightening the tension between them. Andrew tapped his fingers on the desk. 'That's no way to run a business. Answer the damn phone!'

She was surprised how rattled he sounded. Usually, she was the one who panicked; he was the voice of calm. His anxiety made hers even worse. When the phone was picked up, they both spoke at the same time, then he held up his hands and let her take the lead.

She tried to keep her voice calm and business-like. 'Hello. I'm enquiring about a property that you manage in Aldeburgh on Clarence Street. We think our daughter is staying there and wanted to confirm it.'

The girl at the other end of the phone sounded about seventeen. 'I don't know if I'm allowed to tell you who is staying there. It's private information.'

Gripping onto the edge of the desk, Andrew leaned towards the phone and practically growled at her. 'I'm a Detective Inspector and I'm telling you that you can.'

Erica didn't know if this was true or not, but Andrew in work-mode wasn't to be argued with. She felt a little guilty at how nervous the girl at the other end of the phone sounded. 'I only started yesterday. I don't know what the rules are. I'm looking after the office while my boss is out. When they get back—'

Andrew's growl became a bark. 'We need to know now. Our daughter could be in danger.'

Erica's heart nearly came out of her mouth. What was he imagining? What could be going on in that apartment?

The voice on the other end of the phone was nearly in tears. 'My boss will be back in a moment and I can ask them if—'

Andrew snatched up the receiver and then slammed it down again to cut off the call. 'That was a waste of time. I'll call someone at the local station and get someone round there.'

But Erica couldn't just wait. 'I want to go there now.'

He nodded. 'I'll get my keys. I can call the local station on the way to my car.'

Andrew's navy BMW was large, clean and comfortable, the doors solid and the seats leather. It was very different from her Renault Zoe, which was small and messy. It'd been a long time since she'd sat in the passenger seat beside Andrew and she couldn't help but remember the times they'd driven with the children in the back, Benjamin with his earphones on and Mollie glued to a book.

He must've been thinking similar things. 'It's been a while since we did this, eh?'

Nostalgia squeezed her heart. 'Yes. Do you remember when they were tiny and we had that mirror thing set up so that I could see them in their car seats?'

He glanced at her. 'It felt so huge back then, having twins. If only we'd known how that was the easy time. The baby books didn't warn us, did they?'

Tears threatened at the back of her eyes. If only they could return to those early days. Would she have done anything different? 'I don't think it's like that for everyone.'

He nodded acceptance and they drove in silence for the next few moments. According to his satnav screen, it was going to take another thirty-two minutes before they arrived in Aldeburgh. Thirty-two minutes before she had even a chance of seeing her daughter.

Staring out of the window, she was trying hard not to picture all the terrible things that might've happened when Andrew's voice made her jump. 'I can't help but think about the last time we were there. At that apartment.'

They'd always loved Aldeburgh. Andrew had been at university in Norwich, so he knew that coastline well and had taken Erica there when they were first together. Back then, they'd spend long evenings in one of the pubs drinking Adnams beer and then sit on the pebbly beach eating fish and chips from the paper. When they had the twins, they'd taken them there a few times. With the children in the double buggy, they walked two miles along the coast to Thorpeness to take them out on the boating lake. Life had felt so good. So simple.

Once Benjamin began to struggle, things changed. Andrew spent much more time with Mollie than he did with Ben. The last time they'd come to Aldeburgh, he'd taken her out to the bookshop, then they'd walked on the beach looking for the sea glass she wanted to collect. Then they'd had cake in the tea shop.

When they got back, Erica had followed him into the bedroom so that the children couldn't hear them talk. 'You're playing favourites and it's not fair, Andrew.'

But he wouldn't accept it. 'How can I be playing favourites? Benjamin doesn't want to do any of those things.'

She'd seen the pile of books that Mollie had returned with. 'What did you get for Benjamin?'

He'd looked at her as if she was mad. 'Nothing. What could I have got for him?'

She wasn't proud of how she'd erupted at that. It was as if everything she'd been holding in since they'd arrived was pouring out of her. Her anger at the way he never spent time with Ben. How Mollie got so much more from him than their son did. In turn, he'd accused her of wanting to control everything, of telling him what he could and couldn't do.

Maybe it was the sound of them arguing, but something startled Ben and stressed him out. Mollie shouted for them, fear building with every syllable. 'Mum! Dad! Can you come? Now!'

They ran into the sitting room of the apartment. Ben was pacing up and down and he'd started to hit himself. His palms rained down on his head and he was crying like he'd done as a small child.

Mollie, as always, was trying to calm him down. 'It's okay, Ben. It's okay.'

But he was beyond her soothing voice. He was in his own world now and it was going to be hard to reach him.

When Mollie tried to grab his arms and begged him 'please don't hurt yourself, Ben', he'd tried to shake her off and, without meaning to, his knuckles made contact with her nose. A fountain of blood burst from her face and she cried out.

Erica was next to her in a second. Ben saw the blood – some

of which was on the back of his hand – and his distress dialled up even further: he hadn't meant to hurt her. His waving hands were changed into clenched fists and turned on his own body. The blows he rained down on himself got harder. She could hear his knuckles hitting his skull. It was truly awful. They had to stop him.

From behind, Andrew circled his arms around Ben. It hadn't been easy. Even at eleven, Ben was getting strong and when he was upset, that strength increased. It took at least ten minutes for him to stop struggling and calm down and, by then, sweat poured from Andrew's forehead. He looked absolutely exhausted.

He looked exhausted now, too, with his hands gripping the steering wheel, eyes fixed on the road ahead. She resisted the urge to reach out for his arm. 'That was a tough day.'

That was the understatement of the century. That day had marked a turning point in their lives. It was after that episode that Andrew started to really push for a new school with an option for residential care. A year ago, a colleague of Andrew's had been the one to tell him about Woolifers. Her niece was there and she'd told him that it was amazing. Her exact words – which had encouraged Andrew and made Erica want to cry – were 'My sister said that the support they provide has given her her life back.'

'Ben *is* our life.' She'd argued with him 'til she was blue in the face. 'Our kids are our life.' She hadn't been able to understand how he could even contemplate sending him away, her beautiful boy. It took another six months before he wore her down enough for her to go and see it.

She wondered if Andrew was thinking about the same thing. 'We didn't have another holiday together after that one, did we?'

'No. I think the idea of a holiday is that you come back

feeling better than you did before. Wasn't really working out for us, was it?'

He wasn't wrong. Holidays were actually worse for Ben because of the change and disruption. 'No. It wasn't really working out.'

The sign for Aldeburgh came into view and Andrew signalled to leave the main road. The satnav spoke her directions into the quiet and Erica looked out of the passenger window at the houses on her side of the road. How many happy holidays might they have had here if things had been different?

Turning the volume down on the satnav, Andrew cleared his throat. 'Before all of this, I was thinking about taking Mollie away. It's not fair that she misses out, is it?'

Erica snapped her head around to look at him. 'Just the two of you?'

He looked a little embarrassed. 'Well, Ben won't appreciate it and you won't go without him, so, yes, just Mollie and me. Or maybe with some friends or something.'

Friends? Did he have a particular friend in mind? Erica could almost feel the fraying edges of their marriage, their family, pulling apart. She had to hold them together. 'Well, maybe I would come. I mean, if Ben does okay tonight. Just a weekend or something.'

A raised eyebrow showed what Andrew thought of that idea. 'I'll believe it when I see it.'

Was he not even going to try and meet her halfway? 'What's that supposed to mean?'

The phone rang out in the car and Andrew pressed a button to pick up the call. 'Hello?'

'Andrew, It's Mac from East Suffolk.'

This was the officer Andrew had spoken to earlier about checking the holiday let. Erica held her breath. Did they have Mollie?

Andrew's voice was calm and clear. 'Hi, Mac. What's the situation?'

'We've spoken with the manager of the holiday let office and they've confirmed the booking in Mollie's name on your credit card.'

That was something. At least they knew where she was. Andrew was waiting for something else. 'Can you go there and check that she's okay?'

'We're there now. But there's no answer. Someone's coming from the office to let us in. I'll call you back as soon as we gain entry and update you on what we find.'

'Thanks. We'll be there as soon as we can.'

After Andrew ended the call, Mac's words swirled in Erica's brain. *Gain entry. What we find.*

In profile, Andrew's face was pinched with the same sharp anxiety that gripped Erica. In his time on the force, he'd been in a wide range of these situations – some so awful that he wouldn't speak about them, not wanting to bring that evil into their home. Mollie wouldn't be the only runaway he'd ever dealt with. Though it filled her with fear to know what was going on in his mind, Erica had to break the unbearably heavy silence between them. 'Andrew. What do you think Mollie's gone to Aldeburgh for? What are you expecting to find in that apartment?'

TWENTY-FOUR

Andrew's knuckles whitened as he gripped harder onto the steering wheel. 'It's not a good idea to try and predict what's going on, Erica. It'll drive you mad. We'll deal with whatever it is when we get there.'

There was another phrase to join the others in the whirl-wind of her mind. *Gain entry. What we find. Whatever it is.* She couldn't bear it. 'But what do you think she's doing? Is she going to find whoever it was? This boy?'

Andrew glanced at her. 'The boy doesn't exist, Erica. They would have lifted those photographs from some kid's Instagram account. He was unknowing bait.'

It was so creepy. Out there, that boy was completely obliv-ious to the fact that his face and body had been used to lure a vulnerable thirteen-year-old girl. Her girl. Her precious, beauti-ful, naive girl.

In the immediate shock of being told what had happened, it'd been hard to take in everything she'd been told at the police station. Now she was trying to shuffle these events in her brain to try and make sense of them. 'This blackmailing gang uses photographs that they've stolen online and then, once they've gained the trust of whoever they're speaking to, they coerce them into sending them naked photographs?'

It took so much effort not to picture Mollie in this situation. From the twitch in Andrew's jaw, he was probably doing the same. 'Yes.'

'So could she be going to meet with someone from this gang, then? To give them money?'

As her dark thoughts became words, she shivered. For a whole host of reasons, this possibility was so much more dangerous. Meeting an adult man? Or men? And Mollie didn't have any other money that they knew of so what would she do? What might she be forced to do? *Please God, don't let her be meeting anyone.*

Andrew shook his head. 'These animals are in another country, Erica. They're not on their holidays in a twee English coastal town.'

She could do without his sarcasm. Could he not see how bad this might be? Did he not realise how huge this was that Mollie had even been talking to someone online that she didn't know. Much less sending revealing pictures of herself. 'It's just so out of character. I can't believe that Mollie was sucked into this. She always talks to us about things. Why was this such a secret?'

Clearly, she was wrong. Mollie didn't talk to them about things. Or at least, not to her. She hadn't known anything about what was happening in Mollie's life. And last weekend, she hadn't even been able to see her because Mollie had been out when she came. Why hadn't she realised that something must've been seriously wrong? Why hadn't she tracked her down, spoken to her? Why hadn't she been there?

But Andrew had been there. Every day throughout it all. Why hadn't he noticed? Was he not watching her closely enough? 'According to your colleagues, Mollie was talking to this... *fictious boy* all last week.'

He nodded. 'Yes. According to the information they have, it all started last Monday.'

Could he not see where she was going with this? Did he not feel as riven with guilt as she did? 'And there was nothing unusual in her behaviour? She didn't seem different at all? Preoccupied? Happier – or unhappier – than usual?'

He glanced at her before focusing back on the road ahead. 'What are you trying to say, Erica? Don't skirt the issue. Are you saying this is my fault?'

She would never be that cruel. 'Of course not, but you were the one living with her. Did you not notice anything?'

He shrugged. 'She's a teenage girl. She doesn't confide everything in her father. Isn't that what mothers are for?'

That was a low blow, stoking the anger she was trying to contain. 'I think you'll find that fathers are just as capable at listening to their children. If they're there, that is.'

Another twitch in his jaw; she knew she was getting to him but, right now, she didn't care. His voice was cold and hard. '*I'm* there every day.'

This again. 'Really? So where were you on Sunday night when you told me you were going into work? When she was about to start her suspension from school and would've maybe been open to talking about what was going on?'

His face flushed. 'It's none of your business where I was and, anyway, where were you?'

None of her business? Wasn't he still her husband? The face of the young receptionist at the police station came back to her mind. Was she reading more into the way she'd blushed when Erica introduced herself? 'You know where I was. I had to go back to Ben because he didn't have his cup.'

She was acutely aware of how indulgent that sounded, but Andrew should know as well as she did how small things like that could escalate quickly with Ben. Being able to anticipate and avert were the most powerful tools she had in managing his emotions and needs. Picturing Ben, she checked her phone for the tenth time in the last minute. No messages. 'I might call the school again to check that he's okay.'

His eyebrow twitched, but he kept his eyes on the road. 'They'll call you if there's a problem.'

Irritation itched at her. 'It doesn't hurt to check, though.'

He sighed. 'Surely you can trust the school to look after him if you don't trust anyone else.'

'What do you mean by that?'

He shrugged but kept his eyes on the road. 'What I said. You don't trust anyone to look after Benjamin other than you.'

She swallowed, tried not to bite. 'Well, there is only me to look after him, isn't there?'

'Because you've made it that way.'

How convenient for him to make it out that this was her doing. 'Really?'

'You always took everything over. It wasn't that I couldn't do it. I wasn't allowed to.'

She couldn't believe what she was hearing. He wasn't *allowed* to? What was she, his mother? 'You were too busy all the time. Any time I asked you to help you had something urgent at work.'

'Because you always asked me to do things at inopportune times.'

She almost laughed at that. Everything children needed was inopportune. They didn't get sick to a schedule. 'You were always working, Andrew.'

His laugh was sarcastic. 'No, I wasn't. But when I was home there was always a reason that you had to be the one who took care of Ben.'

'Ben had – has – a routine. Your shifts would throw him out of that. I had to be the constant. I had to make sure that he had what he needed.'

She could see the veins on Andrew's hands bulge as he

tightened his grip on the wheel. 'You prioritised Benjamin over all of us – including yourself.'

'Because he needed me!'

The phone rang again and Andrew pressed the button to pick it up. 'Hello?'

'Hi, it's Mac. The landlord has arrived with the keys, we're just getting in now.'

'Go ahead. We're five minutes away.'

Was it possible for her heart to actually stop? It sure felt like it. They drove the last few streets in silence.

TWENTY-FIVE

The apartment was on a residential street a few hundred yards behind the main high street. Seeing the police car outside made Erica's heart thump in her chest. Without thinking, she reached for Andrew's hand.

He gave it a squeeze and then dropped it so that he could shake hands with the officer who walked towards them. 'We've gained access to the apartment. There's no one there.'

Erica closed her eyes for a moment. At least the first of the terrible pictures in her head hadn't come true. But that didn't help the fact that they didn't know where she was.

Andrew turned to speak to her. 'Do you want to have a look inside? See if there's anything that might give us a clue as to what's going on here?'

The apartment looked just as she'd remembered it. A long hallway with a living room and kitchen to the left and two bedrooms to the right. Glancing in to the living room with its heavy wooden table, dark-green walls and a fireplace, it was impossible not to remember that awful day when Benjamin had accidentally given Mollie a nosebleed.

The row she'd had with Andrew after that had lasted days.

He was so angry that Mollie had been hurt that he didn't stop to think about what it was like for Benjamin. How overwhelmed he'd been. How sad he'd felt for hurting his sister. He loved her. Awful though it had been, if they could go back to that day, would they – could they – have done anything differently?

She made for the bedroom at the end of the hall, the one she and Mollie had shared the last time they were here. The bedclothes were dented as if someone had lain there and – beside it – an open backpack spilled clothes onto the floor. Other than that, there was no trace of Mollie. Where was she? What was she thinking? Planning?

Heavy footsteps heralded Andrew's arrival at the top of the stairs. 'I've spoken to the officers. They've put the word out and posted a picture on their social media asking for people to keep a look-out, but it's too early for a search party. I'm going to go to the high street to see if anyone has seen her. Do you want to stay here in case she comes back?'

The unravelling ball of anxiety inside Erica would take her over if she sat here doing nothing. 'No. I want to look, too. We can cover twice as much ground that way, I'll leave a note in case she comes back while we're gone.'

Andrew was in police mode. 'Won't that just alert her that we're here, though? I don't want to risk her running away again.'

She wasn't going to be the one to wait here doing nothing. 'You stay, then.'

She held his gaze until he nodded. Gave in. 'Okay, leave a note and let's go. I'm going to start at the top end of the high street and work my way through the shops, ask if anyone has seen her.'

'Okay. I'll go to the beach.'

'Do you have an up-to-date photo to show people?'

Was he making some kind of point? Maybe not. His face looked as if he was checking on her. It'd been strange to hold his hand earlier. Comforting, though. She hadn't realised how long it'd been since someone had hugged her rather than her being the one giving out the hugs. She'd missed his solid, protective arms around her. 'Yes. I have a photo.'

He nodded. 'Let's go, then.'

It was about a ten-minute walk from the holiday let to the high street. The last time they were here, it'd taken twice that with Ben wanting to stop at every pebble that caught his eye. Now – walking as fast as they could – they were likely to do it in half the time. Every so often, Erica had to almost jog to keep up with Andrew's longer legs, her breath becoming ragged with the combination of the effort and the fear filling her lungs. The silence between them left her brain free to imagine the worst of outcomes: Mollie being attacked, Mollie being abducted, Mollie's body washed up on the beach. Each image was another stone heaped on top of her. Only the adrenaline pumping through her veins prevented her from dropping to the ground under their agonising weight. In an attempt to ward them off, she pushed herself to walk faster, ignoring the burn in her chest, her voice coming in short, breathless sentences. 'She wouldn't have packed a bag... if she was planning... on doing something... awful... would she?'

Without so much as a glance in her direction, Andrew kept thundering onwards, 'I don't know, Erica. I don't know anything.'

Fear wrapped its bony fingers around her throat. Concern about the kids was a constant companion for Erica. But Andrew was always pragmatic, stoic, rational. If he was considering the worst, it made this even more brutally possible. 'You don't really think... that she'd... hurt herself, do you?'

Even voicing her greatest fear seemed a risk, that she might cause it to happen. Up until now, Ben was the one she worried about hurting himself. Not Mollie. Never Mollie. How could this be happening?

With a grey face, Andrew glanced at her, picking up speed. 'I don't know.'

A whimper broke free from Erica's throat. He couldn't mean that. Her fears streamed from her mouth, burning her tight throat. 'But she wouldn't, would she? She's such a happy girl. She has so much going for her. She knows we're here for her. She wouldn't do something to herself.'

Practically begging him to reassure her, to tell her that – of course – Mollie would know that there was always a way to fix things, that nothing was unsurmountable. That she wouldn't be so ashamed that she couldn't see a way out.

By the grim tone of his voice, it was clear that Andrew was as blindsided by all of this as she was. 'I know that you think I have the answers here, Erica, but I don't. I've been a police officer for years, I've seen a thousand cases, but this is different. This is Mollie. My little girl.'

His voice cracked and her heart echoed in response. She wanted to comfort him as much as she wanted his reassurance for herself. 'I know. I'm just trying to make sense of it all. To think like she would think. And I'm so scared, Andrew. Really scared.'

When the twins were babies, she'd worried about so many things. When they slept, how they ate, what they touched. And she'd worried so much for Ben and what he needed, how to care for him best. But all of those fears became background noise to this cold, hard, visceral terror that Mollie was out there, vulnerable, scared, in danger.

To her shock, a sob came from Andrew. 'I'm supposed to protect her, Erica. I'm her dad.'

Hot tears welled in her eyes. Even as they kept walking, she reached out for his arm. What could she say? 'I know. I know.'

'All I ever wanted was to keep you all safe, Erica. You never seemed to understand that. All three of you. I was doing my best. I tried so hard, but it was never enough. Never enough.'

Between the tightness in her throat and the shock of his raw honesty, she couldn't reply. It'd been so long since he'd spoken like this. Here was the man she'd married. Who was kind and thoughtful and made everything work. The man who'd sat up all night with a two-year-old Ben when he had a cough that stopped him from sleeping. Who'd spent hours constructing a Tudor house out of cereal packets to Mollie's strict architectural plans for her history homework. Who'd cheered her up when she was drowning in grading assessments by slipping her favourite chocolate bars between some of the piles of papers.

Not the man of the last couple of years who'd shut down on her, refused to listen, pushed her to make decisions she wasn't convinced were right. Could they ever get back to the way they were?

There was so much to say, to unravel, to unpick. But now they had to focus. His show of fear galvanised her to wrench her thoughts towards the positive. 'We will find her. I know we will. She has to be here.'

In another few steps, they would hit the high street. Wiping the tears from his eyes with the back of his hand, Andrew pointed across the road. 'The beach is that way. I'm going to turn right up towards the shops. I'll go into each of the cafés and shops and ask if anyone has seen her. Let's check in every ten minutes or so.'

As they got to the corner, they turned instinctively towards one another. For the first time in months, he reached out and pulled her into a quick, tight hug and she nearly crumpled to the ground.

Then he was gone and she kept going past the pub to the pebbly beach. Praying silently – over and over – that they would soon have their baby girl in their arms.

TWENTY-SIX

As Erica moved away from the shelter of the buildings on the high street, the wind grew stronger and she was grateful for the sweater she'd brought. Walking on the large pebbles was tricky, even in her trainers. They gave way under her feet so that extra effort was needed just to put one foot in front of the other. Glancing left and right along the shoreline, she tried to pull her mind back from imagining Mollie wading out to sea.

Andrew's tears had rocked her fragile confidence in them finding Mollie: his rare display of fear infectious. When had she last seen him cry? It'd been so easy to see him as the bad guy since she'd left to live in the apartment with Ben. To ascribe her own interpretation – stubbornness, selfishness, control – on his relentless push towards respite care for Ben. Why had he never spoken to her like he did just now? *All I ever wanted was to keep you all safe.*

She took a left towards Thorpeness. At nearly nine o'clock, only a few brave souls were still on the beach in the dusk and it took longer to reach them than she'd thought it would. They shook their heads at the photograph of Mollie on her phone; they hadn't seen anyone that looked like her. Regarding her with sympathy, they promised to keep their eyes peeled and to tell her daughter she was looking for her. One of the women, older but robust in a thick gilet and walking shoes, patted her hand. 'They like to worry us, don't they? I'm sure she'll turn up soon with a story to tell.'

Erica thanked them and continued walking along the beach. How was it that some people could be so calm about parenting? So accepting of the fact that accidents happen and problems occur and dangers might cross their path? Anxiety had been her constant companion for so long, like an inflatable ball of stale fear which expanded and contracted inside her body. At all times, vague worries floated around her head like wisps or sprites. Sometimes intangible. Unclear. Yet filling her head with so much noise that – at its loudest – rational thought couldn't fight its way through.

Her phone rang in her hand and she almost dropped it. Her heart soared in hope then fell when she saw the number. Her mother.

Fighting an irrational anger at the intrusion, she let it go to voicemail. For most people, she'd imagine, a call from a parent at a time like this would be a welcome comfort. But that had never been her experience with her own mother. Any communication between them turned Erica back into an unhappy teen, fighting to be understood, to be listened to. Talking to her now, when she would just be trying to put more pressure on her to come home, or to tell her the latest 'amazing' thing that her brother had done, was the last thing she needed.

The adrenaline of the last couple of hours was starting to seep away and her legs felt heavy as she continued to trudge up the beach. She'd been determined that she would have a better relationship with her daughter than she and her mother had had. When Mollie was tiny, she'd imagined being the one to listen to her news over a cup of milky British tea or wipe her tears when she'd had her heart broken. Not to be her best friend, but to be her best support. Hearing from Amelia about all the things Mollie had gone through in the last couple of weeks and knowing that she hadn't chosen to confide in her... it had really stung. It didn't help that Andrew had known nothing about the boyfriend or the failed school council application either. This wasn't a competition. 'Oh, Mollie. Where are you, baby? Please be okay.'

If she closed her eyes, she could picture a younger Mollie running down this beach towards the sea. Falling, laughing, picking herself up again and carrying on. She'd been such an easy child to look after, such an easy child to love. Is that why they'd missed this?

Still trudging through the pebbles, she scanned from the coastline to the road and back again. Ben had loved this beach, too. Even that awful day, he'd spent the morning happily selecting pebbles for his collection. She glanced at her watch. It'd been almost four hours since she'd left him at the school. Should she call again and check that he was okay? She could still keep looking for Mollie at the same time.

It wasn't until she had her phone out of her bag and was about to find the school's number that she spotted a figure sitting on the wall at the back of the beach, arms wrapped around herself, legs dangling over the side: she'd know her daughter anywhere. Her heart almost burst from her chest to get to her.

'Mollie!'

TWENTY-SEVEN

Mollie looked up at the sound of Erica's voice. For a moment, a flash of recognition, of pleasure in seeing her mother, crossed her face. But then it was replaced with a scowl. 'How did you find me?'

Erica was level with her now and every inch of her wanted to throw her arms around her daughter and keep her close. 'We were so worried about you.'

Mollie looked doubtful. 'Who's we?'

'Me and your dad. We've been looking everywhere. How did you know how to get here?'

'I'm not stupid, Mum. And I am thirteen.'

She said thirteen in the tone that you might use for 'adult' or 'grown woman'. If only she knew how Erica still saw her as that tiny little girl who loved to throw tea parties for every toy in the house 'because it's not kind to leave anyone out, Mummy'.

How she'd navigated the trains in to London and out again to get here was not important right now. She was just overjoyed to see her. Braving the anger on her face, she reached an arm around her shoulders. 'I'm so glad to see you, sweetheart. I need to call Dad and let him know you're okay.'

'Okay?' Mollie practically spat at her. 'I'm not okay. Everything is awful. Everything.'

Though her voice was dripping with anger, there was a vibration to it that suggested tears weren't far away. 'We know, love. We know that there's been some awful things that've happened and we want to—'

Mollie leaped away from her as if she was on fire. 'What do you know?'

She didn't want to have this conversation out here, but she needed Mollie to know that none of this was her fault. 'We know why you needed the money, sweetheart. It's going to all be okay. Dad's here, too and we're going to sort everything out.'

If she'd thought that this would be a relief to Mollie, she was quickly proved wrong. She practically roared her response. 'You don't know anything. You think you do. You and Dad think that you can sort everything out the way you think is best, and me and Ben just have to go along with it. But you don't know.'

Erica had never seen her daughter this angry. She had to let Andrew know that she was found, but she couldn't just call him while Mollie was exploding in front of her. Quickly she fired off a text.

I've got her. She's safe.

Towards the shoreline, gulls cawed at each other as they fought over something in the water. Wind whipped Mollie's hair across her face and she pulled it away, her cheeks red with rage.

Erica needed to go carefully. Right now, the most important thing was getting Mollie home. Once they were there, they could work out how they were going to deal with everything that was going on. 'Let's walk back to the high street and find your dad. We can collect your things from the apartment and talk, then go back and pick up your brother and—'

'Of course you want to hurry back to Benjamin. Why would you want to be here with me? I'm so sick of it. I'm so sick of Ben being your favourite child.'

Her words slapped Erica far harder than her open palm could've done. 'He's not my favourite child. I don't have a favourite.'

Mollie's laugh was cruel. 'Yes, you do. I've always thought it, but now I know it. Because now I know what really happened in the fire.'

Fear crept up the back of Erica's neck. 'What do you mean?'

Mollie stamped her feet onto the pebbles like a petulant toddler. 'I know what you did. I heard Dad talking on the phone about it two weeks ago. He told them about the fire when we were younger. And he described what happened. I know the truth now.'

Andrew was talking to someone about the fire? What had he said? 'I don't know what you mean, Mollie.'

'Stop lying to me!'

She was crying hard now as the wind took her breath. She needed to be comforted, held, loved. But Erica didn't dare to try. 'I'm not lying. I don't understand what you're saying.'

Fists clenched each side of her, Mollie's words came out like bullets. 'I know exactly what happened that day. When the house was on fire and Dad was at work. I've always wondered why I have scars and Benjamin doesn't and now I know.'

Erica couldn't bear this. What had she overheard from Andrew? Please don't let her say it. 'Mollie, whatever you think you heard—'

'I don't think! I know! Dad said it on the phone and I got every word. I know that you chose to save Benjamin over me.'

TWENTY-EIGHT

MOLLIE

It was the Friday before last. The same day that Amelia was appointed to the school council. Feeling embarrassed and stupid, I just wanted my mum. Dad is great and everything, but I just needed to speak to her. I got home from school, changed out of my uniform and checked the clock in my room. It would be about another fifteen or twenty minutes until she was back at her apartment after collecting Ben. I might as well get myself a snack.

I had my foot on the top stair, about to go and see what was in the fridge, when I heard Dad in the kitchen on his mobile. Even though he was speaking quietly, his words travelled up the stairs to where I was standing.

'No, I'm at home. But Mollie is upstairs, so a Zoom call would be tricky. I don't want her walking in and seeing me talking to you.'

Interesting. That made me stop and wait. Who was Dad talking to that he didn't want me to see? As quietly as I could, I lowered myself to sitting so that I could lean close to the banister. The door to the kitchen was right below me and, despite seeming to want to keep this call a secret, Dad had left the door ajar.

His voice was low, but he's never been very good at whispering, so I heard every word. 'We've been living in different houses for three months. Does that count as separated?'

He was talking about Mum. This didn't feel right. Why was he telling someone that he and mum were separated? They weren't, were they? Not that they'd told me. It had all been explained as being necessary for Ben's school. Nobody had said anything about splitting up. All of a sudden, my upset over the school council was pushed aside by the thought that they'd lied to me. Were Mum and Dad getting a divorce?

I barely wanted to breathe in case he heard me listening in, but when – after about thirty seconds of silence – he laughed, it made me jump.

'No. Nothing like that.'

There was something about the way he spoke – especially after the laugh – that made me suspicious. I don't know why, but I suddenly thought that maybe he was talking to a woman. For a start, he was using a softer voice. Not the bark he used for dealing with people trying to sell him car insurance on the phone. Whoever it was on the other end of that call, Dad was definitely trying to make a good impression. Surely he wasn't planning to start seeing someone behind Mum's back?

There was another long pause before he spoke again. 'Well, there was what happened at the old house. We had a fire.'

I don't have the strongest of memories about the fire. Me and Ben were only eight when it happened. It's probably old enough to remember but it's like I only have scenes from that day and I can't really join them up into a film. I do remember the smoke and how much it made me cough. And I remember being very scared. Whenever we talk about it – which isn't often – Mum gets really upset and Dad changes the subject.

What was Dad going to tell this mystery woman at the other end of the phone?

I shifted myself even closer to the banister, holding on to one of the spindles as I tried to catch what Dad was saying. It was like he had a stutter; he was hesitating and not really making sense. He was explaining that Mum was there on her own with both me and Ben because he was on a night shift. He doesn't do those anymore now he's more important, but he did when we were small. Now he was telling the woman about the fire. That it had started in the kitchen. He's telling her that Mum had to get us both out before the firefighters came. I know all this, so it's a bit disappointing. But then he says the thing I didn't know. The part that had never been mentioned to me before. That hit me like someone had slapped my face then punched me in the stomach.

He clears his throat, then says the words as clear as anything. 'She chose to save Ben first. Erica left Mollie in the burning house.'

I gasp so loud, that I'm sure Dad is going to hear me, but he doesn't come out of the kitchen, so he can't have. I form my hand into a fist and jam it against my mouth to ensure that I don't make another sound. I want to hear more, but there's wind rushing in my ears and I feel sick. My fingers wander under the sleeve of my t-shirt to the bumps of my burn scars. Faded now, but still there.

When Mum left to live in the apartment near Ben's school, I missed her so much. She used to call me every single day and tell me that she was missing me, too. She said it was only for a few weeks. A couple of months at most. That she'd be back before I realised she was gone. But it was almost three months now. And there'd been no mention of when she might be coming back.

She chose to save Ben first. Erica left Mollie in the burning house.

This isn't the first time she's left me behind. Not the first time I've been her second choice.

She chose to save Ben first.

I always suspected that Ben was her favourite child.

Erica left Mollie in the burning house.

Now I know for sure.

TWENTY-NINE

ERICA

All the while that she was telling Erica what she'd heard, Mollie stared straight ahead, looking towards the sea. With every word, Erica wanted to beg for her to stop, but knew that she couldn't do that. As soon as she finished, she tried to explain. 'Oh, sweetheart. That's not what happened. If I'd known... I should have told you. I should have talked to you about it.'

When she turned to face her, Mollie's face was hard, defiant, but her voice trembled. 'Why did you leave me behind?'

Pain contracted Erica's heart at the agony in Mollie's face. 'It wasn't like that.'

'Then, what was it like? Tell me.'

Sometimes Erica was back there in the middle of the night, her nightmares pulling her into the worst day of her entire life. Stood at the top of the stairs, smoke creeping towards them, reaching for her babies with its evil fingers. Eyes stinging, she'd tried to push words of comfort from her ash-dry throat. 'It's going to be okay. Mummy won't let you go.'

Why, of all the times, had she left her phone downstairs that evening? She'd been trying to break the habit of doomscrolling when she woke in the middle of the night, hoping it would help her lack of sleep. Now, with fire raging through the house, she had no way of calling the fire service or Andrew or anyone.

'There was only me there.' She had to make Mollie understand. 'Your dad was working nights. You and Ben were only eight. I had to work out how to get you downstairs, through the fire and out of the front door.'

Mollie frowned. 'What about the neighbours? Why did no one come to help?'

Of course, Mollie would only think of Lynn when she thought of neighbours. Lovely kind Lynn who'd taught her to make paper dolls and fairy cakes. 'I don't know, Mollie. Maybe they didn't know about the fire. Maybe they were out. I just know that I had to do something. And do it really quickly.'

Within moments, both children had been coughing. In her arms, Ben's body had flinched with every splutter. Beside her, Mollie had barked between her whimpers of terror at the scene before them. Fear had gripped Erica. What should she do? Could they make it through the flames without anyone being hurt?

There was no choice, she'd realised. No one else to help. She needed to do this. They had to go.

Back in the very recesses of her brain, she'd remembered seeing something about draping a wet towel over your head to keep the smoke out. The bathroom had been behind them on the landing. She had tried to keep her scratchy voice as calm as she could. 'Mollie, sweetheart. Can you help Mummy and bring two towels from the bathroom?'

'You were so good, Mollie. Always such a good girl. I could see that you were absolutely terrified, but you were so brave and did everything I asked. You hurried to get towels from the bathroom and put them in the sink, ran the taps so that they were wet through.'

Mollie frowned. 'Why did I do it? Why not you?'

'I had to keep hold of Ben. He was trying to get back to his bedroom. I couldn't make him understand.'

Mollie's face was unreadable. 'What did you do next?'

Trying to keep Ben close with one arm, Erica had wrung a towel out and passed it back to Mollie. 'Okay. I need you to hold one of these around you, baby girl. I'm going to wrap the other one around Ben.'

It had been no surprise when Ben had recoiled at the sensation of the cold, wet towel across his back. He'd always been so sensitive to anything that doesn't feel right. They'd spent a fortune over the years on clothes without seams and labels to irritate him. Sensory issues is the wording they use. It doesn't come close to describing the meltdown that ensues from a top or shorts or pyjamas that don't sit right with him.

Between the wet towel and the fact that he hadn't wanted to be carried, Benjamin had fought Erica to release him every step of the way down, his fear tangible in her arms. She hadn't been able to risk putting him down, though. If she couldn't communicate to him how vital it was that they got out of there, she'd known, she'd have to physically take, drag, carry him herself.

'You were such a bright little thing, even then. I was able to reason with you, make you understand. But you were terrified, too. Each step down, you tugged on my arm.'

She could hear Mollie's tiny little voice even now, heard it often in bad dreams. 'No, Mummy. I don't want to go down there. I'm scared, Mummy. Stay here with me.'

Every maternal instinct is rooted in keeping your children safe, shielding them from harm. Aren't those the very phrases used to signify the strength of a mother's protective love? *I'd step in front of a moving train to save you. I'd fight a bear. I'd run through fire.* As a parent, your own safety, your very life, is secondary to that of your child.

Yet, there she'd been, in a situation where she had to take her children through danger to get them to safety. She remembered tightening her grip on Mollie's hand. 'It's going to be okay, baby. We just need to get through the door.'

Now she watched thirteen-year-old Mollie closely. The next part was the most difficult to tell. 'At that point, I didn't know whether the fire was at the front of the house or the back: all I was focused on was getting you both outside. Then you tried to pull away, so I had to grip harder to keep you close.'

If she closed her eyes, she'd be back there, trying to make a decision which way to go, with Mollie pulling at her arm. 'Mummy, you're hurting me.'

The sound of her cries had made Ben even more stressed. She'd had to shout over the noise of the crackle and whoosh of the flames to make Mollie understand. 'Mollie! Stop it! You have to come with me!'

Somehow, she'd managed to drag Mollie down after her without letting go of Ben. Her thighs had screamed with the effort needed to make it downwards. Ben's heels had kicked into her hips as he'd tried to get down. She couldn't risk it, she'd realised; he would run.

At the bottom of the stairs, she'd looked left and right, up and down the hall, trying to work out where the fire was through the black acrid smoke. At that point, she'd had no choice but to lower Ben to the floor. 'Keep down. We're going out the front door.'

'That was the moment I heard the sirens and I was so relieved. I knew that someone must've seen the fire and called the fire department or whatever you call it here.'

She saw the merest flicker of a smile on Mollie's face at that. She and Andrew liked nothing better than teasing Erica about the fact that – after so long in the UK – she no longer remembered which were the American words and which the English.

Maybe it had been the sound of the sirens that'd made her loosen her vice-like grip on Mollie's hand... Or had Mollie got a surge of strength because she'd heard something else through the crackle and pop of the fire which seemed to have spread to the kitchen at the back of the house. 'Mummy! It's Joanie. We have to save Joanie.'

Joanie. The cat who had somehow adopted them the year before because, clearly, Erica didn't have enough to be doing. Mollie had loved her with the passion of an eight-year-old girl for anything fluffy and warm. Joanie had actually been a wonderful distraction for her when Erica's eyes were on Ben. She'd been a lifesaver.

Until then.

Mollie's eyes were round. 'I thought Joanie had run away. You said that she'd probably found another family. Did she die in the fire?'

Quickly, Erica shook her head. She didn't need to add more upset to this story. 'No, she didn't die in the fire. She was a stray, sweetheart. She would've found someone else to feed her.'

Back then, Mollie had been distraught at the thought of leaving Joanie behind. 'We have to get Joanie, Mummy!'

'No, darling. Joanie will find a window. She'll be fine. We have to get outside now.'

All at the exact same moment, Ben had kicked at Erica to try to get away and Mollie had twisted her hand out of Erica's damp, sweaty grip and fled towards the sitting room where Joanie liked to lay across the back of the sofa, legs and tail dangling below her large well-fed body.

Erica had lurched towards Mollie's departing back, trying to grab her arm, her hand clasping hot air. 'Mollie! Come back! Come back right now!'

She was gone.

Ben was pulling away to get back upstairs.

She had to make a decision.

A choice.

The sirens were getting closer. If she could get Ben outside, ask a neighbour to keep hold of him, she could come straight back in for Mollie. She had to move. Quickly. Right that moment.

Still screaming for Mollie to come, to follow her, Erica had unlocked the door, Ben almost overpowering her as she'd reached up to the high lock they'd had to put in to keep him from letting himself out of the front door. Burning her fingers, she'd turned the red-hot key once, twice.

She'd continued to shout back over her shoulder. 'Mollie! You have to come, baby! You have to come!'

With a crash, she'd pushed open the front door, pulling Benjamin with her. There was a neighbour from across the street, wringing her hands and behind her – thank God – was a bright-red fire truck.

Throat hoarse, she'd practically thrown Benjamin in her direction. 'Take him! Mollie's inside!'

As soon as she'd known that the neighbour had hold of Ben's arm, that he wouldn't be able to escape, she'd turned to go back in, but a thick bulk of a man in a yellow helmet had barred her way, his bright plastic jacket as impenetrable as the fire truck itself. 'Stop. You have to stay here. It's okay. We've got this. Who's inside?'

Panic had choked her more than the smoke had. She had to get back inside to Mollie, she had to get past him, through him if necessary. 'No, no. I have to go in. My daughter.'

Now he'd held her in the same firm grip as she'd held the children moments earlier. 'We are on our way in to get her. How old is she? Where in the house will she be?'

She hadn't known. Words had ripped from her raw throat. 'Downstairs. The cat. She's looking for the cat. She's eight. She's only eight. Please, let me go. I need to go and get her!'

What had she done? Why had she left her inside? Mollie would be terrified. She wouldn't know who the firemen were. Erica should be the one to go and get her. Behind her, Ben had whimpered like a baby. His twin sister was in there. Could he sense something she couldn't? What did he know?

The next two minutes had been the longest of Erica's entire life. Unable to get anywhere near to the house, she'd held fast to Ben. Behind them, the street had filled with neighbours and onlookers, out to see what was happening. In front of her, fire-fighters had battled to rescue the house from the greedy flames.

She'd loved that house but, right then, she couldn't have cared less if the whole thing had burned to the ground: as long as Mollie was safe. She'd sent prayer after prayer upwards. *Please let her be okay. Please let her be okay.*

The relief when the firefighter had carried Mollie out of the front door had made her fall to her knees. Erica had held out her hands for her precious baby girl, but the firefighter had carried her straight to an ambulance which she hadn't seen arrive. Stumbling to her feet, she'd followed. 'What's happening? Is she okay?'

Mollie's voice had been thin and plaintive. 'Mummy? Where are you, Mummy?'

Erica's legs had felt as if they belonged to someone else. 'I'm here, baby. Mummy's coming.'

The paramedic had called out to her from the back of the van. 'Are you her mum? Mollie's been calling for you. She's been super brave. There are some burns on her arm. We need to get her to the hospital. You can come in the ambulance.'

As she'd opened her mouth to speak, Andrew's voice had boomed from behind her. 'I'll go. You stay with Ben.'

He'd been in the ambulance before Erica had known what was happening. Later, she'd learned that a neighbour had called him. All she'd been able to do was wrap her arms around Benjamin and watch the blue light of the ambulance as it had screamed its way towards the hospital.

THIRTY

Once she'd finished explaining, Erica searched Mollie's face for her reaction. If anything, she looked lost, cast adrift on a sea of uncertainty.

She tried again to make her understand. 'I can't even begin to explain how guilty I have felt since that day, Mol. I still dream about it. The feeling of your hand slipping out of mine is something I will never ever forget.'

Mollie broke her gaze and looked down at her own hands in her lap. 'Why didn't you tell me before? Why didn't you talk to me about the fire?'

'I didn't think you'd remembered any of it. You were in hospital after the fire, and afterwards it wasn't something we wanted to dwell on. But every time I see your scars, I think about it and wonder if I could have done it differently. Did I not hold your hand tight enough? Did I not shout loud enough for you to come back? Could I have managed to get the two of you out at the same time?'

Though these questions had taken up residence in her head for the last five years, it was the first time in a very long while that Erica had said them out loud. They'd become whips to torture herself with in the dead of night. Speaking them into the air, into Mollie's ears, seemed to lessen their power.

For the next few moments, they were silent. Erica needed to let the lump in her throat loosen before it choked her. Mollie seemed to be taking everything in. She scooped up pebbles in her hands and threw them, one at a time, in the direction of the sea.

While they were silent, Erica relived that moment again. The loss of Mollie's tiny fragile fingers from her grasp. Was it the heat? The sweat of fear in her palms? Why hadn't she been able to hold on?

Mollie's voice was small and Erica had to strain to hear her words. 'I did used to wonder. Why I had scars on my arm and Benjamin didn't. I thought maybe he was quicker than me or something.'

Though Andrew had gone in the ambulance with Mollie, Erica had called Celeste to come and take Ben and then followed on behind. To this day, she could still hear the sound of Mollie's cries as they'd cleaned and dressed her burns at the hospital. She'd gripped Erica's hand, tried to pull herself off of the bed and into Erica's arms. In the end, the nurse had had to ask Erica to hold her still so that she could make sure they hadn't missed any debris that could cause infection. Though she knew it was the only thing to do, it had been a fresh torture to have to hold her in place while someone caused her pain. Her cries of 'No, Mummy, please make it stop' still woke Erica at night in a cold sweat.

Now she'd started to tell her about it, everything was bubbling to the surface. 'I still don't know if I did the right thing. Whether I could've put Ben down and dragged him to find you.'

Was it a good idea to be this honest? Would it be worse for Mollie to think that her mother had got it wrong?

For the first time, Mollie looked as if she didn't absolutely hate her. 'I get it, Mum. I can see why you did what you did. I suppose it's my fault for running away.'

No way did she want this turned around so that Mollie was to blame. 'No, sweetheart. You were so little. And it was terrifying in there. The heat. The smoke. I was yelling at you. And you wanted to save Joanie. You always had such a big heart for saving everyone else.'

It was true. How much time had Mollie spent with her brother? Even when each year made the gap in their abilities widen further. When she'd long outgrown the toys he wanted to play with, the TV shows he wanted to watch, she'd sit alongside him, watching *Octonauts* for the hundredth time, passing him coloured blocks to stack into piles.

Mollie picked up a large grey pebble and stroked it with her thumb. 'And now I've run away again. No fire this time, though.'

The attempted joke in her voice squeezed Erica's heart. Though she wanted to pull her close, she knew she needed to wait and listen, give Mollie a chance to speak. Hadn't she been trained to support a child by listening and letting them use the words they had? Not to ask leading questions or put words in their mouths.

But Mollie wasn't a student. She was her precious daughter. 'I'm sorry you felt you had to run away. Whatever you need to tell me is fine, Mollie. I'm not going to be shocked or cross or feel any differently than I do now, which is that I love you and want to make everything okay.'

Mollie pulled her knees up to her chest. 'I don't think you can.'

Erica shifted her position; the stones were hard and made an uncomfortable seat. 'Try me.'

Head on her knees, Mollie's voice was muffled by her sweater. 'I sent some photos. To a boy I was talking to online.

Before you say anything, I know it was stupid. I know that I'm a complete idiot.'

At least it was out in the open now. That was the first step. 'We all do stupid things sometimes. That doesn't make us stupid.'

By the look on Mollie's face when she raised her head, Erica's attempt to keep even the merest trace of judgement from her voice had rendered it trite. 'Seriously, Mum, stop using teacher speak. I know what an utter idiot I've been.'

She wasn't a teacher right now, but she knew what Mollie meant. 'It's not teacher speak. Well, I suppose it is. But it's also true. We all make mistakes, Mollie. I've made more than there's pebbles on this beach.'

After a pause, Mollie changed the subject. 'I didn't get onto the school council. I had an interview. I didn't tell you because I didn't want you to say anything to Miss Winters about it.'

Why did she think she'd go to Celeste? 'I wouldn't have done that.'

The eye roll was exaggerated. 'You wouldn't be able to help yourself. You're always chatting to her about me.'

That wasn't true, but now wasn't the time to get into that. 'So you didn't tell me about it.'

'No. And also because... no, it's stupid.'

'What?'

'I wanted to surprise you with it. You get a really big badge and I thought I'd wait for you to spot it and then it'd be a nice surprise.'

Tears pricked the back of Erica's eyes. She could almost taste the disappointment coming from Mollie. 'I'm sorry you didn't get it. But I'm only sorry for you. I'm so proud of you. I don't need to see a badge to know how wonderful you are.'

Shaking her head, Mollie discounted her last words. 'It was even worse when Amelia got it. I know that you say we have to be happy for our friends. And it's part of the sisterhood to lift up other women. But I really deserved it more than her. I've never had a detention and I help out the teachers all the time.'

She wanted to pull Mollie onto her lap like a baby. She did deserve it more than Amelia. She worked harder. Was more diligent. More empathetic to other students.

But Amelia was more outgoing. More confident. Students like Mollie, who always quietly did the right thing, were often easy to take for granted, to overlook. It wasn't intentional, no teacher wanted to overlook any child. But school life was so busy, so full of deadlines and events and it was too easy to just be grateful for the quiet studious students who didn't demand attention. It was also easy, she was realising now, to do the same as a parent.

'It's okay to be disappointed, love. It's also okay to feel that it was unjust. Maybe it was. Teachers – and head teachers – get it wrong, too. I just wish I'd known about it. I would've taken you out and treated you. Tried to cheer you up.' She paused, not wanting to push too hard. 'You can tell me anything, you know.'

Mollie took a deep breath. 'I had a boyfriend for a few weeks. It wasn't anything serious. We only hung out a couple of times on our own. Mostly we were with the whole group. But it was nice. He used to hold my hand.'

How had her baby got to this stage already? 'That does sound nice.'

'But then he finished with me and I just felt really really... shitty.'

She glanced up at her mother, obviously expecting to be reprimanded for swearing, but that felt as important as one of these pebbles plopping into the sea. Erica let it go. 'I'm sure it did. It's horrible to feel unwanted, isn't it?'

Even when she was really small, Mollie would hold her emotions tightly beneath the surface for as long as she could before they came out of her in a rush. Now her face crumpled into tears as she blurted her feelings at Erica. 'I'm so sorry I sent that photo. I've made such a mess. He's going to post it online, Mum. Everyone is going to see it.'

Her fingers itched to take her into her arms. 'We know, Mollie. Your dad and I, because the person who is doing this to you has done it to other people. The police are aware. They told your dad.'

Mollie looked mortified. 'Everyone knows?'

Erica shuffled closer, something sharp cut into the back of her thigh. 'Not everyone. Just a small team of police and us.'

Mollie let her face fall into her hands and groaned. 'I didn't want Dad to find out. I didn't want anyone to find out. It's so humiliating.'

'I get it, sweetheart. But we're going to help you to sort this out. I'm here now. You're not going through this on your own.'

When she raised her head, Mollie's face was red and wet with tears. 'You're never here. I never see you. You want me to talk to you but you're never there.'

She deserved this. 'I understand how it seems, Mollie. And I'm so sorry for that. But Ben needs me so much.'

Mollie punched the stones with her fists. 'But I needed you, too!'

THIRTY-ONE

Out to sea, a small sailboat was being buffeted by the wind. One way, then the other, its white triangular sail whipped in both directions. On the boat, a small dark figure leaned this way then that in order to keep the little vessel on course. Watching from her seat on the pebble beach, Erica tucked her skirt around her legs and tried to stop herself from crying. This wasn't about her.

'I'm so sorry, Mollie. I'm so sorry I haven't been here for you.'

How many hours of safeguarding training had she sat through in her teaching career? Being instructed – mostly by interminable online training – on the warning signs that a child was being coerced online. If she'd been living in the same house as Mollie, wouldn't she have picked up that something was going on?

'I never see you anymore. When you do come, you're checking your phone in case Ben needs you back again. He gets you all the time.'

There was no way to respond to this other than to admit the truth of it. 'You're right.'

Agreement made her even angrier. 'If you know it's true, why haven't you done something about it?'

Why, indeed. It'd been too easy to think that Mollie was okay. Better than okay, that she was happy with the arrangement. 'You could've come to stay with me and Ben at weekends, but I thought you didn't want to leave your friends. I thought you were happy at the house. That it was best for you to stay with Dad.'

Even this wasn't the entire truth. After the fire, she'd carried the fear that she wasn't capable of looking after both of them on her own. Love wasn't enough. Hyper vigilance wasn't enough. She missed Mollie with an ache that never left, but if that's what it took to keep her safe, it was a small price to pay.

'I did want to stay with Dad. But I wanted you to be there, too. It was like you got divorced and didn't tell me. How was I supposed to choose? That's just not fair, Mum. It's not fair.'

The accusation in her voice was painful to hear. In profile, the twins were so alike. Erica hadn't noticed that recently. They had the same nose, the same delicate chin. Where Ben's hair was straight, Mollie's had a gentle wave, made almost curly in the damp salty coastal air. Though she wanted to reach out and brush it away from her face, Mollie's expression almost dared her to try. 'I thought I was doing the right thing. I was trying to do the best for everyone. You and your dad have such a good relationship, I thought you were okay without me for a while. It was only supposed to be for a while.'

Three months to get Ben settled, that's what they'd agreed. But it had been even harder than she'd expected to try him staying overnight without her. Feeling like she was abandoning him; it'd been too easy to keep putting it off. With just the two of them, it had also been easier to construct their life and routine to make life calm for him. Now, seeing Mollie like this, she had to question whether she'd sacrificed one child to appease the other.

'The thing is, I get it. I understand that Benjamin needs more help than me. But why does it have to be all the time? Why can't there be times when I get to be the one who gets the attention? It didn't matter what I did. Getting good results in tests, passing my ballet exams, learning to play the saxophone. It was like, "Yeah, well done, Mollie, but we expected that" and then if Ben did anything like, just trying peas for the first time, the whole family is expected to put on a parade for him.'

Memories fell like acid rain of the times she'd praised the smallest things that Ben could do. Had she not praised Mollie? Had she not been pleased for her? She searched her mind for examples, but couldn't escape the creeping suspicion that she *had* taken her daughter's achievements for granted. Or, worse, had minimised them in the light of Ben's difficulties. 'Oh, sweetheart. I'm so sorry.'

Mollie dug her fingers into the pebbles beside her, making them rattle as she clenched and unclenched her fingers. 'Sometimes I get really angry about it. I feel frustrated and I wish he was okay, you know. Not autistic. But then I look at him and it's Ben and I love him so much and I feel really horrible for thinking that. So guilty. Like a really terrible sister.'

Erica's heart felt as if it might tear in two. 'You don't need to feel guilty, sweetheart. You don't need to feel bad about that. It's normal. I feel it, too.'

Surprise flashed across Mollie's face. 'You wish that Ben was different?'

That question had a million answers and none of them would capture the complexity of how she felt. 'I love Benjamin – I love both of you – with a passion that almost knocks me over. But do I think our lives would be easier if he didn't have the difficulties he has? Do I think *his* life would be easier? Yes. But then, like you, I feel terrible about even thinking that.'

Mouth open, Mollie was searching Erica's eyes, as if to

check that she was telling the truth. 'Do you mean that? You're not just trying to make me feel better?'

The salty breeze cooled one side of Erica's face; the other cheek burned with the honesty she needed to share with her daughter. 'It's a kind of grief. A loss. A bereavement. Not for Ben – he's my son and I love him for all that he is. I wouldn't change him for the world. But when the two of you were babies, I imagined a life for you both and – for Ben – that's not the way it's going to be. I grieve for the fact his life will be more difficult. That you and he won't be going off to college at the same time. That he isn't going to bring someone home that he loves.'

As her voice cracked, she paused. How honest should she be? Mollie was barely thirteen. She was expecting her to understand complicated emotions that she didn't fully understand herself.

Mollie's hand crept across the stones and took Erica's into it. 'Oh, Mum. I didn't know you felt like that. You were always so... positive about it all. I didn't know you felt sad, too.'

Sad? That didn't even begin to explain the tides of feeling that'd washed over her, buffeted her, even almost drowned her, over the years. 'I'm not sad often, sweetheart. You and Ben have brought me so much joy. Before I became your mum, I had no idea how deep that feeling could go. You are my everything, both of you. You're my beautiful clever girl who can do anything she sets her mind to. Who has a heart big enough for the whole world. I can't wait to see what you will do and where you will go and I will be here cheering you on until I'm hoarse. Ben's life is going to be different. His world will be smaller. But he is brave and sweet and he makes me laugh so much. He's made me more patient and taught me so many things. You both have. But I want you to know, really know, that it's okay to wish that things were different sometimes. I wanted to make the world easy for both of you and I am so so sorry that I haven't done that for you.'

The breeze around them had dropped and, for the first time since Mollie had gone missing, Erica felt as if she could breathe. Honesty was hard, but it could set you free.

Gently, Mollie's hand squeezed hers. 'I'm sorry, Mum.'

'Oh, my darling, you have nothing whatsoever to apologise for. I let you down. But I promise I am here and I will do everything I can to make this right.'

She pulled her daughter into her arms and rocked her like a baby, not letting go of her hand this time. She was never going to let her go again.

They'd just wiped away their tears with a tissue from Erica's handbag when they heard a clatter of stones behind them as Andrew joined them on the beach.

'There you both are. You gave us a real fright, Mol.'

As he enveloped their daughter in his arms, Erica remembered how it had felt earlier to be encased by his strength and support. She stood and dusted herself down and Andrew released Mollie. He looked about ten pounds lighter than he had on the way down here. He even smiled at her. 'Shall we go and get a drink in the bar down the road before we head for home?'

It sounded like a perfect idea, but before she could answer, her phone rang in her bag. She knew before she checked the screen that it would be the school.

'Hi. It's Helen. We've just started our routine to prepare for bed, but Ben is asking for you. We're very happy to manage this, but you asked us to call if there were any issues at all so we're letting you know.'

What was the expression that you're only as happy as your unhappiest child? Right now, it was a tough call which that would be. 'Thank you. I'm about ninety minutes away at the moment, but can you tell him we're coming?'

'Are you sure? We can give it a bit longer if you want to let him try to deal with it?'

She knew that they were being kind but she also knew her son. They should have worked up to this – she should have worked up to this – not just thrown him in at the deep end. 'No, it's fine. If you can make sure he has his letters to play with, we'll take him home to bed.'

Andrew looked at her. 'We need to get Ben?'

She nodded. 'He hasn't settled. It's too much in one go.'

He held out his hands. 'I can go and get him. I'll drop you and Mollie back to ours first?'

Mollie shook her head. 'It's okay, we can all go.'

It was a learned response, this effacing of her own needs in favour of her brother's. How had she never noticed it before? Though this particular beach was full of stones, Erica needed to draw a line in the sand. 'No. Dad can drop us home. It'll be too late to go out for dinner by the time we get there, but you and I could order in a pizza from that place you like? You can even get one of those milkshakes which are full of sugar.'

Mollie's face opened up like a flower in the morning sunshine. 'Are you sure? I'd love that, Mum.'

It was heartbreaking to realise how precious this tiny thing was to her daughter. Half of Erica wanted to go to Benjamin, but for now, the half of her that belonged to Mollie needed to be with her. No matter how she felt, it was impossible to actually tear herself in two. There was always going to be a choice. There was no escaping that.

Andrew looked from one of them to the other. 'Okay, then. Let's be on our way. I'll drop you back to the station so you can pick up your car, then go straight to the school. I'll call you when I get to him to let you know everything is okay.'

He was jittery, like a child who's been entrusted with an errand. Erica forced a smile, tried to convey her confidence in him. 'Great. I'm sure he'll be pleased to see you.'

His smile seemed different. Less assured, but... happier?
'I'm not totally sure about that, but thanks.'

As they walked back from the beach, Mollie slipped her
hand into Erica's and she gave it a squeeze. She had no idea how
she was going to rearrange her life to make sure that Mollie
never felt like second best again, but she was determined to.
They also needed to sort out this issue with the photo and
whether the police could stop it being released online, but that
could wait until tomorrow.

In the car home, the three of them kept up a constant
chatter about Mollie's saxophone lessons and Andrew's work
and what she and Mollie were going to choose from the pizza
menu she'd found online. Keeping the conversation on safe
topics meant she didn't have to think about Ben being upset or
how they were going to help Mollie with the fallout from her
online blackmail.

It was only after they'd arrived home – and Mollie had gone
to get changed into pyjamas while they waited for the pizza –
that Erica remembered how Mollie had discovered the details of
what had happened in the fire from overhearing Andrew
talking to someone on the phone. Why was he talking about the
fire after all this time? And who was it that he'd been talking to?

THIRTY-TWO

Hunger – and guilt – had ensured that Erica had totally over-ordered from the pizza place. Fresh bread and garlic filled the air as they ate straight from the box. There was also tiramisu in the fridge and ice cream for Ben – vanilla, of course – in the ice box.

The sight of Mollie, cross-legged on the sofa, tipping her head back to get the end of the pizza into her mouth, made Erica smile. It felt like a second ago that she was sitting in a high chair and wearing a bib. Now she was so grown up. 'Since when did you start ordering the super spicy pizza?'

Mollie wrinkled her nose. 'I think it was about a month ago. Celeste was here and she ordered it. She told me to try it and it was really nice.'

The glass of white wine Erica was drinking turned acid on the back of her tongue. 'Celeste?'

Oblivious to Erica's tone, Mollie sipped at her Coke and nodded. 'Yes. She came over to help me with some homework. She ended up being here for ages so Dad invited her to stay for dinner with us.'

Erica's heart thudded in her chest, but she tried to keep her voice clear and light. 'I noticed a photo of you and her on the cork board in your bedroom. Was that the same night?'

Closing one eye, Mollie thought for a second, then her face cleared. 'Oh, that photo. No, that was a different time.'

Desperately, Erica wanted to ask her why Celeste was coming to the house. How often. For what purpose? And why no one – including Celeste herself – had ever mentioned this to her before. There could only be one reason. How had she been so blind?

But before she could even begin to phrase a question, Mollie brought her back to what was more important here. 'Mum. What's going to happen? With the photos. I mean, he must've sent them out now, mustn't he?'

All thoughts of Celeste and Andrew were moved to the back of her head. Her daughter was far more important right now. 'The police have got them, Mollie. Your dad has spoken with the team who work on that kind of thing and they confirmed that they've been able to track them down. It was never a boy, honey. These horrible people just sent photographs of someone your age. The person you were speaking to would've been an adult, tricking you into thinking he was a boy.'

Even though she'd avoided using any phrases that would make this even more unpleasant, Mollie winced. She could only imagine how humiliating this was for her. 'So, Roman doesn't exist?'

'No, sweetheart. They would have made him up.'

She watched Mollie's face as she processed all of this. It was too much, too horrible. But she couldn't leave any doubt in her mind that the boy she'd been speaking to was real. Mollie looked down at the pizza, picking off a piece of pepperoni but not eating it. 'Does Dad hate me?'

Where had that come from? 'No. Oh, sweetheart, no. Your dad could never hate you. He hates them, the people who did this to you. We both do. But he loves you.'

Andrew did love her. Very much. He'd been a wonderful father: so much fun and love and laughter. The polar opposite to her own dad who'd been distant and prickly and only spoke about school or whether she'd done her chores. When the children were young, it would bring her to tears to see how much he cared for them both, for all three of them. Hadn't she also congratulated herself on the two of them creating a home for their children that was filled with love? A love she'd rarely felt herself before meeting Andrew.

Still picking at the pizza, Mollie frowned. 'But it must be so embarrassing for him. The people he works with all know about this. They must've seen...'

She didn't need to finish that sentence, the pain in her face was evidence enough. Erica reached out and rubbed her arm. 'These people aren't your dad's friends. They work in a special unit. And they see these things all the time, Mollie. Worse things. No one is judging you. They know how these despicable people work. They are evil, but they are also clever. Anyone can end up in this position. There are grown adults who get tricked into these things. No one thinks anything bad about you.'

Mollie didn't look up as she started to tear at the crust of the pizza. 'But the picture is out there, isn't it? Online.'

There was no getting away from an honest answer. 'Yes, it is. I believe they've taken down the main site. But they said that they can't be sure where else it might be.'

The tearing was getting more aggressive. 'And everyone is going to see it. My friends are going to see it.'

If only she could protect her from this. 'They might.'

Mollie's mouth began to tremble in the way that, since she was small, preceded her rare tears. She'd always been so private with her emotions. Too private.

This time, Erica took her hand. 'You're going to get through this, Mollie, I promise.'

But the look in Mollie's eyes wasn't one that believed her. 'I can't ever go back there. To the school. I don't want to see anyone. I want to move. I want to leave and go somewhere else where nobody knows me.'

Erica's gut twisted in sympathy. She knew that feeling well. Hadn't she been desperate to leave home? To go away – to a whole other country – to start her life again? And after the fallout from the school trip, when she'd been suspended for the duration of the investigation, hadn't she taken the opportunity – the excuse – of Ben starting his new school to run away to the apartment she now lived in? Maybe the urge to run away had been passed down to Mollie with her DNA? 'I understand, Mollie, I really do. But you have all your friends here. What about Amelia? I know that she's desperate to hear from you.'

Mollie's voice was sharp. 'How do you know? Have you spoken to her?'

If Erica could have swallowed the words with her wine, she would've done. 'Only briefly. When I saw her at the school. And then I called her to see if she'd heard from you.'

Mollie groaned. 'Why did you do that?'

'Because we didn't know where you were. And because Amelia is your best friend. She cares about you.'

In that moment, sticking out her chin, Mollie looked just like Andrew. 'I'll make a new best friend at my next school.'

It wasn't as easy as that. First hand, Erica knew how long it could take to find a special friend who would be there for you no matter what. It wasn't until she'd been in England a while, and met Celeste, that she knew she'd found a friend she could rely on. At least, she *had* thought that. Now she had to face the possibility that she'd lost that friend, too.

Mollie had abandoned the pizza and was wiping her hands with one of the stiff serviettes. At a loss of what to say, Erica folded over the box and did the same, in silence, with the weight of unresolved thoughts hanging between them. It was awful. How many family mealtimes had Erica passed in silence back with her own family in the US? Her brother across the table, trying to make her laugh which – they both knew – would make their father lose his temper. Even as a young girl, she'd vowed that – when she had a family of her own – they would have the kind of messy, noisy, family dinners that she'd watch on her favourite sitcoms. How had she come to this?

She tried again. 'What about if you ask Amelia over? Once you've spoken to her you might—'

'Mum. You're not listening to me. I'm never going back. I don't want to argue. I'm going to go and take my make-up off so that I can go straight to bed after Dad and Ben get home.'

Erica hadn't realised that she was wearing any make-up. Girls these days were so good at it with their YouTube tutorials. She knew nothing at all about how to apply cosmetics properly at that age. Even if her father had allowed her out of the house with it. 'Okay. They'll be here pretty soon, I think.'

Andrew had sent a text to say that he was about to leave the school. She could only hope that it'd gone smoothly when Ben realised it was his dad not his mum coming to collect him.

Alone in the sitting room, thinking about Mollie and Ben and the mistakes she'd made, she had the urge to speak to her own mother. Before she could talk herself out of it, she pressed her mother's name on the screen.

She answered in three rings. 'Hello?'

'Mom. It's me, Erica.'

'Erica? What's wrong?'

Either her mother had a sixth sense about these things or she was just amazed that Erica was calling. Either way, where did she start? 'Everything's okay. We've just had some upset with Mollie. It made me want to call you.'

There was quiet on the other end as her mother seemed to be taking this in. Her voice trembled a little as she spoke. 'You wanted to call *me*?'

Wouldn't it be the most normal thing in the world for a

daughter to call home when she was upset? But that wasn't the relationship they'd had in a very long time. Was it too late? 'Yes. I realised today that I've made some mistakes. I don't think I've been a very good mother.'

It was like the wind had been taken out of her mother's sails. Her voice was small and tentative. 'And you want to ask me about being a mom?'

That wasn't exactly what she'd meant. 'I think I just realised that it's easy to get things wrong. And, when I left home, I was pretty angry. Not just with Dad. But with you. Because you never stood up for me.'

Her mother sighed. 'Your father was a complicated man, Erica. You know that.'

That was a misleading euphemism. 'He wasn't a nice man, Mom.'

Her dad had always been in charge. It was that simple. What he said, went. When he wasn't around, Erica and her mom got on pretty well. She'd taught her to bake and they liked the same TV shows. But Erica just couldn't stand the way her mom changed when her father was around. Like suddenly she didn't have an opinion on anything. She'd wait to hear what he wanted and then chime in her agreement. Was it any surprise that she'd vowed to do things differently in her own house?

As expected, her mother defended him. 'He did love you. And your brother. He just didn't know how to show it.'

What an understatement. Erica couldn't remember one time when he'd shown her any real affection. Not that she'd seen him be affectionate with her mother, either. 'Why did you stay with him?'

Her mother sounded surprised. 'Because he was my husband, Erica.'

She remembered her mother's response when she'd sought her opinion on Ben changing schools. *If Andrew thinks it's a good idea, you should definitely look at the school, Erica.* Hadn't she deferred to a man her whole life?

This wasn't going to change. She'd spoken to Celeste – even thinking of her name made her feel bad right now – about her relationship with her mother. Like Celeste had said, if her mother admitted now that it had been a mistake to stay in a marriage that had constricted her life, damaged her relationship with her children, it would be unbearable for her.

No. If Erica wanted a relationship with her mother, she would have to accept that side of her. And she did, she realised now, want a relationship with her. 'I miss you, Mom.'

There was a heavy silence at the other end of the phone. Was she crying? 'I miss you, too. And I've been thinking. Maybe I can come out to you. Come and see the children. If you want me to?'

It had been so long since she and her mother had been in the same room that Erica had no idea how that would go. Especially when you threw in a troubled teen, a son with additional needs and a marriage that was hanging by a thread. But she did know that she wanted to try. 'I would like that, Mom. I would like that very much.'

Mollie appeared at the doorway and she called her over to say hello to her grandmother. Watching her daughter smile down the phone at whatever her mother was saying gave her a warmth in her heart that she hadn't felt about home in a long, long time.

Just as they were saying their goodbyes, the window was flooded with the sensor lights from the driveway. Andrew and Ben were home. She crossed her fingers that it had all gone smoothly.

THIRTY-THREE

Spending time with Mollie – just the two of them – had been the absolute right thing to do, but Erica had been nervous about Andrew collecting Ben without her. Whether Ben would resist leaving with Andrew when he was expecting her and how he was going to cope with the hour-long journey when he was already tired. Though it had been the right thing to stay with Mollie, again she felt the impossibility of providing what they both needed.

Thankfully, when they arrived at the house, all seemed well. Underneath his favourite warm dark-green hoodie, Ben was still wearing his planets pyjamas. The rest of his clothes must have been in the bag that he was clutching to his chest. She reached out for him. 'Hey, Ben. Good job trying the sleep-over. I'm so proud of you.'

Ben let her put her arms around him but didn't put down his bag. He probably thought they were going to leave soon for their apartment. Andrew kicked off his shoes and dropped his keys onto the hall table with a clatter. 'He was all ready for me when I turned up, weren't you, buddy?'

After releasing him, Erica held Ben at arms' length; he

looked absolutely exhausted. 'We're going to stay over with Daddy and Mollie tonight. Is that okay? I've made up your bed in your old room. Mollie's going to take you up there. Do you want to go now?'

Over her shoulder, Ben smiled at Mollie and she grinned back at him. 'Let's go up, Ben.'

Surprisingly quickly, Ben made for the stairs. She'd been expecting much more resistance to staying here. 'Do you want me to come up with you?'

Mollie shook her head. 'No. We'll be fine. Once Ben's settled, I'm going to go to bed myself. I'm shattered.'

She kissed Erica, then Andrew, goodnight and turned to go upstairs. Erica watched Ben follow her. It was way past his bedtime: he was almost asleep on his feet. Despite the emotional upheaval of today, it felt good to have both of her children under the same roof. Once they were gone, she joined Andrew in the sitting room where he was pouring himself a glass of red wine.

He held up the bottle to her as she walked in and she nodded. 'Yes, please. Just a small one.'

He brought the glasses over to where she was sitting on the sofa. 'What a day, eh?'

It felt like a week had passed since finding out Mollie had disappeared. 'I've definitely had quieter afternoons. How was Ben when you picked him up?'

Andrew took a large gulp of his wine and she watched his Adam's apple move in his throat. 'A little confused to see me rather than you, I think, but I told him Mollie was waiting and he couldn't get in the car quick enough.'

Despite the familiar sweep of guilt at keeping them apart, that made her smile. 'What did they say about him getting upset? Was it my fault for just leaving him like that?'

He shook his head, took another gulp of his wine. 'The woman I spoke to was very kind. She said it's common for it to

take a few attempts for some children before they're comfortable staying the whole night. She said we can try again with a
sleepover for Ben whenever we're ready.'

She wasn't sure she'd ever be ready. She liked to have him
with her, where he was safe. 'It's strange all being back here
together. Nice, but strange.'

Andrew nodded. 'Yes, I think Mollie has really missed
living with Benjamin. I don't think I'd really considered how
close they are.'

'Well, they are twins.'

'Yes. I suppose so.'

She wanted to ask him if he'd missed living with her. But,
bearing in mind the arguments that had punctuated their last
months in the house together, she was afraid of his answer. She
sipped at her wine. It was strong and fruity. She drank so rarely
these days.

Andrew broke the silence. 'Do you remember that first
holiday we took them on? When they were only a few months
old?'

In her mind, a picture postcard of rolling Yorkshire hills
from the windows of their car, tea and cake in small gingham-
clothed cafés in picturesque villages, a visit to the James Herriot
Museum where they'd bought each of the children a toy lamb.
'Yes, of course. It was lovely. Just the four of us.'

It hadn't even mattered that Benjamin had woken them up
at 4 a.m. each morning, that they'd taken it in turns to sit up
with him, bleary-eyed and coffee in hand, so that the other one
could catch another couple of hours sleep before Mollie joined
the party. The faraway look in Andrew's eyes suggested he was
remembering it the same way. 'I thought we'd won the jackpot,
you know. One of each, first go. I remember looking at the two
of them in that double buggy and thinking we've cracked it.'

Erica swallowed down the lump in her throat which the
memory of her two babies in that double stroller had brought.

She'd felt the same, basking in the admiration from strangers on the street: everyone was interested in twins. And her babies had been beautiful. 'I know what you mean. It was hard work, but...'

Andrew raised an eyebrow. 'Not as hard as it is now, right?'

She knew what he meant but didn't want to agree that fast. 'It's just different.'

He frowned at the deep burgundy wine as he swirled it in the glass. Whether it was the relief of finding Mollie or the fact of him collecting Ben or just being here in this warm familiar room with a glass of wine, there was a connection between them that she hadn't felt in a very long time. He was still, two decades after they'd met, the man she found most attractive in this world. She thought about that picture in Mollie's room of Celeste and fear crept into the edges of her contentment. She took a larger sip of her wine. 'Mollie was asking about the fire.'

He didn't look up. 'Was she?'

She needed to work up to asking him about the telephone call that Mollie had overheard. 'Yes. We had a long conversation on the beach about it. I explained why I had to get Benjamin out. And why I couldn't get back in to her.'

Was he even listening? He'd barely moved. Did he still not understand what'd happened that day?

She kept talking over his loud silence. 'She understood. I mean, I had to explain what'd happened because she didn't remember it, but it made sense to her. I think she's forgiven me.'

When he spoke, his voice was harder. 'Has she?'

Surely, he knew how important this was to her? He knew how guilty she'd felt about that night. How she'd relived it again and again. 'You can imagine how that feels for me.'

Finally, he looked up at her, but his eyes were dark and unreadable. 'Of course I know, Erica. I was there when you woke up with a loud gasp in the middle of the night for months afterwards, listening while you talked about it – relived it – over and over again. Do you not think I felt it, too? That guilt. That I hadn't protected you – any of you?'

The force of his voice was a shock. She knew that he'd taken it hard when they'd discovered that the fire had been started by a young boy he'd arrested the year before. He'd found out where Andrew lived, where his family lived, and thrown a firework through the letterbox of their old house. He'd never talked about this though. Never spoken about feeling guilty the way that she had. 'I didn't know you felt—'

'And I was angry, Erica. So angry at you.'

She put a hand to her throat; it was hard to breathe. 'Angry? At me?'

'How could you have let go of Mollie? She was so tiny and fragile. How hard could it have been to just drag her behind you?'

'I told you... I had Ben... and...'

'Of course you had Ben. Those scars down her arm are a constant reminder of the fact that you saved Ben first. That you always put him first. I was just thankful that Mollie didn't remember much about the fire afterwards. But I did, Erica. And that night – sitting beside her as she sobbed with the pain of having her burns dressed – I swore to make sure that nothing like that ever happened again.'

Hot tears pricked the back of Erica's eyes. How many times had he told her not to blame herself. That it had been an impossible choice. And now he was saying that his anger against her had smouldered all of these years? She couldn't speak; she could only watch as he unleashed all the words that had festered unsaid in the last five years.

'I tried to do it your way, Erica. I tried all the strategies you came up with. But then, that day in Aldeburgh, when Ben gave Mollie a nosebleed...'

'He didn't mean to do that. He was so upset—'

'I know he didn't mean to do it. Do you think I'm a monster?

But it still happened. She was still hurt. Again. Mollie just keeps on coming off worst. For me, it was the fire all over again.'

The fire. Clearly, they couldn't move on from that day, either of them. Thinking back to Mollie's explanation of how she'd found out what had happened, it was time to ask him outright what was going on. 'Why were you talking about the fire on the telephone a few days ago, Andrew? Who were you talking to?'

That made him turn towards her with a start. 'How do you know about that?'

'Mollie told me. She overheard you.'

He returned to gazing at his fingers, picking at his thumbnail. 'We don't need to talk about that right now.'

Her heart thumped in her chest at the way he was avoiding her eyes. 'I want to talk about it. Who was on the other end of that call?'

He took a deep breath and then looked at her. 'If you really want to know, I was speaking to a lawyer. I was asking what I needed to do to file for a divorce.'

THIRTY-FOUR

It was as if he'd punched her in the stomach. 'Divorce?'

Andrew held out his hands in supplication. 'What did you expect me to do? How long did you expect me to wait, Erica? I'm here on my own all the time. Mollie is a thirteen-year-old girl. She doesn't want to hang out with her dad. I'm just supposed to stay home and wait until you decide to come back?'

How had they seen this so differently? 'You make it sound as if I left you for another man. I'm living there, in that tiny little apartment, because I'm looking after our son. We agreed that I would rent somewhere closer to his school. It was for Ben.'

Andrew's sigh went down to his boots. 'Yes, we agreed to it but it wasn't supposed to be permanent, was it? The idea was that you would stay there for three months at the most, gradually get him settled into the school and then we'd work out a way to combine some residential care with the day school. But aside from today, you've never tried him overnight. I doubt he's even visited the residential wing. It feels as if you're never going to do it. It feels as if you don't want to come home.'

Was he right? If she was really honest with herself, the move to the apartment hadn't only been a good decision for

Ben. Living somewhere else, not having to see familiar faces around town, she'd also been able to keep anxious thoughts about the investigation at a manageable distance. And life had been calmer, easier, with only Ben to worry about.

But when she'd told Andrew it would be temporary, she hadn't been lying. She really had hoped that over time – once she'd got to know the teachers at his new school and he was happy there – the fear of what might happen if he was out of her sight would recede. But it hadn't. She couldn't keep the tears spilling from her eyes. 'I know that I agreed to some residential care. I know, Andrew. But he wasn't ready for that. I couldn't force him. What did you want me to do?'

'I wanted you to accept that we needed time together without Ben's needs twisting our family out of shape.'

'You expected me to find it easy to just send my son away?'

'Our son. And no, I never said it would be easy. I just wanted Mollie to have some time, too. And yes, maybe I'm selfish, but I wanted to have my wife back. Is that so wrong?'

They were going round and around again. The same arguments with no solutions. 'You have no idea how hard it is, Andrew. This feeling that you have to pull yourself in so many different directions that you're failing in all of them.'

'I do understand, but I also know that we all deserve a life here. Not just Ben. I've waited a long time, Erica – more than just these three months that you've been living elsewhere – and, at some point, I realised that I need to just accept that you're not coming back. Literally and metaphorically. Our marriage is over.'

She was surprised by the break in his voice. She'd never considered it this way, that he felt abandoned. Then the picture of Celeste with Mollie that she'd seen in her bedroom flashed up in her mind. 'Have you met someone else? Is that what it is?'

At least he had the decency to look uncomfortable. 'Not exactly.'

Her hand was so tight on her glass of wine that she wouldn't have been surprised if it had shattered under the pressure. 'What does not exactly mean?'

'I've been out a couple of times. Just for a drink. Nothing happened between us. It was nice to be with someone who enjoyed my company, who wanted to be with me, who actually gave me their full attention. I wasn't asking a lot, Erica. We've got two children. I'm not a baby. I was just asking for something. A little tiny piece of you.'

Erica wanted to throw herself on the rug and beat at the floor with her fists like a child. She didn't have a tiny piece left to give Andrew when every gram of her felt used up by the end of every day. It was impossible not to raise her voice along with her anger. 'You expect me to believe that all you've done is have a couple of drinks with *someone* when you've taken off your wedding ring and called a divorce lawyer?'

Andrew's right hand moved instinctively to cover the fingers of his left. Had he thought she hadn't noticed? 'Calm down, Erica.'

Has anyone, in the whole history of the world, felt calmer after someone says that to them? 'I am perfectly calm. Can you answer my question?'

'I just thought that, if you suspected that I was seeing someone, you might try and take Mollie to live with you. The lawyer I was speaking to is someone we know at the station. She's not a divorce lawyer, she's a family lawyer. I was asking her about custody of the kids. She wanted to know if I had any evidence that Mollie would be better off staying with me and...'

He didn't need to finish that sentence. She felt sick. Five years on from that terrible day and he'd use it to keep her daughter away from her? 'I can't believe it.'

He looked so ashamed. 'I jumped the gun. I'm sorry. It's just, I was talking about our situation at work and... things were said and I thought I should be prepared.'

She could just imagine what things were said. Almost none of his colleagues had marriages that'd lasted. The strains of the job. And that was without a child with special needs in the mix. 'Did you really think I would take the children away from you?'

He shrugged. 'You're already an hour away. What if you decide to go back to the States? What if you find a school there for Benjamin and Mollie wants to come with you? Where does that leave me?'

How could he give up on their marriage so easily? 'I think you'll find that you were the one who found this school for Benjamin, not me.'

'Because I thought it'd be good for him, good for our family. I didn't expect you to just divide the household.'

She pressed her lips together tightly. Not trusting herself to start speaking because a terrible tsunami of words was threatening to flow from her the minute she began to tell him what she thought.

Andrew slid his glass onto the table. 'I can't do this again. I'm going to bed. We need to focus on Mollie and school. All of this can wait.'

As soon as he'd gone, Erica let her head fall into her hands. Everything was such a mess. The last few months had been so difficult. Through everything, though, she'd thought that they would work it out someday. Maybe once Ben didn't need her as much. Or when Andrew wasn't working so hard. Or Mollie...

But none of that was real life. Ben did still need her. Would always need her.

And Mollie needed her, too. Much more than she'd realised.

And Andrew? His anger had taken her breath away. Maybe there was no coming back from this. She hadn't had the courage to ask him outright if he was seeing Celeste, unsure whether she'd actually survive him telling her that she was losing both her husband and her best friend at the same time.

Celeste was the one she needed to speak to about Mollie and school. She'd call her tomorrow. And maybe she would feel brave enough to ask her about Andrew and why there was a picture of her with her daughter on a visit to the house that she knew nothing about.

THIRTY-FIVE

The next morning, Andrew and Erica kept their distance like two opposing magnets. Using a jar of instant coffee while he was making something frothy in his stupid new machine was petty but satisfying. Determined not to ask him outright whether the woman he'd been 'for a few drinks with' was Celeste, she opted instead for cool politeness which was the exact opposite of the burning rage in her gut. Did their marriage mean nothing to him? How could he move on so quickly and easily?

Today was the planned back-to-school interview after Mollie's suspension, but when she and Andrew floated the idea to Mollie of taking the rest of the week off to get over the events of yesterday, she was more than eager to agree with them. 'Yes, please. I can't face going in and seeing everybody.'

Across the kitchen table, trying not to be irritated by the hiss and clunk of Andrew still making himself a coffee, Erica began to lay the groundwork for what she planned to do next. 'I think I should go in anyway and explain what's happened.'

Mollie reddened. 'No. I don't want my teachers to know.'

Erica could understand why she'd feel like this. 'I know,

sweetheart. But we need to keep the school informed. And it also explains why you were acting so out of character.'

Everything she said was true. What she wasn't saying was that she had a second motive for wanting to go into the school alone: to meet with Celeste and have it out with her. Was she the woman Andrew had been meeting for 'just drinks'?

Pushing cornflakes around the bowl with a spoon, Mollie's face had darkened. 'I just don't want my teachers knowing what I did.'

That, she could help with. 'They won't tell all the teachers. With an issue like this, it's kept strictly on a need-to-know basis. I could make an appointment to talk to Celeste. You know her. She's not going to judge you or make you feel embarrassed about this.'

Looking sideways at Andrew, she waited to see his reaction at Celeste's name, but he had his back to her. Mollie continued to stare into her cereal bowl. 'Okay. You can tell Celeste. She'd be okay.'

It was a good thing she'd agreed, because Erica had already sent a text to Celeste last night to ask whether she had any free time tomorrow and Celeste had offered to squeeze her in at the beginning of period three.

Erica arrived at the school just as the students were streaming out of the building for break time. There was such a huge difference between the youngest and oldest students in a school this size. They began as small children – blazer arms longer than their fingertips, backpacks as big as they were – and left at the end as fully fledged adults. School felt like a lifetime to kids, but it was a blink of an eye in their whole life. Friendships that had been everything at school were often lost before they even hit twenty. That's what she'd tried to convey to students who were having a tough time. But it was impossible to understand without the benefit of age and hindsight.

Celeste was waiting for her in reception and walked her straight to her office. 'I only have about thirty minutes. I'm sorry. It's a full teaching day normally, but my class are in the hall for a road safety presentation with the rest of their year group so I can sneak out for a short while.'

Erica's priority was Mollie and how they were going to navigate her return to school. The other issue would have to come second. 'No problem, I probably should've just called you, but I wanted to see you. Sorry.'

Pressed for time, Erica got straight to the point as soon as they'd sat down, explaining in more detail than she had on the phone what had happened and what they'd discovered about why Mollie had needed the money she'd stolen.

Celeste looked as if she might cry herself. 'That's awful. Poor Mollie. We had no idea she was struggling. It's so difficult: things like this are going on a lot more than we're aware of. I know that the internet is a wonderful thing but sometimes I do think it would be a lot easier if it never existed. Especially for kids. I could tell you so many stories of the issues that we're having right now because of Snapchat and Instagram and whatever other fresh hell of an app that's about to appear next.'

It was so difficult: trying to stay one step ahead of what was going on. Celeste had always been such a brilliant teacher. She cared as much as Erica had when she was here. She worked as hard, she was as diligent, but she had an ability that Erica had never mastered. The ability to switch off. Erica had always struggled. If something happened with one of the kids at school, she would lay awake worrying about it, playing it over and over in her mind to see if she could have done something different or helped them more. Andrew had tried to help her. As a police officer he'd told her that he'd had to find a way to leave cases at work. He said that, if she didn't manage to develop that ability, she'd drive herself crazy. Maybe that was one of the many reasons that Celeste had been a much better fit for senior leadership than she had been.

Maybe it was also the way she'd managed to spend time with Erica's husband and daughter without considering that she should tell her best friend. 'How do you do it? How do you manage to switch off and not let this job completely take over your life?'

Celeste smiled. 'I've learned to compartmentalise. When I leave here, everything stays in my in-tray. I can't allow it to travel home with me in my brain. It's not always possible; some things really do get to me. But if I let everything from here – every petty parental complaint, every argument with a student – take up residence in my head, I would never be able to do this job.'

She wanted to stay focused on Mollie. On a strategy for helping her through the next few months, but she had to get this suspicion out of the way. 'What were you about to tell me last time I was here?'

For a moment, Celeste looked wrong-footed. Then she blushed. 'I'm not sure how to say this.'

Erica's heart plummeted: she'd really wanted to be wrong. 'You've been seeing Andrew.'

When she nodded, Erica felt sick. 'Yes. I mean, not really Andrew. It's Mollie. Andrew asked me to come and spend some time with her. I know it's a little weird, because I'm her teacher. But I'm also friends with her parents.'

Friends? 'You're not dating Andrew? You haven't been out for a drink with him?'

Celeste's eyes widened. 'Dating Andrew? Absolutely not. What made you think that?'

Momentary relief flooded through Erica. 'I just thought... well, he said he had been out with someone and then

I saw a picture of you and Mollie... I'm sorry. I jumped to conclusions. But why the secrecy? Why didn't you tell me?'

Celeste blushed again. 'I wanted to. Twice, I saw your neighbour on the way in and I was sure it'd get back to you, but Andrew begged me not to say anything.'

That would be what Lynn had wanted to tell her about Andrew when she spoke to her in the front garden on Sunday. 'Why didn't Andrew want me to know?'

'He said you'd think he wasn't coping. I think he's struggling, Erica. I think he really misses you and Ben. They both do. When you were in here last, I almost told you, but you seemed so laden down already that I thought it might make you feel worse.'

Erica swallowed hard. If only she had been as good as Celeste at compartmentalising. Teacher. Wife. Mother. School. Andrew. Benjamin. Mollie. Where did one end and the next begin? And where was she in all of it? 'I've made such a mess of all of this, Celeste. I've let Mollie down so badly.'

Celeste looked amazed. 'What do you mean? You're a fantastic parent!'

The kindness in her tone only made Erica feel worse. 'I'm not. I've tried to do everything right and I've ended up letting everybody down.'

That's how it felt. She tried so hard to do right by all three of them, to sacrifice everything that she had wanted to ensure that everybody else's lives could run smoothly but that hadn't been a solution, had it? Her marriage was in ruins, Mollie was going through this awful thing and even Benjamin – she couldn't help but think – might be making more progress if she wasn't too frightened to let him experience anything without her.

Celeste was shaking her head. 'You need to stop thinking that right now. You know as well as I do what some parents are like out there. You've done nothing but the best you could at every stage.'

'I've spent so much time trying to help Benjamin that Mollie has felt completely abandoned. And I had no idea.'

There was a pause while Celeste considered what she'd said. 'Like glass child syndrome?'

'What's that?'

Celeste rested her elbows on the desk, steepled her hands and dropped her chin onto her knuckles. 'Okay, I am not saying this is you for a moment, but glass child syndrome is a term used for the sibling of a special needs child who is unseen – looked through like glass – because their parents' attention is focused on the child with the needs.'

Erica's stomach lurched. 'It's a thing? There's a name for it?'

'Again, I'm not saying this is you or Mollie, but often the child without the additional needs tries to be as well behaved as possible, becomes a people pleaser, because they don't want to give their parents any more work to do.'

Hot tears burned at the back of Erica's eyes. 'And I've done that to her?'

'The twins have two parents. This is not all on you, Erica.'

Guilt flooded through her. 'But maybe that's my fault too? That Andrew isn't more involved? Because I shut him out?'

Celeste's face reddened. 'Okay, you need to stop heaping hot coals on your own head. Andrew is big enough and ugly enough to have made you listen if he felt that was happening. He needs to take responsibility for the fact that he didn't do more.'

Of course, she was right. Erica knew that. But she also knew that sometimes you had to leave space for somebody else to fill. Like in class when you asked a question of a student and you had to wait for them to answer before rushing in to put words in their mouth. You need to leave the step empty so somebody else can climb onto it.

'I want to make this right, Celeste, but I don't know how. I don't know how to untangle any of this and make it work.'

Her friend's face was sympathetic and kind. 'What about starting with what *you* want for a change? If you know how you want things to be, you can aim for that. What do you want?'

What did she want? The easy answer was that she wanted her whole family together in one home. She wanted Ben and Mollie to have the best life they could. She wanted her and Andrew to be able to repair their relationship.

If she wanted to sort out this mess, maybe she needed to go back to where it started.

THIRTY-SIX

Home isn't where you're born, it's where you want to be. Third in a terrace of four, the terracotta Victorian house was quintessentially English. From its large bay window, which looked out on the street, to the navy front door with its stained-glass window and brass knocker. When they'd moved here, Erica, newly pregnant with the twins, had been entranced by all the traditional features. The tiled front step, the ornate white coving, the cast-iron fireplace. It's a cliché that Americans in England want to live in a house with history, but for Erica, it had been true. She'd loved it from the moment they'd walked inside.

After leaving Celeste's office, she'd needed some time to clear her head before returning home to Andrew and the children. Not knowing where to go, she'd ended up here. Their first family home. Parked outside, she had an unsettling sensation of familiarity and strangeness. It was their house, but it wasn't. Whoever had bought it had clearly spent a lot of money on restoring it to its best. Looking at it from the road, no one would know that it had once been ravaged by fire.

Speaking about the fire to Mollie, and to Andrew, had

brought it all back again. The memory so vivid of standing almost exactly where she was parked right now, searching the windows of the house for movement as smoke billowed from the front door, waiting for her daughter to be brought to her, not knowing if her mistake – letting Mollie's hand slip from hers – had been fatal. Erica pressed her clenched fists into her stomach to try to stop the churning there. It was a nightmare that she'd tried to push down and not think about. But pushing it down had just made its effects more potent.

A face came to the bay window, a woman maybe a decade younger than her looked out at her car, maybe wondering who was this stranger staring at her house. Erica avoided her gaze by turning her head forwards, placing her hands on the steering wheel as if she were about to leave. Legs trembling, she didn't trust herself to drive away yet. Five more minutes and she'd go.

One of the things she'd loved about this street was the trees. Strong oaks lined the pavement, so different to the young saplings on their new housing estate. Many afternoons, she'd walked back along these pavements with the twins asleep in the buggy after attending a music group or storytelling at the library. Before the fire, they'd been so happy here. Even after Ben's diagnosis, after he'd started at a different school and she had to try to split herself in two every afternoon at pickup. They'd still been together, still been a family.

It wasn't Ben. She knew that now. His needs weren't the thing that had cracked their family open. Her sweet, sensitive boy had not been the catalyst for all that was to come. It was that night. The fire. The moment where she'd had to make the decision that haunted her to this day. She pictured Andrew's face yesterday when his anger, suppressed for so long, had come to the surface. Her guilt, his anger, their inability to listen to one another. That's what had caused this.

After the fire, she hadn't been able to even think about coming back here. It didn't matter that Andrew had promised that the insurance pay out would ensure that all the electrics could be redone and they wouldn't have to worry about anything like that happening again. Even stepping into the hallway afterwards – seeing the destruction first hand, the children's toys blackened by smoke, the wooden banister eaten by flames – had made her feel nauseous. Nothing on earth could have persuaded her to bring her precious children back here again.

Buying the new build was supposed to be a fresh start for them all. Somewhere modern and safe. She'd wanted to put that nightmare behind them. Start again. Learn how to manage the needs of both her children. Keep her marriage alive.

But juggling everything had been so hard. Fighting the system for what Ben needed was a full-time job in itself. And she also had Mollie and a job that demanded a lot from her. Some days she felt overwhelmed, overwrought and it was no surprise that she had so little energy left for Andrew. Why hadn't he understood that? Why hadn't he seen how much she was struggling?

When the accident happened at Easter – and a boy had been hurt on her watch – it fed the fear that had been lying in wait since the fire. It grew inside her until it was all that she could see. How vulnerable Ben was. How no one else could keep him safe. How much he needed her to be his advocate. His voice.

Erica knew that every mother worried about their child going into the world. Who among her friends hadn't lain awake thinking about how it was going to be when they let their babies walk to the corner shop alone, meet their friends at the park without them, catch a train unsupervised, learn to drive a car? It didn't matter if your head tried to tell you that everyone does those things – that you did those things once for the first time – you still worry about how your child, that tiny little person still in front of you, will ever be safe in this world.

For most people, though, it was a natural process. As their child grew older, they become more separate from them. Independence made them brave and they took tentative, increasingly confident, steps into the world.

But when your child has special needs, that doesn't just evolve. They don't say, *Mum, can I go to the shops with my friend* or *everyone else's mum lets them do it* or *I promise I'll be back before it's dark.* No. That change won't – can't – come from your child. It has to come from you. You have to be the one to decide when they're ready for the next stage, for something other than you. People can suggest, advise. Teachers, educational psychologists, carers. But they can't make the decision for you. And they can't tell you that your decision will be the right one. For him or for you. Because what mother is ever really ready to push her child – however gently, however lovingly – from her nest?

Andrew had accused her of being happy to move out of their home, to leave him and Mollie alone. That wasn't true: she'd missed them both as if two slices of her heart had been left behind. But she'd be lying if she didn't admit that there was a relief, too. With only Ben in the apartment, she would never again be forced to make a decision between the two of them. She closed her eyes and let her forehead rest on the steering wheel. How she'd failed Mollie, her beautiful girl.

After the events of the last few days, she knew that things had to change. Mollie needed her more than she'd realised, and Ben needed her to be braver about what she expected from him. And Andrew? He had his own mistakes to own. She still loved him, but Celeste was right. He'd let her take everything onto herself. He did need to take responsibility for the fact that he didn't do more. And if he wouldn't? Maybe it would be over between them.

She glanced back at the house again. The woman had gone from the window. The house was back to its best. It'd survived the fire and was now the home for another woman, maybe another marriage, another family. Could her family get back to its best, too?

She turned the key in the ignition and the car engine roared into life. At the end of their meeting at the school, Celeste had tried to make her understand that everything could be fixed. She'd offered counselling for Mollie at the school and also – tentatively – suggested that it could be something Erica and Andrew might want to consider for themselves. 'Please can you stop beating yourself up about all of this? There's no guidebook to parenting. This thing that's happened with Mollie could easily have happened anyway, it's rife. I know it's scary, but this could be the beginning of a whole new level of honesty that lots of teenagers and parents don't have.'

Maybe that was the solution. Honesty. Transparency. Truth.

And asking for – and accepting – help.

She couldn't fix everything at once. And Mollie – her glass child – deserved to be seen first. In bed last night, she'd thought about something that might help her take control of what had happened to her. It might be crazy, but it was time to start taking some risks. Before pulling away, she called Celeste's mobile to leave a voicemail.

'Hi, Celeste. It's me, Erica. Do you still have that friend that works at the local TV station? I might have an idea of how I can help Mollie.'

Tomorrow she had to attend the Teacher Misconduct Panel to determine her professional fate. Whatever the outcome, she would need to make some big decisions about the next stage of her life.

THIRTY-SEVEN

The Teacher Misconduct Panel took place in a nondescript office building in East London. On the third floor, a small meeting room with a large oval conference table gave little space for movement. Erica sidestepped along the far side, following her union representative – Richard – to their seats. Cleaning fluid, ink and paper: it smelled like a classroom. Anxiety crept through her and she tried to push her shoulders down, clear her mind, breathe.

Richard was a nice guy, but more suited to sending peppy group emails than face-to-face situations. Meeting her outside the room this morning, he'd smiled hopefully at her. 'Let's do this.'

Opposite them, on the other side of the conference table, sat a panel of three people who would decide her fate. Before they introduced themselves, she knew that the panel had to include at least one current teacher and a lay member – someone who'd never been a teacher.

The chair of the panel – Polly Wood – was a deputy head, around fifty, she'd guess, and wore a long floral dress with a black jacket. Her smile was kind. 'Thank you for coming in today, Erica. I can imagine that this has been a very difficult time.'

That was the understatement of the century. Erica squeezed her hands into fists under the desk to stop them from trembling. 'I just want to get this over with, to be honest.'

She tilted her head to show her understanding. 'We'll try and get through it all as quickly as we can. We've already been through all the information sent to us. But there was something new that we were sent late yesterday, which I'm not sure you'd have seen?'

Erica glanced at Richard, who shrugged and shook his head. She turned back to Polly. 'No. We haven't.'

'Okay, then. I presume, though, that you know that the referral to the Teaching Regulation Agency came from parents at the school and that, because a child was physically injured, the decision was made to undertake an investigation?'

Bile burned the back of Erica's throat. She hadn't been able to stomach anything to eat this morning. Though she'd had weeks to digest this, it was still so hard to hear. She'd always been a popular teacher. Never had a parental – or pupil – complaint in the whole of her career. It was one of the reasons the head had been so keen for her to attend the trip in the first place: she was well known for being firm but fair. These three people wouldn't know that, though, would they? It was so humiliating. 'Yes. I'm aware of that.'

'Our job today is to make a decision whether there is a case to answer and, if so, whether the alleged misconduct is potentially serious enough to result in prohibition from teaching. This can come under one of three headings: unacceptable professional conduct; conduct that may bring the profession into disrepute; or that you have been convicted of a relevant offence.'

Though it was part of the process that all of this was explained again, it was like water torture, each word was a drip more painful than the last. Erica swallowed and glanced at Richard. He shuffled some papers.

Polly clasped her hands together and leaned forward in her chair. 'According to the parents who made the referral to the TRA, on the day of the accident, you'd been—' she glanced at the paperwork '—victimising their boys. Following them around when other children were allowed the freedom to explore on their own. The boys claim that you effectively chased them into the road, resulting, unfortunately, in quite a serious injury for one of the students. We also have your written statement explaining that you were asked to keep a close eye on one of the boys in particular due to past challenging behaviour.'

There was nothing in her tone to give any kind of clue, so Erica tried to read Polly's face. As a teacher herself, surely Polly had understood the need for her to tail a child who might – *had* – put himself and others in danger? Again, she ran the events of that day in slow motion through her mind. Had she been too close? Had she made the boys uncomfortable or been too strong in the way she spoke? As she had many times in the last three months, she saw again Luke's face, the deliberation whether to follow his friends or his teacher's instruction, the decision to dart across the road, the screech of the car, the metallic thud...

'Mrs Mason?'

She looked up and saw a raised eyebrow on Polly's face. Clearly, she'd missed a question. 'Sorry. Could you repeat that?'

'Of course. I asked if there was anything you wanted to add to your statement at this stage?'

What could she add? That she'd woken in a hot sweaty mess at least twice a week ever since? How she wished with every ounce of her that she'd stuck to her guns and refused to go on the trip? Explain the impact of that day – that guilt – on every part of her life since? She shook her head. 'No. Nothing to add.'

Polly nodded. 'Okay. Now I've got all of that out of the way,

I can tell you about this new evidence. Another child on the trip, who will obviously remain anonymous, actually filmed the whole thing.'

Erica's gasp was involuntary and dramatic. It was on film.

Polly continued. 'The student has said that they were recording the student who was arguing with you. For comedy value. Then obviously the accident happened and they were afraid that they would get into trouble. The date of this panel is being shared on various parent WhatsApp groups and, when he confessed to his parents, they got in touch.'

It was difficult to breathe. The room was so hot. Erica's face burned. 'What does it show?'

'The whole thing. Because of the sensitive nature of the recording, it was decided not to send it to you on email. But you can request to see it. However, the important part is that the recording shows that you were not physically close to the boys and that, at no point, do you raise your voice in a way that could be seen as threatening.'

Erica had to hold tight to the arms on her chair to stop her from sliding from it. Warped from so many replays, her memory of what she'd said and done – or not done – had been completely unreliable.

She could barely whisper her next question. 'What does this mean for the investigation?'

Polly smiled. 'It means that the investigation will be closed. There will be no further action. You are free to return to your teaching position.'

It took a while for the words to filter through to Erica's brain. It was over? As easily as that? All those weeks of self-recrimination and guilt and worry and anxiety and it was 'you can come back and be a teacher again'? She wanted to leave, to find somewhere quiet, to weep. 'Thank you.'

The final bits of paperwork and closing remarks passed in a blur. Then they were outside the room, Richard shaking her hand and wishing her well. Not trusting her legs to carry her too far just yet, she sank down into one of the plastic chairs in the waiting area to catch her breath. That's when she saw the woman looking at her. Slight, dark-haired and pretty, there was something familiar that she just couldn't place.

Tentatively, the woman approached. 'Hi, Mrs Mason? Is that you?'

Erica pasted on a smile for, she assumed, this must be a parent of a child she'd taught in the past. It was an occupational hazard to live in the same area that you worked. Over her time as a teacher, she'd often been caught at the most inopportune times by a current or ex-student. 'Hi. Yes, it's me.'

When the woman smiled, though, recognition chilled Erica's spine. She looked just like her son.

'Thank goodness. It is you. Otherwise, I'd have looked a complete fool. I'm Amanda. Amanda Taylor. Luke Taylor's mum.'

After the accident on the trip, Erica had gone in the ambulance with Luke and stayed with him until his parents arrived. The last time she'd seen Amanda Taylor's face, it'd been ashen with worry. After that, she'd had to return to the accommodation until another teacher could be sent to replace her.

Now Amanda was standing in front of her in a pale-blue shirt and smart trousers, with a face she couldn't quite read. 'How are you here? I mean... did you have to...'

Amanda shook her head. 'No. I wasn't required to be here. But I've seen the film. And I knew the hearing was today. I just wanted to speak with you.'

This still wasn't over. What did she want? 'How's Luke?'

Despite the screech of car tyres and the thud of impact that still woke Erica in the night, Luke had been extremely fortunate that the worst of his injuries was a broken arm. That hadn't stopped her replaying her actions over and over along with the catastrophic anxiety about what might have happened.

'He's healing really well. He's back at school.' She frowned. 'I don't know if you already knew that?'

Surely she knew that Erica had been suspended until the investigation was complete? Or did she wonder if Mollie had told her? Or one of the other teachers? 'No. I didn't know. That's great.'

Amanda's voice was hesitant, but she clearly had something she wanted to say. 'I should've spoken to you. Before it all got out of hand. By the time I asked, we were advised not to. I still don't really know why.'

Erica nodded. 'I was told the same.'

Amanda's eyes dropped to her hands, where she was fiddling with her wedding ring. 'I was terrified when we got that call from the school. It's every parent's worst nightmare, isn't it? Being told that your child has been hurt. My husband drove so fast that night I thought that we were going to have an accident ourselves. We just needed to get to him as fast as possible.'

Still raw from the panel, Erica didn't know if she could take this. But what else could she do? Whatever had been concluded in there, she was still present when this poor woman's son was hurt. 'I can imagine.'

All of this still weighed on her, but when Amanda looked up, it was her eyes that looked guilty. 'We should never have done this. It was never your fault. I knew it wasn't your fault.'

A hard knot of a sob rose from Erica's chest and almost choked her. She wanted to speak, to thank her for these precious words, but it made it impossible to open her mouth without risking letting it escape.

Amanda's eyes begged her to understand. 'It was one of the others. Vinnie's mum. She was so fired up with it all. Said the school had treated her son so badly. We kind of got swept up in it. But later... my husband says he thinks she was just trying to get some sort of payout. Now we've seen the film, she'll have to drop it. It's clear that the boys ran out in the road. You weren't to blame.'

Again, that knot in her throat threatened. She knew this now. And she'd been completely exonerated. Andrew had been through this with her over and over again. But still... 'If I hadn't been there. If I hadn't spoken to them.'

Amanda shook her head. 'You can't think like that. The what-ifs will destroy you. The boys need to take responsibility for what they did.' She paused. 'And so do us parents. It's us who owe you an apology.'

Pressing her lips together wasn't enough to stop a solitary tear from escaping. Erica brushed it away with the back of her hand, but wasn't fast enough to prevent Amanda from seeing it.

Her hands flew to her mouth. 'I'm so sorry. I've upset you, haven't I? And that really wasn't my intention.'

'No.' Erica shook her head. 'No, you haven't upset me. I'm glad you came. It's just... I'm struggling a bit with my son at the moment and I'm terrified that something like that might happen to him. If I take my eye off him for one second.'

Face softening again, Amanda held out her hand. 'I get it. I really do. After the accident, I wanted to wrap Luke up in bubble wrap, but you can't, can you? However terrifying it is, we have to let them find their own way in the world.'

Someone else telling her the same thing. It wasn't as easy as that, though, was it? 'I have to go. My family need me at home.'

'Of course. And I really am sorry that we put you through all this. If it's any comfort, Luke was terribly upset when he found out. He really liked having you as his teacher. Will you go back now?'

Go back? How far back would she need to go to make everything okay again?

THIRTY-EIGHT

If you were asked to describe your ideal head teacher, Fiona Bixby would be it. Always immaculately dressed – often in a crisp dark suit and brightly coloured shirt with matching pumps – and so professional that you could easily imagine her holding her own with a combative parent, a panel of Ofsted inspectors or a room full of government officials. At the same time, she was kind and gentle and could often be seen crouched down next to a child listening for as long as they wanted to talk – or sign or gesture – about whatever they wanted to communicate to her. And they did. When Erica and Andrew had taken their first ever tour of the school, children in every classroom had wanted to take her hand and show her what they were working on. As a teacher herself, Erica was also aware of the way the staff responded to her. It was clear that they were as happy to be working for her as the children were.

For all of these reasons, she trusted Fiona to be honest about what would be best for Benjamin. 'Thank you for seeing us at such short notice.'

While Celeste was working on Erica's idea to help Mollie, she'd pushed ahead with the second part of her plan by arranging a meeting here for her and Andrew. Behind Fiona's large desk, hand-drawn pictures and cards were pinned to a cork board. In places, they were three deep. 'No problem at all. What can I help you with?'

Beside her, Andrew – also in a dark suit – was poker straight. Erica kept her hands in her lap, trying to hide the fact that she'd managed to pick the polish from half of her nails this morning. 'We wanted to talk about Benjamin. To get some advice, really.'

Fiona tilted her head, her chin-length black hair swung below her ear. 'I had a quick chat with Ben's teacher this morning. She said he's making great progress with communication and is developing his independence. Hasn't he been selected to go on the trip next week?'

This was harder than she'd thought it would be. For so many years she'd been the one sitting on the other side of the desk. The one with the answers to concerned questions. Now she had a head full of them. 'He has. And that's one of the things we wanted to discuss. We've...' she glanced at Andrew '... or, more accurately, *I've* been quite cautious about what I've expected from Ben. I know that the expectations are higher here and I, well, I think I just wanted to have a chat about it.'

It sounded weak, she knew that. Andrew was probably chomping at the bit to jump in but, as usual, he let her do the talking.

Fiona leaned back in her chair. 'We do have high expectations for our students, but I hope that we always ensure that they're achievable. We want to lead them onto new experiences. Not push them where they don't want to go. We want the best for our children. The best that they can be.'

They'd heard this phrase before, it was a favourite of hers. But this time it twanged something in Erica. Though she hated herself for it, her throat tightened and tears threatened. 'The thing is, I don't think I know what's best for Benjamin. I don't know what's the right thing to do. I've tried to keep him safe, but I might have stopped him from... from...'

Andrew reached into her lap and took her hand. 'You've done a great job of looking after him, Erica. No one can say you haven't.'

His unexpected praise, the warmth of his touch, squeezed her heart so tight that she couldn't breathe. Instead, she tried to communicate it all – her fear, her guilt, her desperation for guidance – through the tear-filled eyes she directed at the woman in front of her.

As if she'd understood all of this, Fiona's tone was kind. 'There is no "right" thing. Especially for children with additional needs. That's what makes it difficult. Every child is different and needs different things. Part of our job here is to support you as much as Ben. We know how hard it can be.'

Tears were impossible to control when she was asking for help. 'I don't want to put him at risk. He finds it difficult to be away from me.'

Nodding slowly, Fiona looked from Erica to Andrew and back again. What was she thinking? Clingy mother? 'Sometimes we have to let our children do difficult things.'

The truth of her words hit Erica in the chest. Had she tried to make Ben's life easy? Or was it her own comfort zone that she was too scared to step out of? Her voice came out like a whisper. 'I don't know how to do that.'

Andrew's grip on her hand tightened. Was he finding this as difficult as she was?

'I understand that you gave Ben the opportunity to try an overnight stay with us. How did that go from your perspective?'

Awful. Terrible. 'He struggled to settle.'

'It can be quite a challenge the first time. But I think it would be worth trying again. Some of our children thrive in the routine of boarding here all week.'

'We're not planning on doing that.' Andrew's voice was firm

and not open to negotiation. It was difficult not to show the shock on her face. Wasn't that what he'd wanted?

Fiona smiled. 'No. I know that. And I think that's the right decision for now. But things change over time. His needs will change, like they do with any child as they approach adulthood. And it won't end when he reaches eighteen. Children – and adults – with special needs are lifelong learners. As he grows up, Ben might want more independence. Overnight stays here are a way to gently move in that direction. One day he might be ready to try assisted living with other young adults.'

On some level, Erica hadn't really thought of Ben becoming an adult. She'd worried about it in a kind of foggy way of wondering how that would look for them as a family. But she always pictured him as he was, maybe a little taller, and that she would care for him in the same way that she did now. Had the limits of her imagination – of her fear – limited him too? 'So you think it's a good idea? Him staying here sometimes?'

'You have to do what's best for your family. I know that you have to take so much more into consideration when you have a child who needs extra support and that can take its toll, particularly on the primary carer, but on everyone in the family. Ben has a sister, I believe?'

'Yes. A twin sister. Mollie.'

'Well, we have groups here for the siblings of our students. And we have parent groups. I could tell you what I think would be good for Ben, but I don't have the perspective of a parent to share with you. I know that a lot of our parents and carers have found it really helpful.'

What had she expected? That the head teacher would give her a list of instructions on how to navigate this? She just needed to hold her breath and take that step. 'Could we try again? With him staying over?'

Fiona smiled. 'Of course. We'll work with you as and when you and Ben are ready.'

She was about to stand when Andrew cleared his throat. 'What kind of provision is there for... later on in Ben's life? When we're gone.'

There it was, the biggest fear of every parent of a child like Ben. What will happen to them when you die?

'One of the most important parts of our role is our students' transition to their next steps at the end of school. For some of our students, that is into assisted living accommodation. Ben has several years before we need to think about that, but I can promise you that we are here to guide and help.' She looked at Erica. 'Right now, we want to build his confidence and independence. The trip next week to the café is one of the steps towards that.'

Erica nodded. It didn't matter how terrified she was – how many scary situations she could imagine – she needed to let her son take his first steps without her. 'Thank you for seeing us. We really appreciate everything you're doing for Ben.'

Fiona Bixby smiled. 'Thank you. I know that these kinds of transitions can be difficult, so can I give you one more piece of advice? Don't look at Ben's world through your eyes, look through his eyes. He has parents and a sister who love him very much. That makes him a fortunate young man.'

Five minutes' drive from the school, the coffee shop on the high street was quiet after the morning rush. Andrew came back from the counter with two cups of coffee. 'They're bringing the bagels over once they're ready.'

She'd been here several times on her own, a few times with Ben and once with Mollie. It felt nice to be here with Andrew. How long had it been since the two of them were on their own like this? 'I was surprised in there. When you said you didn't want Ben to board at the school. I thought that's what you wanted?'

Andrew shook his head. 'I just wanted you to consider that we could get some extra help. That you didn't need to be the one looking after him all the time. As soon as I said anything, it caused arguments between us. I just gave up in the end.'

It was the time for truth. 'You shouldn't have. If you wanted to be part of Ben's life, do more for him, you could have done so. I hold my hands up and admit my part, Andrew. I did take over; I did think I was the only one who could look after him. But you let me. You needed to step up and be his dad.'

She held his gaze, waiting for him to reply. She didn't expect to see tears form in his eyes. 'You're right. I did.'

She'd only ever seen Andrew cry three times in their marriage: once when he lost his father and again two years later when the twins were born. The third time was now. She kept her tone gentle. 'Why didn't you try harder?'

It took him a moment to compose himself to speak. 'In the beginning, I thought that Ben was just going to be a bit of a handful. All the times you said you thought there was something wrong, I was convinced that you were just overthinking it. Mums worry, don't they?'

His mum worried, he meant. Andrew's mother was a warm, kind woman who had a place at the table for anyone who turned up and made you give three rings when you got home even when you had children of your own. 'I tried to tell you.'

'I know. But I didn't want to hear it. I didn't want to accept that there was anything wrong, anything that we couldn't fix for him.'

This wasn't news. Andrew had been determined that Ben would go to the same school as Mollie, adhere to the same rules at home. It didn't matter how many times she'd told him that they had to do things differently for him, he hadn't wanted to hear. 'I know it was hard. But it was hard for me, too.'

'But you were so good with him. So patient. I used to watch

you and think that I could never be like you. And then, at the same time...'

She was expecting him to finish his sentence, but he clearly needed prompting. 'At the same time... what?'

'I was angry with you. I thought you were babying him. That he'd never cope in the real world. He was – he is – so vulnerable.' When he looked up at her, his eyes were haunted. 'I see the real world every day, Erica, and it's not a nice place. I see adults with special needs being taken advantage of, being treated... terribly. I just want him to be safe.'

Why had they never spoken as openly as this before? Why had their marriage had to be taken to the edge of the precipice before they'd communicated properly? 'I want him to be safe, too. I want them both to be safe. But I'm worried that you're right. That I have held him too close.'

He rubbed away his tears with the heel of his hand. 'You're an amazing mum, Erica. Really amazing. And I'm sorry. I'm sorry for everything I've said to you in the last few months. I'm sorry that I blamed you for leaving Mollie behind that day. For my anger. It wasn't your fault.'

Now her eyes filled with tears. 'Do you really mean that?'

He nodded. 'Watching you in there, with Ben's head teacher, I realised how much you've done for him. How hard you've had to fight. And I'm so sorry that you've had to fight me, too.'

Erica's throat was so swollen with emotion, that she couldn't answer.

He hadn't finished. 'I'm going to make it up to you. I'm going to step up. Be a better dad. I'll speak to Mollie about what she overheard. And I'm going to try harder with Ben. I'm his dad and I've let him down.'

It was everything she'd wanted to hear for so long. 'Thank you.'

He shook his head. 'You don't need to thank me. I should be

thanking you. We need to be a team. We need to work out what we're going to do next. For Mollie, too.'

He was right. They would need to help Mollie deal with this issue before she went back to school. 'How about Ben and I come and spend the day with you both tomorrow? Under the circumstances, it won't hurt for him to miss a day at school. We can talk to her then.'

He smiled, looking more like the man she'd fallen in love with than he had in a long time. 'That's a great idea. I'd like that very much.'

They chinked their coffee mugs and she was happy that they were coming together to do the best for both of their children. But she also realised that this was about being good parents. There'd been no mention about being a husband and wife.

THIRTY-NINE

Behind the house, beyond the patio, a small yard was mostly laid to lawn bordered by shallow flower beds. Ben was on the patio outside the back door, picking the largest stones out of the gravel that bordered the grey stone slabs and straightening them into a line. The morning was warm and fresh sunshine bathed him in an ethereal light. He was content.

At the other end of the garden, the atmosphere was decidedly less calm. With a hand wrapped around an oversized mug, Mollie's face had darkened. 'I'm not going back.'

The metal garden chair Erica was perched on – part of the bistro set she'd bought about five years ago – was cold and hard, but at least it meant that she and Mollie were both facing back towards the house rather than staring at each other in some kind of stand-off. 'Tell me what's worrying you.'

Mollie twisted towards her. 'Half the kids at school might've seen that picture. They've all seen my naked body. How can I face them?'

It was undeniably awful. Erica could remember the inner turmoil of going to school with an unsuccessful new haircut when she was around Mollie's age. For her classmates to have seen her vulnerable naked body was unthinkable. How was she going to help her daughter come back from this?

The back door opened and Andrew emerged with two cups in his hand. One of them was Benjamin's bright-green beaker.

He was really making an effort to compromise. When they'd lived together, he'd argued that they should be forcing Benjamin to drink from different cups. 'You're pandering to him, Erica. I know he doesn't like it, but we need to teach him that it's okay to drink from a different cup, for goodness' sake. How is he going to get on in the real world?'

That had always been his mantra. This idea that they had to force their little square peg into the round hole that the world expected him to fill. She'd seen things very differently. Tried to create a world – even if it was a safe little square – where he could be who he wanted to be. Was there a middle ground?

She tried again with Mollie. 'Do you think you need a few more days at home until it dies down? Or even a week? Maybe we could ask if you could go in just for mornings to start with?'

Mollie slammed her mug down onto the small round table and it rocked on its spindly legs. 'You don't understand. I'm not going back to school not ever ever ever.'

She ran from the table in tears and back, Erica assumed, to her bedroom.

She closed her eyes for a moment. This was totally new territory. Mollie had always been the most gentle and amenable of children. In fact, she'd often joked that Mollie was her gift to make up for the extra help that Ben needed. Had all this anger and upset just been hidden beneath the surface for years? And what kind of mother was she that she hadn't noticed?

She opened her eyes to find Andrew sitting beside her, holding out a cup of coffee. 'That didn't go too well, then?'

The warmth of the cup was a comfort. 'Nope. I get it. It must be terrifying for her to have to face up to everybody. She made a mistake. It happened. But the trouble is that that mistake will be there forever.'

Andrew nodded. 'I know. It was different when we were her age. If we did something stupid, there was no lasting evidence.'

There was no getting away from that. It didn't matter that the school had given a stern warning to every student about the consequences – legal consequences – of having inappropriate images on their phones; now that the photograph was out there, there was no possible way of clawing it back. 'It's going to follow her around, isn't it? She's always going to be that girl. Even when she applies for a job or college or meets new people.'

Andrew's mouth was a straight line of anger. 'It makes me want to hunt down those...'

She held up a hand to stop him. 'I know. I feel the same.'

They sat for a few more moments in the quiet. From the upstairs window – Mollie's bedroom – the plaintive wail of her saxophone curled out into the open air. Melancholic yet beautiful, it reached its fingers into Erica's heart. Her daughter was in pain. What could she do to soothe it?

The idea she'd mentioned to Celeste was still taking shape in her mind. 'What if she took control of the narrative?'

He frowned. 'What do you mean?'

'At the moment, everything is outside of her control. This is being done to her. Those... blackmailers have taken something from her. But what if she is given the chance to have control again?'

'You're speaking in riddles. What do you mean? What do you think we should do?'

The strains of the saxophone were practically weeping. 'I don't think we should do anything. I think it's something Mollie needs to do.'

. . .

'Are you crazy? That is *not* going to happen.'

Mollie's bedroom had changed a great deal in the last couple of years. Gone were the teddy bears and floral bedspread. In their place, discarded clothes fought for floor space with hairbrushes and make-up bags spilling their contents. Erica perched on the end of her bed. 'Just let me explain what I'm thinking.'

Clutching a cushion to her stomach, Mollie shook her head. 'I know what you're thinking. You just told me. You want me to go on the local news and talk about the fact that my whole school has seen a naked picture of me. Is it not bad enough already? You want more people to know about it?'

Put like that, it did seem a little off. 'It might be too much, I get that. It was more that I want you to have control of this situation. They've tried to frighten you and hurt you. I thought that, maybe, if you had the opportunity to stand up and tell them that you haven't been beaten by it, you might feel a little better?'

Mollie's face looked very similar to Andrew's ten minutes ago when she'd suggested this to him. 'Wouldn't it make everyone just go and look for the photograph?'

Andrew's colleagues at the sexploitation task force had assured him that the original site had been taken down and arrests had been made. Of course, that didn't guarantee that someone connected with the blackmailing gang didn't still have a copy of Mollie's picture. And, of course, plenty of other people had taken screenshots of it. 'Because of your age, they wouldn't use your real name and your voice would be changed and face blurred out. Only the people that you tell will know that it's you.'

'Then what would be the point of that?'

It had made sense when she'd thought about it last night in bed. Or had she just been clutching at straws? Trying to think of anything to distract Mollie from how terrible she must feel. A desperate desire to make this better for her. 'If you think it's stupid. It's fine. Let's forget it. I'm sorry if I've made you feel worse.'

Mollie laughed. It almost sounded genuine. 'I'm not sure I can feel any worse, Mum. I know you're trying to help me.'

That precious face looked up at her. How long did she have before Mollie was out in the world, finding her own way, facing challenges that Erica hadn't even thought of? It'd been difficult to be a thirteen-year-old girl when she was one herself – teetering on the line between girlhood and womanhood, wanting freedom yet scared to cut her ties – how much harder was it to parent one? Everything she said and did would sculpt the way Mollie would face the world.

Honesty was the only way. 'I'm so sorry that I didn't give you what you needed, Mol. I think I just saw you as having everything under control. You've always been such an independent little girl. Once, when you were about five or six, we were out shopping and you were determined that you didn't want to hold my hand. At one point, you were getting too close to the road and I told you to take my hand because the cars weren't going to stop for you and do you know what you did?'

Mollie did know, because she'd enjoyed this story plenty of times. A smile tickled the edges of her mouth. 'I held up my hand to stop the cars?'

With a laugh, Erica nodded. 'You held up your hand like a traffic cop and the car coming towards us literally stopped in the road and let you cross.'

Thank goodness it had been a one-way street. It had been very difficult to explain to Mollie afterwards that this wouldn't happen every time.

Though she started to laugh at the story, Mollie's face quickly crumpled. 'I wish I could hold my hand up now and stop all of this. Stop myself from sending that stupid photograph.'

Pulling her close, Erica wanted to fold Mollie inside herself, carry her next to her heart as she had as a baby with a sling wrapped around her chest. She pressed her lips to the top of Mollie's head, breathed in the familiar scent of her coconut shampoo. 'I wish I could take this away from you, sweetheart. I really do.'

Once she'd released her, Mollie grabbed a tissue from the box on her dressing table and blew her nose. 'You know, maybe the TV idea isn't so terrible. I mean, how would it work?'

She'd already asked Celeste to run the idea past her friend, who'd said that this was a very topical subject right now. It'd made Erica shudder to think of all the other young people who'd been targeted in this way. For many of them – she knew from her late-night googling on the subject – it'd led to even greater tragedy. 'I don't really know how they'd approach it. I'm pretty sure that they'll do whatever you're most comfortable with.'

From the pile of make-up and sponges beside the tissue box, Mollie slid out a small green tin of Vaseline without its lid, wiped a finger across its surface and then on to her lips, her eyes scanning the posters on her wall. 'Would I get to meet anyone famous?'

Erica stifled a smile. This was the first glimmer of her daughter coming back to herself. 'I don't know. It's only regional TV so maybe not. Although you never know. A local celeb maybe?'

Mollie pulled herself up to sitting, her eyes on Erica now, an eyebrow raised. 'And would I need a new outfit? Something expensive?'

This time Erica didn't hide her smile. 'Definitely. Really expensive.'

Mollie's smile was tentative. And tempered by the tears that filled her eyes. 'This is all so horrible, Mum. Is anyone going to ever forget it?'

'Yes. They will. Because, you know what, all of your friends are going to make mistakes. With boys, with girls, with jobs, with nights out gone wrong. And you will make more mistakes, too. Hundreds of them. Thousands. That's how we learn, Mollie. By getting it wrong. I've got a lot of things wrong. With you and your brother.'

Mollie's face clouded over. 'I'm sorry, Mum. All that stuff I said.'

'No. Don't be sorry. You were right. I messed up. I should've been there for you.'

'But I know it's difficult. He does need more looking after.'

'He needs different looking after. But I'm working on it. I'm working on how to make sure we all get what we need.'

'And you.'

'What do you mean?'

'You need to get what you need, too. Not just me and Ben. You should have some time for you, too.'

Her kindness made Erica's eyes sting. How was her daughter wiser than her? She brought Mollie's hand up to her mouth and kissed it. 'And time for me, too.'

'And you can get some new clothes for the TV show. Make Dad sit up and look.'

What was behind Mollie's smile this time? Did she know about her and Andrew's marriage problems? What else had she overheard eavesdropping on Andrew's telephone conversation about the fire?

Their marriage was going to take a lot more fixing than a new dress and a pair of shoes. But she smiled nonetheless. 'Great idea. A new set of clothes for each of us. I'll call Celeste and see if she can set it up with the news show.'

FORTY

The shopping mall was quiet on a weekday and they already had an armful of bags each. The shopping trip had been fun – and an eye opener. 'Why is everything so short and tight and low cut?'

Not for the first time that hour, Mollie rolled her eyes. 'It's called fashion.'

At thirteen, Erica had been wearing oversized band t-shirts and baggy jeans. Flicking through the dresses and tops on the rails in New Look, she wondered how many of these items it would take to make one thing that she had worn back then. 'This looks more like underwear than clothes.'

Jutting out her hip, one hand on her waist, Mollie held out a scrap of fabric with more holes than a tea bag and pouted to make her laugh. 'Are you slut-shaming me, Mother?'

Amused and amazed in equal measure, Erica held up her hands. 'I know I'm doing penance, and saying yes to everything, but I'm still your mother and you're still thirteen. You can put that one back for at least another three years.'

Mollie grinned as she dropped the hanger onto the rail. This new ease between them was like the first warm day of spring. Erica wanted to bask in it as long as it lasted. 'I miss the days when I could dress you in pretty things. You used to want to wear the same as me. *Be my twin, Mummy.* That's what you used to say to me.'

The eye roll was back. 'There's a reason that five-year-olds aren't fashion designers.'

Once Mollie was in the changing room, Erica checked her phone for a message from Andrew. He'd promised to keep her up to date on how his day with Ben was going. They'd decided to stay over at the house last night and, without his Gro Clock to tell him when it was okay to get up, Ben had woken her as soon as the light had come through the curtains of his bedroom. They were sharing: him on the bed, her on the floor. To her surprise, Andrew had met them on the landing, scratching his head and yawning. 'You go back to bed. I can watch cartoons with Ben and get him some breakfast.'

Having resisted the urge to check her phone for the last hour, Erica's heart plummeted when she saw there were five WhatsApp messages from Andrew. Was he not coping? Had something happened?

Mollie called through the changing room curtain. 'I won't be a minute.'

Opening the most recent message from Andrew, a photograph filled the screen. She almost dropped the phone. Before she could call him, Mollie emerged from behind the purple curtain across the changing cubicle. 'What do you think?'

Wanting to give Mollie her full attention, Erica slipped her phone between her thighs and smiled at her. The pale-blue dress she'd chosen had spaghetti straps and a darker blue floral pattern, ending just above her knees. She looked incredible. At thirteen, she could already pass for three years older. She was so beautiful. 'You look amazing. That's the outfit. That's the one you should wear.'

Twirling slowly in front of Erica, Mollie's smile lit up the thin corridor. 'I love it. Can I get some blue shoes to match?'

Today, she could have whatever she wanted. 'Yes. As long as you can actually walk in them.'

As soon as Mollie was back in the cubicle, Erica looked at the photograph again. Yes, she hadn't imagined it. The photograph had been taken at the park local to the house – she recognised the houses beyond the fence from when she'd taken the twins there. On the tarmac path, there was a bike – or a trike? – with Ben sitting on it.

Quickly, she fired off a text.

Have you bought that?

The reply came back.

Yes. I'm teaching Ben to ride.

She had a hundred questions, but the scrape of the curtain on its metal rail heralded Mollie and her excitement about the new dress. Today was all about her. The conversation about how ridiculous – and possibly dangerous – it was that Andrew had bought this bike for Ben, and taken him to the park with it, would have to wait.

After the dress had been paid for, and the perfect shoes – pale-blue Mary Janes with a sole that looked like it was made from tractor tyres – had been found, Erica took Mollie to the John Lewis cosmetics department for a makeover. It took a lot of effort to wrench her mind away from whatever was happening in the park back home. Imagining Ben falling from the bike, Andrew getting frustrated, Ben having a meltdown... no. She had to stop thinking about it. Benjamin was with his dad. She was here to be Mollie's mum.

Make-up was another area where Mollie was so much more

advanced than she'd been. Long gone were the claggy electric blue mascara and Heather Shimmer lipstick of Erica's youth. Mollie knew what she wanted and how to apply it. Watching her talk with confidence to the young make-up artist was a reminder of how fast her baby girl was growing up. She wouldn't have her forever; it was vital that they share as much time as they could while Mollie still wanted to be with her.

By the time they got home, Mollie had enough bags to start up her own boutique.

'Wow.' Andrew's eyes widened. 'Someone did well.'

Mollie waved the bags. 'I'm going to go upstairs and try them on. Shall I come down and show you? It won't be for about half an hour because I want to do my hair. Get the full effect.'

'Can't wait.' As soon as she'd gone, Andrew raised an eyebrow at Erica. 'She seems a lot happier.'

'Nothing beats the power of a new outfit. It was really nice to spend some time with her on my own. Wait until you see how amazing she looks in her new dress. Thanks for having Ben.'

Andrew frowned. 'You don't need to thank me for spending time with my own son. What did you think about the trike I bought today?'

It was a trike, then. That made her feel marginally less terrified. 'I was surprised. I assume that's for Ben?'

He laughed then. That abrupt staccato laugh of his that sounded like a cough. She hadn't heard it in a while. 'No, Erica, It's for me. I just need to get the blue light fitted and then I'm good to go.'

The image that presented made Erica laugh, too. 'To be honest, that would actually surprise me less. What did he make of it?'

Andrew rubbed at his chin. 'He took it on a walk around the park. When I suggested he get on it, he looked at me as if I was insane.'

That look was already well known at Ben's school. It was a relief that he hadn't forced Ben to do anything he wasn't comfortable with. 'It was nice that you tried. Can you get your money back on the trike?'

Andrew turned to her in surprise. 'I haven't given up. We'll try again tomorrow, when you're at the TV station. What you said the other day, about me not stepping up? You were right.'

Try again? She wasn't sure about that idea at all, but her face burned at the memory of their argument and she didn't want to start it up again. 'You were right, too. I did take over.'

'But I should've done more. I think I let you take the lead because I thought I wasn't up to it. That you knew best because you were a teacher.'

'Not a teacher of special needs, though. That's a whole other skill set.'

'I know. But you still knew more than me. Either way—' he held up a hand to stop her from interrupting again '—I know that I need to step up now and take my share of the responsibility.'

That was a good thing, wasn't it? So why did she feel so anxious?

FORTY-ONE

'I don't think that I can do it.'

To be honest, looking at how small and fragile her daughter seemed in that large office chair, Erica was beginning to question how she'd thought this was a good idea. 'It's fine. If you don't want to do it, we'll just tell them.'

As Mollie didn't get up from the chair, Erica assumed that she hadn't fully made up her mind. 'I'm worried that I'm going to make an idiot of myself. Make it worse. I know they said they won't be able to tell it's me, but people at school will know it's me and I don't want to tell all the details about what happened.'

Erica could've slapped herself. In her rush to empower Mollie, she'd actually set her up to relive what'd happened. And so soon, too. 'I'm sorry, sweetheart, I shouldn't have suggested it. We'll tell them we've changed our minds.'

Mollie's bottom lip trembled. 'I don't want to let them down.'

Erica crouched on the floor in front of her. 'You're not letting anyone down, love. This is only a good idea if you think it is. If not, we'll leave right now. I'll tell them it's me.'

The door opened and a young woman with long dark hair

and an easy smile joined them. 'Hi. You must be Mollie. I'm Savita, pleased to meet you.'

Mollie took Savita's hand, her own smile hesitant. 'Hi.'

'I'm the producer for this segment. I wanted to come and have a chat with you and tell you how it all works. See if there's any questions you want us to avoid, that kind of thing.'

Erica opened her mouth to explain that Mollie had changed her mind, but Mollie shook her head at her to be quiet. Didn't she want her to speak for her?

Savita's words came out in a gush of enthusiasm. 'First of all, I just want to say how amazing I think you are. You are so so brave to do this. And I can't believe you're only thirteen. You are way cooler than I was at your age.'

That can only have been a handful of years ago. Was the praise going to persuade Mollie into doing something she didn't want to do? She certainly seemed to be enjoying it.

Savita was still going strong. 'Your friends must think you're amazing, too?'

Mollie shifted in her seat. 'I haven't really spoken to them about it.'

To give her her due, Savita was clearly high on the emotional intelligence scale. 'Yeah, I guess it's tough. What you've been through, in one way or another, it's something that a lot of women have to go through. But maybe you're the first to experience it among your friends?'

Everything she said was the same things that Erica had said, but Mollie was listening as if all of this was brand-new information. To be fair, Erica wasn't a twenty-something beauty with silver Doc Martens and a diamond stud in her nose.

Still, she was worried that Savita's charisma – coupled with Mollie's desperate need to please – might lead her to do something she'd regret.

But she'd misjudged her child. 'I don't want to do it. I'm sorry if I've messed you around, but I just can't.'

For a moment, Savita paused. Then she tilted her head to the side. 'Why?'

Mollie took a deep breath. 'I don't want to talk about what happened to me. I feel ashamed. I feel stupid. And I'm not ready to share that with the world.'

Erica's heart was fit to bursting. She knew how difficult it was for Mollie to stand up and say no. Savita was nodding slowly. 'Okay, but if you were on the show, what would you want to say? What do you want people to know?'

Pausing to think, Mollie looked down at her fingers. 'That it can happen to anyone. You think it's not going to be you, but it could be. Easily.'

And it could easily be your child. Even if you were an ex-teacher who'd had all the training in the world about online grooming and exploitation. It could still happen to your vulnerable baby, right under your nose.

'Anything else? Any advice that you'd give?'

Mollie glanced at Erica before she spoke. 'Talk to someone. A friend in the real world. Before you do anything like this. Because you don't know who you're talking to. Even when you think you do.'

Savita tapped her nose then her chin as she considered what Mollie was saying. 'I get it. I do. Just give me a minute.'

She disappeared out of the door and Mollie deflated in front of Erica's eyes. 'She probably thinks I'm pathetic.'

Erica was beside her in a moment. 'Absolutely not. I am so proud of you, sweetheart. It wasn't easy to say no, but you did it.'

'I thought you wanted me to do it?'

'No. I thought it might help you to do it. If it's not right, or you're uncertain, you're absolutely right to say no. Savita is probably just letting someone know that it's not going to happen. Maybe they need to know as soon as possible. And then we can go home.'

The door swung open and Savita swooped back inside. 'Right, I have an idea for you. I just ran it past my presenter and they think it's a great idea. How about you present the segment?'

Mollie looked as confused as Erica felt. 'But I just said that I didn't feel comfortable telling everyone my story.'

Erica's heart ached at her daughter's tiny voice.

But Savita was shaking her glossy hair. 'No, sorry, I'm not explaining it right. I mean, we don't tell your story – well, not directly. But you can be the presenter. You'll present the topic to the camera, read off the autocue and all of that. Then the presenter can tell your story as if it happened to someone else. Not you.'

Mollie still looked uncertain, but she was also intrigued. 'So I would be on the screen. My actual face?'

'Yes. As a presenter.' Savita looked at Erica. 'As long as your mum was okay with it and you're happy? I mean, it's all pre-recorded, so if you're not comfortable or you change your mind, we can just go back to the presenter doing the story and we'll cut your bit.'

Now Mollie looked at Erica. 'What do you think, Mum?'

'I think it's up to you, sweetheart.'

A smile twitched at the edges of Mollie's mouth. 'I think I want to do it.'

Mollie was amazing. A complete natural in front of the camera. The segment about online predators was only five minutes long, but Savita took her time with her, patiently ensuring that everything was perfect.

Once the filming was over, she walked them back to reception. 'Really, Mollie, you are born for presenting work. If this segment works out, maybe I'll be getting in contact for some more work.'

Mollie flushed with pleasure at the praise. 'I'd really enjoy that.'

. . .

When they got home, Andrew had bought a bottle of non-alcoholic Prosecco and had it chilling in a bucket. 'How was the first day of stardom?'

'Dad. Seriously.' The smile on Mollie's lips gave a lie to her mocking tone.

When Andrew held her close, Erica heard him whisper, 'I'm so proud of you, love.' And it brought tears to her eyes.

'She was really incredible. Wait until you see her on TV tomorrow night. She sounds so mature.'

'It's a really great thing you're doing, too. You might prevent someone else going through all of this.'

This time her smile was gentle. 'Thanks. I hope so.'

Erica watched her go, taking two steps at a time in her eagerness to go to her room and watch the unedited clips that Savita had sent to her phone. They still had a lot to work through with what had happened, but this felt like a very good start. She turned to Andrew. 'Where's Ben?'

His expression was cryptic. 'Follow me. We have something to show you.'

Outside the back door, Ben was pushing his trike backwards and forwards on the small patio, transfixed by the spokes of the wheels. Erica had to bite her lip to stop herself from warning him not to put his fingers too close. 'Hi, Ben. I'm back. Have you had a good day with Daddy?'

Ben looked up at her, then at Andrew. He waved his hands at the trike.

Andrew stepped towards him. 'Shall we show Mum what you can do?'

Ben slapped the saddle of the trike with his hand, rocking onto the balls of his feet, something he always did when he was eager to go somewhere or do something.

Erica watched Andrew in disbelief as he opened the side

gate and helped Ben to manoeuvre the trike through the narrow space. Ben's hand waving was getting faster. He glanced back to ensure that Erica was following. Surely he wasn't going to actually ride it?

The house was on a close and the road was quiet, but Erica couldn't believe what she was seeing. Andrew held the trike as Ben managed to swing his leg across and sit on the saddle. Then he helped him place his feet onto the pedals.

'Okay, Ben. Remember what we were doing, push down on this one.'

Andrew had his hand on Ben's right foot. It was impossible to see how much Ben was pushing with his foot and how much of it was Andrew, but the pedal went downwards nonetheless.

Encouragement rolling with every vowel, Andrew kept his eyes on Ben's feet. 'Great work, Ben. Now the other one.'

This time it was clear to see that it was Ben. Andrew stayed this side of the trike but sidestepped crab-like to stay in line with Ben as the trike moved.

'Back to this one, Ben.'

His right foot went down again. She put her hand over her mouth to stop the words coming out. *Be careful. Not too fast.*

Andrew was still walking sideways, a little faster now. 'Down with your foot. Now the other one. Back to this one. Good boy, Ben. Good boy. You're doing it!'

And he *was* doing it. Ben was riding a trike.

All the while his feet were moving up and down, Ben stared intently at the crossbar, his face frozen in concentration. But Andrew's face was a picture of joy when he glanced at her. 'Can you see? Can you see what he's doing?'

She could barely get the words out. 'I can see what he's doing. Oh, my clever clever boy.'

Tears flowed freely down Erica's cheeks. This moment was one she would hold dear to her heart for many many years to come. Ben's determination. Andrew's joy. A simple everyday moment for so many children. Today it was theirs.

'We did it. He did it. He learned to ride a trike.'

'You did it too. You taught him.'

She watched as Andrew – tough, solid, practical Andrew – wiped tears away with the back of his hand, his voice a croak. 'I taught my boy to ride a trike.'

Without thinking about it, she reached for him and he wrapped his arms around her. For a moment, she dared to hope that there was still a chance for them.

FORTY-TWO

After both children were in bed – if not yet asleep – Erica watched Andrew load the dishwasher while she sipped the second half of a glass of wine she'd had with dinner.

'It's nice to be back here again tonight.'

The forks clattered as he dropped them into the cutlery holder. 'It's nice to have you here.'

Eating dinner together this evening – Andrew recounting his hilarious early attempts to persuade Ben that he could actually sit on the saddle of the trike, Mollie explaining all the skills Savita had shown her that afternoon, Ben surreptitiously helping himself to a fourth, fifth, sixth baked potato while no one was telling him to stop – she'd felt the togetherness of their family like tucking a cold arm back under the blankets in the middle of the night.

'It feels like ages since we were all around the dinner table like that.'

Andrew glanced up at her as he slotted their dinner plates into place in the rack of the dishwasher. 'It has been.'

He wasn't giving an inch, but his hug this afternoon gave Erica the courage to be bold. 'I always thought we'd get back together, you know. I know we've been living separately, but I never thought that was the end.'

For a moment, he paused, then continued to arrange the crockery on the lower shelf. 'I don't think I ever expected you to actually leave.'

Her stomach squeezed. What did that mean? He was making it sound like she'd made that decision. But they'd agreed to try it, hadn't they? 'You wanted him to try the school. And this was the only way. It was far too far for us to commute. We agreed.'

Though there were no more dirty dishes or pans, Andrew remained in front of the dishwasher, one hand gripping the worktop, not meeting her eyes. 'I did. Something had to change, didn't it? We kept going around and around with the same arguments. We weren't living the life we wanted, either of us. My dad died six weeks after he retired, Erica. He had a whole other lifetime planned that he never got to live. We need to live in the now. I need to live in the now.'

The wine that had tasted so good at the table turned acrid in her mouth. Did this mean he really did want a divorce?

She tipped the rest of the wine down the sink and placed the glass on the top shelf of the dishwasher. 'I see.'

The contents of the dishwasher rattled as he slammed it shut. 'Let's sit down and talk about this properly.'

When the children were small, they'd had a large wicker box in the corner of the living room that they could scoop all their toys into at the end of the evening, in order to relax – just for half an hour – without the chaos. As they'd got older, and bedtime became more of a struggle with Ben, this had happened less and less. It would often only be Andrew in this room while she was upstairs, fighting to resist the clutches of sleep on Ben's bedroom floor. Yet, this room had many comforting memories of evenings spent in each other's company. The deep-blue velvet sofa, the low oak coffee table, the fireplace unusual in a modern built house. They'd known as soon as they moved in, only a matter of months after the fire at the last house, that they would never have a real fire here. In the grate, in place of coals or wood, they'd kept a vase, full of fresh flowers. Though the vase was still there, it was empty and looked lost in that space.

Erica was on the sofa, staring at that vase rather than look at Andrew in the armchair to her right. Something about his expression, coupled with the mention of divorce last week, made her realise that this might be their last shot. If she wanted this marriage to have a chance, they were both going to have to be completely honest with one another.

'It changed me. It changed us. Having Benjamin, learning to navigate his needs. I'm not the same person any longer, Andrew. I have so much fear in me. I worry all the time. It takes so much out of me.'

Though she didn't turn to face him, Erica could feel Andrew moving forward in his seat. 'I know that and I understand that. But if we're going to make this work, you have to let me try. In the past, it was too easy for me to take a step back. And then it felt like you were taking steps forward and I was being left behind.'

She wanted this to work between them, but she was no martyr. 'I *was* taking steps forward, I was trying to wear a path for Ben, so that he could follow.'

Sometimes it'd felt as if she was an Arctic explorer, cutting through ice to find undiscovered territory, weighed down by a pack of fear and trepidation.

'That's what I mean. You dictated the path. You decided where he would go. The rest of us just had to follow.' He held up a hand. 'I know that makes me sound weak and I was weak. I see that now. I should have been stronger. I should have been his dad.'

His voice broke at those last words and her heart broke with it. If he had stood up to her, what would she have done? She certainly wouldn't have rolled over as her own mother had. How much had her own determination not to relive the dynamic of her parents' marriage almost destroyed her own? 'I was trying to be strong. For Ben.'

He reached out then. Took her hand. 'I understand that. And you have been strong. Always. It was one of the things I most admired about you when I met you. How many people uproot their lives and move to another country, start all over again? You've always had a strength that I'm in awe of.'

Her throat tightened. Right now, she felt weaker that she ever had. 'I don't think anyone is born strong. But sometimes life makes you that way. I had to be strong for Ben.'

'We would've been stronger together. I think we both lost sight of that. You took control and I let you. We both made mistakes.'

He was right. They had both made mistakes. Was it too late to recover from them? 'Is it possible to go back to the beginning and start again?'

Her heart plummeted when he shook his head. 'No. We can't start again. But we can start from where we are. We've made mistakes. Both of us. But we can learn from them. We can be like Ben. Lifelong learners.'

She could barely breathe. He was right, they had to keep learning. Would they do it together? 'I like the idea of that.'

A smile curled at the edges of his mouth. 'Seeing Ben learn to ride that trike... he was amazing. It was really difficult, but he kept going.' His eyes clouded. 'We should have kept going. Living apart was the wrong thing to do.'

Not trusting herself to speak, she nodded. He was right again. 'It seemed the only solution. After that holiday... it was impossible. Like you said, we couldn't carry on the way we were. It seemed like the right thing to do. Living apart for a while.'

He nodded. 'But we've learned that it wasn't good for us.'

His smile was infectious. 'Lifelong learners.'

He pulled her towards him. 'Lifelong learners.'

As his lips pressed onto hers, she closed her eyes and let herself imagine another holiday, the four of them, together.

FORTY-THREE

One of the reasons they'd bought this house was that the back garden got the sun for most of the day. When they'd moved here with eight-year-old twins, she'd envisaged summer days spent outside in the fresh air. Though he was less keen on the idea than she'd hoped back then, now Ben had condescended to at least sit on the patio watching cartoons on his tablet, although she couldn't help but think that their company was less of a draw to him than his trike – the prized possession that he liked to be within tapping distance.

Having spent the afternoon weeding the flower beds, she'd invited Lynn over from next door. Sitting around their small table, Lynn looked as if she was on vacation with her sun hat shading her beaming smile and a glass of orange juice in hand. 'It's so lovely to have you back here, Erica. Isn't it nice, Mollie, having your mum back here?'

Mollie, face pleasantly flushed from the heat, grinned at Erica. 'It really is. Although she tells me to do my school work much more than Dad did.'

As if he'd heard his name, Andrew stepped out of the patio doors with a cup of juice for Ben in his lime-green cup with the straw. It had been really great to wake up together this morning and last weekend. Having Andrew there to share the load. And he had been doing it. A few times she'd had to bite her lip when he was doing something differently than she – and Ben – was used to. But he had to find his own way with his son.

It warmed Erica as much as the sunshine to see how much easier he was around Ben. It was still early days, but the difference was palpable. After placing his drink next to the trike and saying something soft to him – Ben nodded even if he didn't look up – Andrew dragged another chair from the patio to join them at the back of the garden. 'Can I get you anything else, Lynn?'

She waved her glass of orange juice. 'No, I'm still full, thanks. Ben seems to have settled back in well. Is he coping okay with the weekends here and the weekdays at your other place?'

Change to routine was always tricky for Ben, and the hour in the car from the apartment to here on the last two Fridays – and back again on the Sunday night – had been a little sticky, but it was worth it to have the four of them together for the whole weekend. 'He's doing really well. He had an overnight stay at school on Thursday and he managed the whole night.'

She could hear the pride in her own voice. Andrew and Mollie had stayed at the apartment with her that night, but she hadn't got a wink of sleep. It'd reminded her of when she'd first brought the twins home from the hospital and she'd been afraid to fall asleep in case they stopped breathing. This time, she'd slept with her phone – the ringer turned up to maximum – level with her eyes on the bedside table.

Lynn beamed at her. 'Good for Ben! How was that for you?'

She looked from Erica to Andrew and back again. Erica looked at Andrew and he laughed. 'I don't know why you're looking at me, but, yes, it was great. We drove to pick him up early the following morning and we had to wait because they had chocolate croissants for breakfast and he didn't want to miss out.'

He reached across for Erica's hand and it made her blush. After so long apart, it felt as if they were starting over and she was still getting used to being affectionate again. 'He did really well. I was worried, obviously. But I didn't need to be. He was happy.'

'That's great news.' Lynn shifted in her seat and turned toward Mollie, who was pretending that she wasn't surreptitiously scrolling through her phone rather than joining in the conversation. 'And how about you, Mollie? How's school been?'

After another week off, they'd managed to persuade Mollie to go back to school. It'd been helped by Amelia telling her that everyone was talking about her presenting on the local news. She'd made her sound like a celebrity. Despite the tears over breakfast on the morning of her return, it'd seemed to go well.

However, Mollie's face wasn't filled with enthusiasm. 'It's okay.'

This was one of the main reasons she'd wanted Lynn to come here for coffee rather than meet in town. Erica was hoping that Lynn might be able to get to the root of this with Mollie better than she'd been able to. 'What do you mean by okay?'

Mollie tilted her head to one side, twisting a lock of her hair between her first two fingers. 'It wasn't as bad as I thought it would be. I mean, a couple of the boys teased me, but most people were more interested in the TV stuff and wanted to know if I could get them to come into school and do a report from there.'

Thank heavens for the teenage obsession with fame. Still, Erica was concerned that Mollie didn't sound totally happy. It was difficult not to jump in and try and fix things, try and persuade her that it'd all be okay eventually.

Lynn adjusted her hat from where it had fallen over her eyes. 'Well, that sounds good. It must be nice to be a celebrity.'

With a weak smile, Mollie slid her hands under her thighs and rocked gently in her seat. 'I want to change schools.'

Erica's heart sank. Clearly things weren't as good as she'd thought they were. Had she missed it again? Assumed that everything was okay only to discover there was something going on below the surface?

Sipping her orange juice, Lynn frowned. 'Why's that?'

Shifting in her seat, Mollie glanced sideways at Erica and Andrew. 'I want us to all live together. And I've found a school near Ben's where they do Media Studies GCSE. And they have special courses in TV and drama at their sixth form. I want to go there.'

From the look on Andrew's face, this was news to him too. When had she researched all of this? Was she just doing this to make life easier for them? Because that wasn't what Erica wanted her to do. 'Are you sure that's what you want, Mol? You're over halfway through school and it'll be a big upheaval to...'

She trailed off. She could feel herself doing it again. Jumping in to solve everyone's problems, second-guessing their needs and wants.

Mollie turned in her seat, her face a picture of determination. 'It is what I want. I want to start again. And I can't do that if I stay at the same place where everyone knows what happened.'

It was going to take a long time for her to get over the humiliation she'd felt, Erica knew that. Nonetheless, she also knew that starting a brand-new school was no walk in the park either. But the choice had to be Mollie's. 'If that's what you want, we can go and look at it.'

Mollie's expression was simultaneously surprised and hopeful. 'It is. And I want Dad to come, too. I want us to all live in the same house again. Every day.'

Since their conversation in the kitchen, she and Andrew

had been spending their time swapping houses and children and trying to be together as a foursome as much as possible. It couldn't continue like that, but she wasn't sure what the long-term solution was going to be. 'Your dad needs to get to work. And the commute is too far from where I'm living right now.'

Andrew raised a hand like he was in class. 'Dad can get a transfer. Someone needs to make a sacrifice and it's definitely my turn.'

She looked at Andrew, then back to Mollie, then glanced at Lynn whose smile echoed the one that was spreading over her own face. They were going to need time to work through all the mistakes and miscommunications of the last thirteen years, but it looked as if they might be travelling there from the same house, together.

EPILOGUE

One Year Later

After a week of rain, everyone had been ecstatic that the sun had broken through and was now bathing the field in brightness and warmth.

Ordinarily, the playing fields behind Ben's school were used for nature classes and sports, but today they were festooned with stalls and rides and ice cream vans. Erica, Andrew and Mollie had been here since eight o'clock helping to erect gazebos and tables. The gates opened at ten and Ben had been on a teacup ride, thrown plastic balls at some skittles and managed to eat three ice creams before he'd been in need of some quiet time; she was getting much better at reading the signals.

In a large tent, a little way from the noise of the main event, they'd set up a quiet space for anyone who needed a calm place to be. There were beanbag chairs in the four corners, tables with paper and colouring pens and a TV in the corner playing cartoons at a low volume. Thanks to a couple of mobile air con units, it was cool in here and Ben sat happily at a table, tipping out the pebbles he carried in a small pouch tied to his belt.

They'd come so far in the last year. Ben now stayed overnight on a Tuesday and Wednesday, which gave her three full days where she didn't have to dash around at both ends of the day. In September, she was going to start back working in a school, taking small groups for literacy support on a Tuesday and Wednesday. Thursdays, she had a long lie-in, and lunch with her husband, before collecting Ben.

Beside her, a woman around her age with a long dark pony-tail tilted her head into Erica's line of vision. 'Hi, I'm Ellie. My daughter Daisy is at the school. She transferred here a couple of months ago. She has Downs.'

It was almost a reflex, introducing your child, then their diagnosis. Erica understood, but she wished for the day that they didn't find it necessary. 'Nice to meet you. I'm Ben's mum.'

Ellie smiled. 'I know. I think Daisy has a soft spot for your son. She's been following him around all morning.'

Looking in the direction of Ellie's nod, Erica spied a small blonde girl in a purple summer dress with the sweetest smile. She hovered behind Ben, watching as he lined up coloured pebbles, as entranced as if he was a celebrity. Her heart warmed at the scene. Why wouldn't she? He was such a handsome boy. 'I hope she likes watching him straightening stones. She might be there a while.'

She turned to grin at Ellie just in time to see the woman's eyes fill with tears. Before she could offer sympathy, Ellie shook her head, sniffed and screwed up her face. 'Ignore me. I'm strug-gling a bit at the moment. Puberty is hitting hard and it's a struggle, to be honest.'

It seemed as if she wanted to say more, so Erica resisted the urge to fill the silence, just nodded and reached out to pat her arm in solidarity.

For a few moments, they watched the two children in

silence. When she spoke again, Ellie's voice was a whisper. 'Does it get easier?'

Easier? That was the question often asked in the parent group that Fiona Bixby had cajoled Erica into joining and, now, running. Andrew was avoiding the head teacher today because he was convinced that she had him in her sights for running a group for dads. 'That woman is impossible to say no to.'

'No.' She smiled at the surprise on Ellie's face. 'It does not get easier. Ben has autism and it's always going to make life more difficult for him. The challenges just get different. But you do get stronger. You do become able to deal with it better.'

Ellie wiped at her eyes with the back of her hand. 'I'm not sure whether that gives me hope or not.'

Erica passed her a tissue from the packet in her pocket. 'I think the hope and sense of failure take it in turns day to day. Believe me, today is a good day and I'm making the most of it. But tomorrow...'

She tilted her head to one side and stuck out her tongue, and was pleased to see Ellie laugh. 'Thank you. That makes me feel less inept.'

'Honey, if you want to feel better about yourself, stick around with me.' She grinned. It felt good to be able to ease someone's mind. 'Let me give you my number. One thing you do need is to be around people who understand what it's like.'

'Thank you. I'd really appreciate that.'

They'd just exchanged numbers when Mollie came bowling into the tent, her arms full with a pile of bright-yellow leaflets and an overflowing bag of yellow button badges. 'I'm going to sit at the front gate and give these out to any of the brothers and sisters who come. They might not know about the Young Carers group.'

She was so proud of her daughter and the work she'd done this year to promote the group. It'd been so good for her to be around other young people who knew what it was like to have a sibling with special needs. The glass children.

Looking at her now, she was a different person to that little girl on the beach all those months ago. She loved her new school and had hit the ground running with a social life once the other students recognised her as the teen reporter on the local news. She'd even brought friends home to meet her brother and a couple of them were here with her today. There were still times when she was frustrated that Ben's needs prevented – or changed – their plans, but she was getting better at telling them how she felt and compromising on a solution.

'Have you seen your dad?'

Before Mollie could answer, Andrew appeared. 'This is where you all are.'

She lifted up her face for him to kiss; Mollie mimed throwing up. You'd think she'd be happy to have her parents so clearly back in love, but no one is as appalled by parental displays of affection as a fourteen-year-old child.

'Ben was feeling a bit overwhelmed so we came in here.'

'Good idea. I was just thinking about lunch.'

At that word, Ben's face flipped up in their direction. That boy did not like to miss the opportunity for a meal. Andrew crouched down in front of his table. 'How are you doing, buddy? Shall we go and get a hot dog?'

Ben didn't need asking twice. He scooped his stones into the bag and was ready to go without a backwards glance at poor Daisy. Giving Ellie a little wave goodbye, Erica put her arm around her own daughter. 'Do you fancy a hotdog, too?'

Mollie shook off her arm and wrinkled her face in disgust. 'I'm a *vegetarian*.'

To be fair to Erica, she'd only announced this three days ago. 'Of course. Let's see what else they've got.'

Mollie waved the leaflets. 'I need to get to the welcome desk. Can you bring me some chips? Please?'

'Okay, I'll bring you some chips.'

Mollie's kiss was so quick, she barely felt it. 'Thanks, Mum. Why don't you tell Dad and Ben to come over, too? Ben can help me give out the badges.'

As she watched her daughter scoot off to join her friends, Erica's mind wandered back to the head teacher's words. 'Don't look at his world through your eyes, look through his eyes.'

Right now, through all of their eyes, life looked pretty good.

A LETTER FROM EMMA

Thank you for choosing to read this novel about Erica, Andrew, Ben and Mollie. I really hope you have enjoyed it. If you did enjoy it and want to keep up to date with all my latest releases, just sign up at the following link. Your email address will never be shared and you can unsubscribe at any time.

www.bookouture.com/emma-robinson

Unusually, the title came before the idea this time and I thought a lot about the different circumstances in which a mother might be forced to make a choice. I was reminded of something my mum said once that you love each of your children the same amount, but you love them differently. Now my children are getting older, I can see the truth in this as they need – and want – different things from me. I think it can be difficult for all parents to get the balance right when they have more than one child. But this can be so much harder when one of your children has complex needs.

Probably due to children within my own family and friendships, I have included a child with autism in two of my other novels. Recently, in *All My Fault*, and also in my fourth novel – *My Silent Daughter* – which followed Sara and her daughter Ruby. Many readers fell in love with Ruby and wanted to know what happened for her as she grew up. Though there are no plans for a follow up story for Ruby and Sara, it did encourage me to write about an older child and the different dilemmas that might arise.

This book is not about a child with autism, but about his mother. In preparing to write Erica's relationship with Ben, I spoke to friends who could give me an insight into her thoughts and feelings. I hope I got it right.

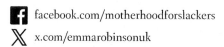

facebook.com/motherhoodforslackers

x.com/emmarobinsonuk

ACKNOWLEDGEMENTS

First thanks must go to my brilliant editor, Laura Deacon. This is the first book that we've worked on together from the start and I know that it is a much better book for your guidance. Ongoing thanks to the lovely Sarah Hardy and the rest of the PR team and to everyone at Bookouture who works so hard to get my books out there. You are all incredible at what you do.

I absolutely love the cover for this book which is the creation of the fabulous Alice Moore. For ensuring that there are no embarrassing errors and typos, thank you to Donna Hillyer and Deborah Blake for your ability to work out which tense I think I'm writing in and then correcting it. Also, to my good friend Carrie Harvey for finding all the mistakes I've missed in the final proofs.

As always, being able to listen to first-hand experience is a huge help in creating characters that react and behave in an authentic manner. To this end, a huge thank you to Nikki Kadwill and Lyndsay Robbins for giving up your time to talk to me about raising your beautiful boys which really helped me to tap in to Erica's feelings. Sometimes other elements are gifted to me by chance. For sharing your knowledge about learning to play the saxophone, a big thank you to Toby Partridge.

Lastly, as always, to my family. This year has been full on, but we made it. I love you.

PUBLISHING TEAM

Turning a manuscript into a book requires the efforts of many people. The publishing team at Bookouture would like to acknowledge everyone who contributed to this publication.

Commercial
Lauren Morrissette
Hannah Richmond
Imogen Allport

Cover design
Alice Moore

Data and analysis
Mark Alder
Mohamed Bussuri

Editorial
Laura Deacon
Sinead O'Connor

Copyeditor
Donna Hillyer

Proofreader
Deborah Blake